THREE BROTHERS

ALSO BY PETER ACKROYD

FICTION

The Great Fire of London
The Last Testament of Oscar Wilde
Hawksmoor
Chatterton
First Light
English Music
The House of Doctor Dee
Dan Leno and the Limehouse Golem
Milton in America
The Plato Papers
The Clerkenwell Tales
The Lambs of London
The Fall of Troy
The Casebook of Victor Frankenstein

NONFICTION

Dressing Up: Transvestism and Drag:
The History of an Obsession
London: The Biography
Albion: The Origins of the
English Imagination
Venice: Pure City
London Under

BIOGRAPHY

Ezra Pound and His World
T. S. Eliot
Dickens
Blake
The Life of Thomas More
Shakespeare: The Biography

ACKROYD'S BRIEF LIVES

Chaucer
J. M. W. Turner
Newton
Poe: A Life Cut Short

POETRY

Ouch!
The Diversions of Purley
and Other Poems

CRITICISM

Notes for a New Culture
The Collection: Journalism, Reviews,
Essays, Short Stories, Lectures
edited by Thomas Wright

Three Brothers

A NOVEL

Peter Ackroyd

Nan A. Talese | *Doubleday*

NEW YORK   LONDON   TORONTO

SYDNEY   AUCKLAND

Copyright © 2013 by Peter Ackroyd

All rights reserved. Published in the United States by Nan A. Talese/Doubleday, a division of Random House LLC, New York, a Penguin Random House Company. Originally published in Great Britain by Chatto & Windus, an imprint of the Random House Group Limited, London, in 2013.

www.nanatalese.com

DOUBLEDAY is a registered trademark of Random House LLC. Nan A. Talese and the colophon are trademarks of Random House LLC.

Jacket photograph © Picture Post/Hulton Archive/Getty Images

Library of Congress Cataloging-in-Publication Data

Ackroyd, Peter, 1949–
Three brothers : a novel / Peter Ackroyd. — First American edition.
pages cm
Originally published in Great Britain by Chatto & Windus, an imprint of the Random House Group Limited, London, in 2013—Title page verso.
1. Brothers—Fiction. 2. City and town life—England—London—Fiction.
3. London (England)—Fiction. I. Title.
PR6051.C64T48 2014
823'.914—dc23
2013033737

ISBN 978-0-385-53861-9
ISBN 978-0-385-53862-6 (eBook)

MANUFACTURED IN THE UNITED STATES OF AMERICA

1 3 5 7 9 10 8 6 4 2

First United States Edition

Contents

I

Cheese and pickle

I N THE London borough of Camden, in the middle of the last century, there lived three brothers; they were three young boys, with a year's difference of age between each of them. They were united, however, in one extraordinary way. They had been born at the same time on the same day of the same month—to be precise, midday on 8 May. The chance was remote and even implausible. Yet it was so. The local newspaper recorded the coincidence, after the birth of the third son, and the Hanway boys became the object of speculation. Were they in some sense marked out? Was there some invisible communion between them, apart from their natural affinity?

The interest soon subsided, of course, in a neighbourhood where the daily struggles of existence were still evident four or five years after the War. In any case, there were other differences between the boys—differences of temperament, differences of affection—that soon became manifest. These diversities, however, were still mild and pliable. They had not yet become the source of great disagreement or hostile division.

The three boys were young enough, and near enough in age, to enjoy the same pastimes. On the pavement outside their small house in Crystal Street they chalked the squares of hop-scotch. They played marbles in the gutter with fierce concentration. They hardened the seeds of the horse chestnut with pickle juice and brine, so that they could compete with conkers. They raced each other on the common, at the edge of the council estate in which they lived. They explored the deserted tracts of land beside an old railway line, and trod cautiously among the debris of an abandoned bomb shelter.

On the common, too, they played the old game "Run Run Away." One of them, with a scarf wound about his eyes as a blindfold, repeated a few well-known words as the others ran as far as they could; when he stopped speaking, they had to remain quite still. He then had to find them, and the first one he touched became "it" when the whole game began again.

On one particular afternoon the youngest of them, Sam, was standing, his eyes blindfolded, and he began to shout out the words.

"When I was standing on the stair
I met a man who wasn't there.
He wasn't there again today.
I wish, I wish he'd go away.
Here I come, ready or not!"

After a minute or two of threshing around he caught hold of his oldest brother, Harry. But there was no real excitement in the game. They had played it too often.

"Listen," Sam said, "what do you both want to be when you grow up?"

"I want to be a pilot."

"I want to be a detective."

"Do you know what?" Sam told them. "I don't want to be anything."

The sky was growing darker, and a cold breeze had started up across the common with the promise of light rain. "Come on," Harry said, pointing to the abandoned bomb shelter, "let's all go under the ground. I've got some matches. We can start a fire. Mum won't miss us till teatime. Let's start a fire that will go on *for ever!*"

"I dare you."

"I double dare you."

So one by one, in single file, following each other, they descended into the earth.

They had a small back garden, in which they investigated the lives of earwigs and other insects. At the bottom of this garden there was an old stone basin often filled with rainwater, and in this they raised tadpoles caught from the pond on the edge of the common. They put their heads together and peered down into the murky water, their sweet liquorice breath mingling with the dank odour of moss and slime. They tried to grow beans and peas in the garden, but the shoots withered and rotted away. It was, in short, a London childhood. They had never seen mountains or waterfalls, of course, but they lived securely in their world of brick and stone.

They recognised by instinct the frontiers to their territory; a street further north, or further south, was not visited. It was not welcoming. But within their own bounds they were entirely at home. They knew every dip in the pavement, every front door, every cat that prowled along the gutter or slumbered on the window sill. They knew, or at least recognised, most of the people they saw. There were few strangers in the neighbourhood. They lived among familiar faces.

Any stranger who happened to walk through the neighbourhood would not have come away with any distinct impression. It was a council estate, built in the 1920s, of two-storey red-brick terraces. That was all. One row of houses was interrupted by some small shops—a newsagent, a hairdresser, a butcher among them—and on the corners of the narrow streets were general stores or public houses. There was a fish-

and-chip shop, and a bakery, in the street where the Hanways lived. The district smelled at various times of dust and of rain, of bonfire smoke and of petrol. Its sounds were not of cars but of trams and milk-floats, with the distinct but distant roar of London somewhere around the corner. It had the forlorn calm of a poor neighbourhood, yet for the three brothers it repaid the closest possible attention. It was the source of curiosity, of surprise, and, sometimes, of delight. The centre of their lives was very small, but it was brightly lit. And all around stretched the endless streets, of which they were largely unaware.

Their first memories of childhood differed. Harry recalled how he had managed to walk unaided across the carpet of the small living room, praised and encouraged by his parents sitting on a yellow sofa. Daniel, between his brothers in age, remembered being taken out of a pram and held up to the sunlight, in which he seemed to soar. Sam's first memory was of falling and cutting his leg on a shard of broken glass; he had cried when he saw the blood. Had their respective memories ever come together, they might have had some understanding of their shared past. But they were content with these fragments.

They attended the same primary school, a red-brick building set beside a grey-brick church, where the signs for "Boys" and "Girls" were carved in Gothic script above two portals. The school smelled of soap and carbolic disinfectant, but the classrooms were always cluttered and dirty with a faint patina of dust upon the shelves and windows.

The Hanway boys were in separate classes, according to their age, and in the playground they did not care to fraternise. Harry was the most gregarious and thus the most popular of the brothers; he laughed readily, and had a circle of acquaintances whom he easily amused. Daniel had two chosen friends, with whom he was always deep in consultation; they collected bus numbers and cigarette cards, which they would compare and contrast. Sam, the youngest, seemed content to remain on his own. He did not seek the company of the other children. And they in turn left him alone. But Sam had a temper. One morning, at the gate of the school, a boy remarked on the fact that Sam had torn his school jacket. Sam struck out at him with his fist and knocked him to the pavement. His two brothers witnessed the event, and adjusted to him accordingly.

Harry Hanway was ten, Daniel Hanway was nine, and Sam Hanway was eight, when their mother disappeared. They returned late one afternoon from school, and found an empty house. Harry made sandwiches of cheese and pickle. They sat around the kitchen table, and waited. No one came.

Their father, Philip, was employed as a nightwatchman in the City. He always left the house in the afternoon, stopped at a pub on Camden High Street, and then took the bus to the financial headquarters where he worked. He would put on his dark blue uniform, kept in a small locker off the main hall, and then sit behind an imposing central desk. He always had with him pencils and paper. After a few minutes of concentration he would begin writing, slowly and hesitantly; then he would stop altogether. For the rest of the night he would smoke and stare into space.

He had been called up for the army, in the third year of the War, but in fact travelled no farther than Middlesbrough where he was assigned to the barracks as a clerk of munitions. He remained in that post until the end of the War when, with army pay in his pocket, he returned to London. He had been brought up in Ruislip, but he had no intention of returning. Ruislip was the place where he had waited impatiently for his real life to begin. Instead he set off for Soho. He believed that he was destined to be a writer. When he was a schoolboy, he had read an English translation of *The Count of Monte Cristo* over several weeks; he had devoured it, page by page, elated and terrified by the turns of the plot. The day after he finished the novel, he began his own story. He never completed it. He put the pages in a biscuit tin, where at the time of this narrative they still lay. Yet he was not discouraged. He began writing other stories, to which he could never find a satisfactory conclusion. The more disappointment he suffered, the more intense his ambition became. He recalled the last words of *The Count of Monte Cristo*, "wait and hope."

So he migrated to Soho in search of publishers, of magazines, of fellow writers, of critics, of any stimulus—he was not sure of his way forward. He rented a small room in Poland Street, and indulged in what seemed to him to be the bliss of bohemian life. He woke late; he drank coffee in dirty cafés; he lounged and sipped Guinness in shadowy pubs. Yet he could not write. He sat down at the folding table in his room, pencil in hand. He could find no subject.

When his army funds were low, he sought work in the neighbourhood. He became a barman in the Horn of Plenty, a pub in Greek Street that was the chosen spot for a group of hard-drinking and sometimes bellicose Soho residents. Philip Hanway was happy here. He called himself a writer, and enjoyed the anecdotes of the journalists and advertising copy-writers who frequented the bar. And then he met Sally Palliser. She worked in a cake shop, or "pâtisserie," in Meard Street. He had passed its window, with a display of almond tarts and buns and pastries, and had seen her delicately picking out an angel cake for a customer. His first impression was of the graceful way she moved behind the counter, her skirt slightly creasing as she bent forward. On the following morning he paused, opened the gaily painted door, and ordered a macaroon. He purchased a macaroon every morning for the next few weeks.

Sally had been impressed when he told her that he was a

writer. He was young, and looked very smart in a grey suit, grey overcoat and grey trilby.

"I like grey," he told her. "I can disappear."

"Now that's interesting."

"I promise you, I will *always* say interesting things to you. I can't help myself."

"But what will *I* say?"

"You just have to smile."

When he first took her out she ordered a pink gin and smoked Woodbines. This delighted him. They went dancing at the Rainbow Room in Holborn to the music of Harry Chapman and his orchestra. After three months, much to her parents' disapproval, she moved into Philip's small room.

"Living in sin is not right," her mother said. "It will come to no good. Mark my words." She was always enjoining her daughter to mark her words. "And what are you going to live on? Spam and baked beans?"

In fact there was a fish-and-chip shop in Dean Street. And the pastries were free. She brought back the stale ones at the end of the day.

After a violent argument with the staff of the Horn of Plenty, Philip Hanway lost his job.

"Where are you going?" the landlord asked him.

"I'm going *outside*. For good." He wanted to slam the door but it swung limply to and fro.

"Well," he said to Sally when he returned home, "at least I can concentrate on my writing." She surmised that he would be happy to survive on her small income.

When she first realised that she was pregnant, she panicked. She enquired about abortionists, of whom there were several in Soho, but the stories of injury and even fatality dissuaded her. "Sometimes," a friend told her, "they stick a knitting needle up your you-know-what."

"Ouch."

"Have you ever seen a dead baby? Looks like a mole."

So Harry was saved.

She informed her parents of the pregnancy before she told Philip. She wanted to present him with a family ultimatum. And so, five weeks later, Sally and Philip were married in the registry office on St. Martin's Lane. Philip then exerted himself to find work, and applied for the job of nightwatchman. The two of them formally requested a council house, as a newly married couple, and to their relief they succeeded. So they moved to Camden, where Harry was born four months later.

The three brothers had been sitting in silence around the kitchen table. Sam was fiddling with two elastic bands he had tied together. "I'm going to have a drink of fizz," Harry said. "Anyone else want some?"

"Where is she?" Daniel asked him.

"I think," he replied, "she's been delayed." An old alarm clock was ticking by the sink. "Dad will know what to do."

Philip Hanway did not seem particularly surprised by his wife's disappearance. "She has gone away for a while," he told his sons. That was all he said. He offered no other explanation. In fact he never afterwards spoke of her. He continued his work as a nightwatchman, and the boys saw little of him. They grew accustomed to looking after themselves. Philip provided them with pocket money that they pooled. After a few months they forgot that their life had ever been different.

In the days immediately following her disappearance, however, Sam was very quiet. On going to school in those mornings the boys encountered a thick smog, and under its cover Sam wept softly without the others knowing. They explained nothing to their school companions or to their teachers. On the matter of their mother, they were wholly silent. Something—something vast, something overwhelming—had happened. But they could not speak of it. The neighbours, curiously, did not seem to notice Sally's absence. The three brothers were left to themselves.

A year after the disappearance Harry progressed, as he had expected, to the secondary modern school on the other side of the borough. He had sat the 11-plus examination, but he had not excelled in any of the papers. He changed from one school uniform to another, and caught a bus in the morning. Then, a year later, Daniel passed the same examination with much higher marks.

Daniel seemed to have a natural propensity for study, and a love of reading. Often, when Harry and Sam would busy themselves with sports or games on the common, he would stay behind with a book. In this he could be said to take after his father. But Philip knew very little of his son's secluded life. Daniel visited the public library on the boundary of the estate, and brought home each week a selection of adventure novels and popular histories. He took out on an extended loan each volume of *Arthur Mee's Children's Encyclopaedia*, and vowed to memorise the contents.

His work was rewarded when it was announced, after passing the 11-plus, that he had won a place at Camden Grammar School. If his mother had been there, she would have danced with him around the kitchen; she would have lifted him up, and pressed her nose against his. Philip simply shook his hand, and gave him half-a-crown. Harry joked with him about a school for swots. Sam never mentioned the subject.

But there was now a change in the Hanway family. Daniel had to strive with his contemporaries. He had to compete. He was given homework every night, and would sit at the kitchen table while Harry and Sam were free to roam. He became more deliberate and circumspect; he saw his life as a series of hurdles over which he was obliged to jump.

Then Harry started playing football for his school team. He enjoyed the exhilaration of the dribble with the ball, the clever pass, and the sudden shot at the goal. He enjoyed the exercise of his own body—the exercise of his power in the world. He called out to his teammates, he shouted at the linesmen, he whooped with triumph at every goal his team scored. It was a world of expressive noise. The physical sensation of movement delighted him. He revelled in the wind and rain and sunlight as he ran across the pitch.

In this, he was different from his brothers. Gradually the intimacy between them began to fade. Sam was left to himself. He spent many hours making elaborate contraptions out of wood and cardboard. Even though he did not know the word melancholy, he began to experience it. He would turn, head over heels, on his narrow bed in order to make himself dizzy and disoriented. He did not prosper at school. As a matter of course he was sent to the same secondary modern school as his older brother. He made no friends there, and Harry seemed to avoid him.

II

The path is clear

HARRY HANWAY left school at the age of sixteen, and was already eager to join the world. He was active, determined, and energetic. At school he had won popularity for his cheerfulness and bravado. He had become captain of the football team. He had retaliated against one notorious school bully by knocking him to the floor. He had his own recognisable phrases, which were instantly imitated. "How the heck are you?" was his standard greeting. He also said, in mock irritation, "What the heck?" So he became known as Harry Heck.

"I don't want to go to college," he told his father as his leaving day approached. "I want to get a job."

"Say that again."

"I want to get a job."

"Just so you're certain." He looked away for a moment. "There's nothing worse than a dead-end job."

It was a Sunday afternoon. Philip Hanway was about to leave for the City. He now worked seven nights a week in order to support his family. "I'll come back with money, Dad."

"It's not about the money. It's about you."

"But what do you think, Dad, of the newspapers? That's a good life, isn't it?" Harry loved newspapers. He enjoyed the appearance, and even the texture, of them. He liked their smell. He relished the size of the headlines and the neat rows of type. He was excited by the thought of thousands of copies despatched from the printing plant into waiting vans. In the evenings, after school, he flattened the *Daily Sketch* on the kitchen table and slowly turned its pages. Sometimes he read out paragraphs aloud, just like the news broadcasters on the wireless.

"Newspaper boy?" Daniel was writing in an exercise book, but now looked up at him.

"Dry up."

"I was only asking."

"Sod off."

"There's no need for a fight," Philip said. "We have to think about this seriously."

"I have thought about it seriously."

So Harry arrived at the offices of the local newspaper, the *Camden Bugle*, and asked if they needed a messenger boy.

He was astonished to discover that the offices of the *Bugle* comprised two small rooms, one marked "Editorial" and the other marked "Advertising," above a row of shops along the high street. Its premises were on the second floor above a barber, and the candy-striped pole could be seen from the desks of "Editorial." The floor was covered with scuffed linoleum, and the interior needed repainting.

The *Bugle*, quite by chance, did need a messenger boy, the previous occupant of that post having just handed in his notice in order to become a gentleman's outfitter in Bond Street. The editor, George Bradwell, prided himself on making his decisions in an instant. And he reckoned Harry to be a lively young man. "Do you run or do you walk fast?" he asked him. He had a gruff voice that seemed to come from his chest rather than his throat.

"I run, sir, when I see the path clear."

"That's good. That's what you must do." He had an emphatic manner of speaking, reminding Harry of the fairground barkers who came to Camden once a year. George Bradwell was not used to being interrupted or contradicted. He explained that Harry was supposed to take the "copy" from the office to the printer, and then bring the "proof" back to the *Bugle*. Copy of what? Proof of what? It was very mysterious. Bradwell then showed Harry some pages of typing, with various scrawls and symbols in the margins. "These," he said, "have been marked up." Harry nodded, as if he understood perfectly what he was being told. The air was heavy with the stale odour of tobacco. "Cadogan Street." Pinned to the wall was a large map of the borough. Bradwell pointed with tobacco-stained finger to the street in question. "On the right is Lubin the printer. Just tell him you're from the *Bugle*. This is Tony, by the way."

Tony was a middle-aged man of florid complexion, with the indefinable air of having been disappointed in life. He boasted a thin pencil-like moustache, and a clump of hair perched precariously on his head. "You can't miss Lubin," he said. "He is the Jew boy." Harry knew at once that Tony wore a wig, and he suspected that the moustache was dyed. Tony looked like a man perpetually in disguise.

Tony, in turn, took an instinctive dislike to the new recruit; any young person threatened him.

Harry soon became accustomed to his duties. He was so exhilarated by his new job that he mastered its details easily enough. He dashed from the *Bugle* to the printers. He ran between "Editorial" and "Advertising," picking up the copy from both departments. In "Editorial" Tony was news. George was interviews and reviews. An elderly man, Aldous, was sports. Aldous hardly ever spoke, and seemed to Harry to exist in a state of self-pitying gloom. Stress and tension were always in the air. Bradwell would answer the telephone and announce himself as "editor in chief." Tony would then give a sarcastic smile. Bradwell would often snatch his hat and coat, and stride purposefully out of the office. Sometimes he would not come back for an hour or more. Then he returned with an air of mystery, and with the odour of alcohol.

In the background there was always the stutter of a typewriter, as Tony or Aldous put together a paragraph. Aldous described the triumphs, or the miseries, of the Camden Rovers. He praised the exploits of a Camden schoolgirl who had won a North London javelin competition. He denounced the closing of the bar of the Camden Cricketers' Association. He typed down all this with the same air of gloom. Tony celebrated a lucky win on the football pools by a Camden pensioner. He described the closure of a cottage hospital in East Camden. He reported the theft of a jukebox from a Camden public house. He sat over his typewriter like a bird of prey.

On the whole, Harry preferred "Advertising." It was run by a small woman with a strong Scots accent. To Harry, Maureen seemed marvellously exotic. She wore a skein of artificial pearls over her hair and, according to Tony, dressed like something out of a shop window. He referred to her as Queen of Scots or Bloody Maureen. She supervised the work of two young men who were, again according to Tony, "slaves at her feet." Maureen had overheard the remark; she had arched her eyebrows and sniffed. She considered Tony to be, as she put it, "a drastic little creature." "Excuse me," she said, "but I think he's a very common type of person. And that wig looks like a dead cat." Harry could not disagree.

Harry enjoyed his time in Lubin's printworks. He savoured the pervasive smell of ink, and the steady metallic beat of the electrotyping machines. He saw the curved plates of metal type being inserted into the presses, and watched as the paper flowed between them. It was a cheerful and good-humoured place, filled with shouts and the noise of the machinery. This was the newspaper world that Harry had envisaged—a strident, exciting, declamatory world.

Harry was walking back from the printer one evening, after delivering the last of that day's copy, when he noticed a man in a dark raincoat walking ahead of him. He was in his thirties, or so it seemed, but he was much smaller and slighter than Harry. He was carrying a shopping bag in each hand, containing something bulky or heavy. He had difficulty in maintaining an even pace, but he looked calmly from side to side. On a whim, or instinct, Harry decided to follow him. The man crossed the road, and then began walking down a street of semi-detached dark red-brick houses. The area was gloomy enough in the day, but on a winter evening it was a place in mourning. It was one of those parts of London that sunlight never seems to enter, an almost subterranean world of domestic privacy and seclusion. Net curtains were hanging at every window, and the gates of the small front gardens were all closed.

Harry knew that the brick church of Our Lady of Sorrows stood at the end of this dark red avenue, opposite a small park. He suspected that the man was about to enter the park, but then he saw him vanish into the deep shadow of the church itself. He followed him through the porch, and then sat quietly in a pew at the back. The church was deserted. The man had walked slowly up the aisle and had halted at the wooden rail before the altar. It seemed to Harry that he had knelt down and, with his head bowed forward, begun to pray. But that was not what he was doing. Harry heard rustling, and noticed that he was taking something out of the bags. He walked towards him silently and cautiously; then, to his alarm, he saw two large cans of petrol. He did not hesitate. He shouted out "Heck!" and rushed at the man, knocking him to the floor before pinning him against the rail. The man looked at him, mildly, and did not try to resist.

The cry had roused the curate of the church, who had been dozing in the sacristy amidst the mild perfume of lilies and beeswax polish. He came running out, and was astonished at the spectacle of Harry straddling the man and pressing him against the floor of the church. Harry suggested to him that he might go in search of a policeman. A glance at the cans of petrol convinced the curate. "I'm in no possible hurry," the man said as Harry continued to sit upon him. "Don't you think this church is rather wonderful?" It was ornate and comfortable, with candles and flowers and images; statues of the saints stood between the Stations of the Cross, and a wooden confessional box was against the south aisle. "My mother used to frequent this place a great deal. She used to sit here with me. I was only a boy, naturally. That was in '44. When the bombing got a trifle on the heavy side." He had a plaintive or earnest expression, as if he were trying to solve a curiously subtle problem. "I can remember the bombs very well. I was never scared, you see. It was the excitement. Glorious feeling." His voice, echoing in the empty church, was very gentle. "I was one of the Blitz boys. Have you heard of us by any chance?" Harry shook his head. The War was, for him, very distant. "We were the ones who put out the fires. We had buckets of sand and a hand-truck. We had iron bars to force our way in. We were absolutely fierce. We were ready to *eat* fires, even if I say so myself."

The curate came back with three policemen. Harry rose to his feet and two officers took the man away. The third remained to take down Harry's statement.

Harry told George Bradwell the following morning. He became so excited by his own narrative that he knelt on the floor to demonstrate the manner in which he had pinned down the arsonist.

"I think," Bradwell said, "that we can make a story out of this."

"But it's true."

"A news story. *Bugle* reporter foils arson attack upon church. Commended by the police for his heroism."

"But I'm not a reporter."

"You are now." He glanced at the unoccupied desks of Aldous and of Tony. Harry sensed, then, that he did not altogether relish their company. "You know how to hold a pen, don't you?" Harry nodded. "That's a good start."

Within a very short time Bradwell taught him how to construct a news story; he explained to him that he should begin with the simple fact, in a short sentence, and then gradually elaborate. He pointed out the places where Harry might acquire news—the magistrates' court, the town hall, the police stations, the office of the coroner. He gave him lessons in typewriting, and even sent him on a course of shorthand. Bradwell seemed to be reliving the earliest stages of his own career; he saw in Harry a version of his younger self. He wished him to succeed. And Harry did. He had a natural gift for vivid description, and a keen eye for a likely story. Another messenger boy was hired.

Tony was furious at Harry's appointment. He believed himself to have been supplanted and, in effect, humiliated. But he did not show his fury to those who had instigated it. He concealed it from Bradwell and Harry, but he vented it to Aldous. "He can't write," he said as they sat in a local public house. "He can't spell. He is an ignorant little bleeder. I think he may be a pansy. What do you think?" Aldous was deeply uncomfortable about any such allusion. He merely shook his head. Tony's anger emerged as genial malice in Harry's presence. He was careful not to criticise him directly, but tried to unsettle him with jokes and insinuations. Harry feigned not to notice his resentment and bitterness.

He spent most of his time, in any case, out of "Editorial." He rushed after stories of burglaries and assaults. He attended weddings and funerals. He waited outside the local police station for the arrival of the Black Maria van. He spent hours talking to the elderly clerk of the magistrates' court, Mr. Peabody, who was a source of local information. Mr. Peabody was a grave and dignified gentleman, with a taste for whisky. He would speak eloquently of the foibles of a certain magistrate, or the surprising conclusion of a certain case; but as he drank he grew more thoughtful, until his conversation came to a lingering end. Harry knew that, at this stage, it was time to withdraw. He would leave Mr. Peabody at the bar, glass in hand, staring solemnly at the row of bottles above the cash register.

"Hanway? Hanway?" he asked Harry one evening.

"Yes, Mr. Peabody?"

"The name is known to me. I can recall it. It is an unusual name. Most unusual." He reflected. "There was a young woman, by the name of Hanway, connected with the court in some way. Some years ago. I seem to remember her crying."

Who was the young woman, crying? Could Mr. Peabody have some vague recollection of his mother? But, then, what had she to do with the magistrates' court? Harry sensed, at that moment, that all this had something to do with her disappearance.

He decided to consult the court's files. He knew the approximate date of his mother's disappearance. It had been in the early winter. He recalled the smog. He had been ten years old. So he turned back to the records of October 1957. It was weary work, going through the reports of cases and incidents long forgotten. But he read on through evidences and judgements—until one name arrested his wandering attention. Mrs. Sally Hanway was brought before the court on 22 October 1957. He started to sweat, and looked away at a printed notice fixed to the wall. With an effort of concentration he turned back to the page, from which he had been momentarily distracted by a pang of anxiety so great that he caught his breath. At that instant, too, Daniel Hanway and Sam Hanway were seized with a sensation close to panic. Harry carried on reading and learned that Mrs. Sally Hanway had been found guilty of soliciting and of offending public morals. The magistrate had sentenced her to a term of three months' imprisonment.

Harry got up from his chair and walked down the long corridor of the building. He came out of the entrance, descended the stone steps, and was then sick on the pavement. He steadied himself against a pillar, and breathed in deeply. He had a sudden image of her, standing on the steps of the magistrates' court, with her finger to her lips. He went back to the library, and replaced the heavy volume on the shelves.

It was only when he had walked out again into the street that he realised something else. His father had known of this. That is why he had evinced no surprise. That is why he had never spoken of her disappearance. And the neighbours must also have known of his mother's arrest. Out of pity or embarrassment, they had not remarked upon her absence to the three young brothers. He realised, too, that with this knowledge he could no longer remain in the house with his brothers.

The life of the Hanway household was not, in any case, as it once had been. The brothers had steadily grown apart. Daniel spent his evenings in study, while Harry pursued his new work. Without the company of his older brothers, Sam had become aimless. He had no friends and spent his time, outside of school, roaming through the streets—in search of what? Their father had changed his job. He gave up his post as nightwatchman, and had become a long-distance lorry driver with a regular run from London to Carlisle; as a result he spent less time than ever at home.

Harry took advantage of his father's absence to leave quietly and quickly. He found a small room in a street close to the offices of the *Bugle*. He had few possessions; what he owned could be carried in a suitcase.

Daniel saw him packing. He asked him where he was going.

"Now that's an excellent question. I'm going away. I'm taking off."

"For good?"

"Nothing is for good, clever boy."

"Dad won't like it."

"Dad will like it. You will have more space. Sam can have my room." He closed the lid of the suitcase. "Dad doesn't even know I'm here. When is he ever at home?"

"Where are you going then?"

"Carver Street."

It was a street of small houses and of small shops. They were some of the first buildings ever erected in the fields of Camden, in the early nineteenth century, but they did not wear their age gracefully. Their yellow brick had faded with grime and decay; the doors were peeling, and the windows were dusty. A sudden gap in the row of houses marked the spot where a stray doodlebug had flattened two houses; they had not yet been rebuilt, and the open site was covered in weeds and refuse. The windows of Harry's room overlooked this waste-ground. He rented the room from an elderly Irish couple, the Stantons, whose son had recently died of poliomyelitis. It was the son's room that Harry now occupied. A crucifix hung on the wall above the bed.

Harry had never been alone before. He had never thought

of himself as solitary. He had lost contact with his erstwhile school friends, but he would have denied ever being lonely. He never once used the word. But now he sat by himself in any number of cheap cafés, where the principal resource was egg and chips and brown sauce. It was the sauce, in fact, that effected his introduction to Hilda. She was sitting at the table next to his in the Zodiac Café for Working Men. He was shaking the bottle of sauce so vigorously that it splattered over her plate of spotted dick and custard.

He offered to buy her an untainted pudding, an offer that she gracefully accepted. It was the least he could do. Then they began to talk.

"I expect," she said, "that you will be laughing at me soon."

"Why would I do that?"

"Everything I do seems to be funny. Not funny peculiar. Funny ha ha. People laugh at me for no apparent reason. I'm *serious*." She had a direct manner, but it was accompanied by a shy smile that Harry found charming; she had a round face, but it was a pretty one. "My name is Hilda. That makes you laugh, doesn't it?"

"No."

"It should do. Hilda is a stupid name. *Everyone* in Southend is called Hilda."

"But they can't all be as pretty as you."

"Now that *does* make me laugh. I don't suppose you've ever been there."

"Where?"

"Southend."

"I have, actually. I felt the need for fresh air."

"Did you find any?"

"No. It just smelled of seafood and candy-floss."

"That's it. That's *it*."

"Yet I enjoyed it. I liked the gloom."

"That's where I *come* from." Then she did laugh. Harry thought that it was a delightful laugh, an innocent laugh. "What's your name and rank?"

"Harry Hanway. First-class."

"Where are you from, Harry Hanway?"

"If you seek my monument, look around you."

"A local yokel?"

"That's me."

So Harry and Hilda became friends long before they were ever lovers. Hilda worked in the "typing pool" of a City bank, from which she emerged every evening with stories about her colleagues. She seemed to be in a continual state of amusement at the absurdities of the world, and often began her sentences with "You'll never guess" or "Don't laugh, but . . ." Harry did laugh. He began to write a short weekly column in the *Bugle*, entitled "Don't Laugh, But . . . ," in which he retold some of Hilda's anecdotes.

"I'm a bit of an orphan, actually," she had told him. "I was found. On a doctor's doorstep in Tilbury. Where the docks are."

"Was your father a sailor?"

"I don't know. That's the *point*. Anyway I was called after a nurse in the hospital. That was before I was taken on."

"Who by?"

"Mum and Dad. Well, *honorary* Mum and Dad. That's why I ended up in Southend, you see. They had an ice-cream van on the front by the pier."

"One of those ones with a chime? A tinkle?"

"'Singing in the Rain.' Mum used to serve ices like Chocolate Melody and Vanilla Creamsicle." She laughed. "The van was the colour of strawberries." She suddenly had a memory of the strawberry van against the blue sea, its melody sometimes drowned by the sound of the waves. "My favourite was Raspberry Wriggle."

She lived now in a hostel for single young women, with a strict rule against male visitors. Harry could hardly have brought her to his little room in the Stanton household, with the crucifix above the bed. So they existed on the fringes of lovemaking. They met in the park. They retreated to the back rows of the local cinemas. They were passionate but furtive. What others might have found embarrassing, they considered to be amusing. It was part of the comedy of life.

Whenever she saw love stories on the screen, Hilda wept. "I can't *help* myself," she said. "It's daft, I grant you that, but there it is. But let's face it. I'm a *girl*. And Robert Mitchum is so handsome. He looks like you." Harry remained dry-eyed, and slightly bored, through the films that Hilda enjoyed.

One late afternoon he had spread the pages of the *Morning Chronicle* over the grass in the neighbourhood park, so that they might be protected from the damp ground. At the beginning of spring they both enjoyed this part of Camden. Harry was just about to roll on his back when he glimpsed an item in the newspaper. It announced a competition, sponsored by the *Morning Chronicle* itself, for young writers. The challenge was to complete a profile of a neighbourhood personality. "Now this is interesting," he remarked to Hilda. "This is just the ticket."

And then he thought of the Blitz boy, the arsonist whom he had forestalled in the church of Our Lady of Sorrows. He was a fine subject for a pen portrait, connecting the carnage and mayhem of 1944 with his own obsession. The arsonist wanted to live in flame. And, in London, there would always be a time when fire broke out.

Mr. Peabody recalled the case very well. Harry himself had wanted to attend the trial, but the man had pleaded guilty to all charges and had thus dispensed with jury and witnesses. He had also confessed to two other offences of arson, connected with a garage and a gentlemen's lavatory. He had been sentenced to three years and despatched to Wormwood Scrubs, where he would be subject to regular medical reports. Mr. Peabody consulted the registers and uncovered the name of Simon Sim.

Harry applied for permission to interview Sim, and the prison authorities obliged. He then wrote to Sim, introducing himself once again, and to his surprise received a friendly response. So, on an early summer morning, he arrived at Wormwood Scrubs. The name itself was sinister. What could be worse than a wood full of worms? It had been designed to resemble a fortress, with a wooden gateway between two great towers. Harry's pace slowed, and he approached the entrance with some hesitation. He had the curious sensation that, once he entered, he would never get out again. He went up to the prison officer on duty, and explained his presence. Doors were opened, and gates were unlocked. He was led into "C" wing, and taken to a small room containing nothing more than a table and three chairs. One chair was at each end of the table, and the third was by the door. The air of the prison smelled of wet paint and stale potatoes mingled.

Simon Sim was accompanied by a warder, who sat by the door. "Wonderful to see you again," Sim said. "I haven't been well. But I wanted to talk to you. I know that I know you. Isn't that peculiar?" Harry did not understand what he meant. "This is a fine place to have a fever, actually." He looked appreciatively at the grey walls and the barred window. "It calms you down. Helps you to think."

"Are you feeling better?"

"Over the worst. Just the occasional shake or two." He fixed his stare upon Harry with the same plaintive force as before, when they had struggled in the church. "May I enquire, I mean, why do you want to see me?"

"I wanted to ask you about the Blitz."

"Oh that's an enormous subject. Vast."

"What was it like?"

"What was it *like*? Golly, that's a hard question." His laughter turned into a cough. "This is what it was like. The glass was raining down. It was raining glass. If you looked up, you would have been blinded. But that was not the worst thing." His voice was curiously melodious. "I'm glad that you caught me. It would just have gone on."

"How old were you when you began?"

"Eleven. Twelve. A ripe old age. Terrific noise sometimes. We were out one night, after the sirens had sounded, when the bombs came down on the high street. I saw one girl. Her face was smashed where pebbles had lodged in her cheeks. One man was running down the slope of Hannaford Street, making for the shelter, when a falling bomb got him. I saw his head rolling along like a football." He paused for a moment. "We were as keen as mustard." Sim then told him of the bombing of a jam factory, where the dead were found covered in marmalade. He told him of a girl whose back was blown off, so that her kidneys were exposed; she had continued talking as she was taken away. There were other stories that he related with a peaceful and sometimes even blissful expression. Harry wrote down all of them. "I told you," Sim said, "that I knew you. As soon as you wrote to me, I remembered. Your name is Hanway." Harry nodded. "I knew your parents. I knew your mother. Lovely lady." Harry looked at him in alarm. "After the War I worked in the grocer's on Sutcliffe Street. Do you remember it?"

"It's still there," Harry said.

"She used to buy bacon for you. Sometimes one of you boys came with her. She was always cheerful. And now you're here. Isn't it curious how things come about? But then, dear me, you found me. I never found you. Isn't it astonishing?"

"I wanted to ask you," Harry said, hesitantly, "about the fires." He glanced at the warder who was clenching and unclenching his hands.

"About my fires? Goodness me, I don't know. I don't enquire into my reasons. I don't like to pry, you see."

"Do you think there is some connection with the Blitz?"

"I wouldn't speculate on that. It might just be an amazing coincidence. Coincidences do happen. Your mother bought bacon from me. There's one. And a fine one. Where is she now, by the way? Your mother?"

"She's dead," Harry replied.

"Is she? We used to talk about the terrible shortage of matches. And of flypaper, actually. There wasn't much of it around. And, goodness me, there were plenty of flies."

So Harry wrote his profile of Simon Sim. He described his fever; he described his calm and melodious voice. He read it out to Hilda on one Sunday afternoon. They had decided to walk along the river at Chelsea. They liked to look into the windows of the houses there, and imagine occupying those large and opulent rooms. "Do you think we ever shall?" she asked him.

"Oh yes. I should hope so." And then he added, after a pause, "I intend it. And I will do it."

They sat down on a bench overlooking the Thames, and Harry took the article out of the pocket of his jacket. Hilda listened intently. When he had finished she put her arms around his neck and kissed his cheek. Someone was walking past them. When they had finished their embrace, Harry looked up. He seemed to recognise the figure. He was taking long strides, and his head was bowed. It was Sam. Harry was sure of it. He called out to him. But Sam—if indeed it was Sam—quickened his pace. Then he began to run. He did not look back.

Harry was unsettled by the unexpected sighting of his younger brother. He had not visited his father. He had not heard from his father. Now he believed that Sam had avoided him out of anger, or disappointment, at his sudden departure. Still, Harry was of sanguine temperament. He rarely thought of his family. He put the matter out of his mind.

After he had sent the profile of Simon Sim to the *Morning Chronicle*, he endured some weeks of suspense. He had told no one, at the *Bugle*, of his intentions. Tony, however, sensed something in the air. "You're nervous, Harry," he said, barely restraining a smile. "Anything up?"

"Nothing at all."

"Just thought I'd ask." Then Tony noticed that he read the *Morning Chronicle* every morning with unusual attention. "Are you thinking of leaving us, Harry?" he asked as soon as he saw that George had entered the room.

"Of course not."

"As long as you're sure."

"Well. I am sure. Thank you for asking, Tony."

Then on a Saturday morning, three weeks later, the *Morning Chronicle* printed his profile of Simon Sim. Harry had won the competition. He looked at his name in ten-point type. He could not bear to stand in the street, but walked into a café and ordered a cup of tea. He was nervous, and his hand shook as he held the cup. He thought that he had seen his future. He had tasted ambition. He received a letter the following week, asking him to collect the £25 cheque in person at the offices of the *Chronicle*. This was his opportunity.

He decided that he would not take Hilda with him. She would laugh, or out of nervousness say something absurd. Harry knew that, to attain his goal of acquiring a job as a reporter on the *Chronicle*, he would need to remain calm and attentive. He would need to convey an air of seriousness and professionalism. Of course they all knew at the *Bugle*. George

Bradwell had shaken his hand, and expressed the wish that he would remain with them. Aldous had looked grave, and nodded. Tony had never mentioned the subject, and avoided Harry's eye. Maureen had embraced him, and congratulated him, while her two young men stood up and clapped. The new messenger boy, Percy, had pretended to blow a trumpet. "That's the bugle," he said, "of the *Bugle*." Percy was a cheerful boy.

In the following week Harry took the 48 bus to Fleet Street. He had passed through it before, but he had never stopped here. He had never been here in earnest. Now he was struck by the pace, and the intensity, of this narrow valley between tall buildings. He found the offices of the *Morning Chronicle* easily enough; they were based in what seemed to be a new building of plate glass and Portland stone. In the lobby there was a constant stream of people coming in or going out. Harry announced himself to a woman standing behind a large desk and was directed to the office of the deputy editor on the fifth floor. Harry could sense the beating of his heart as he entered the lift. He felt faint. He made his way along a corridor. He glimpsed a large room where several middle-aged men were sitting hunched over their typewriters. Telephones were ringing. A small man in a brown suit was standing by the open door, his hands on his hips. "Where," Harry asked him, "can I find the deputy editor?"

"You have found him." His glance was very sharp. "And who are you?"

"Hanway, sir. Harry Hanway. I won the competition."

"Oh did you?" He was very carefully dressed, with a white handkerchief discreetly visible in the upper pocket of his jacket. His tie was tightly knotted, his cuffs crisp. He was short but he seemed to Harry to be plumped up and perky; he looked like a pigeon about to mate. "Well, young man, I have a cheque somewhere about me." He was scrutinising him very carefully. "Where do you work?"

"At the *Camden Bugle.*"

"No! And how's George?"

"Sir?"

"I started on the *Bugle*! With George."

So the connection was made. The deputy editor, John Askew, was immediately impressed by this coincidence. What a tight little world, and a tight little city, this was! He asked Harry if he carried a union card. Harry did. George Bradwell had arranged the matter as soon as Harry had joined the staff of the *Bugle*. "What a chance this is," Askew said, almost to himself. "It is too good." He went into his office and telephoned Bradwell. Bradwell was of course reluctant to part with Harry, but he gladly acknowledged his skills as a reporter. He wanted Harry to succeed where he had failed.

"Arranged, arranged," Askew said as he joined Harry in the corridor. "Just a word with the editor." He came back, twenty minutes later, singing "Oh I do like to be beside the seaside." "You are in," he said, almost casually. "Now where's that cheque?"

So in the spring of 1965, at the age of eighteen, Harry Hanway became a reporter for the *Morning Chronicle.*

III

My life begins

*A*T REGINA *gravi iamdudum saucia cura.*" In his small bedroom, Daniel Hanway was reading the opening of the
fourth book of the *Aeneid* to himself. He repeated the words
out loud, savouring the rhythm of the Virgilian dactylic hexameter. Dactylic hexameter. He was pleased that he knew the
phrase. No one else in the street would know it. He assimi-
lated his school books easily and readily. He was a natural
scholar, and translated Latin with such rapidity that his companions looked at him with suspicion.

Daniel preferred to stay in his room, despite the emptiness
of the house. He did not enjoy the emptiness, and preferred
the clutter of his books and papers. He kept the curtains
closed. He did not like the view of the shabby street, in rain
or in sunshine. In sunshine it seemed angular and obdurate,
unyielding; it smelled of hot dust and dirt. In rain it seemed
mournful and desolate, absorbent, encompassing. When he
walked down this street, and the other streets of the council
estate, he felt contempt and betrayal.

He kept a diary in which he disclosed the feelings he could
not otherwise have expressed. "Today I walked five miles. The
further away I got from this place the happier I became. I
could actually *smile.* I don't belong here. Which is a pretty

obvious thing to say. But sometimes I feel like screaming it out loud. I don't want to be a part of Crystal Street or Camden Town. I *hate* it when someone comes up to me in the street. I am a prisoner of war, planning for my escape. The people here are so *common*. None of them have any manners. God, they *sicken* me with their boring opinions. What's the point of them? Well, I hope I can rise above it all."

He had been given by his father, last Christmas, a gramophone. He had bought a long-playing recording of Beethoven's Ninth Symphony. He played it loudly and, with both arms outstretched, he would conduct the Berlin Philharmonic Orchestra. He twirled around; he jumped up and down; he leapt onto the bed, and conducted from there. He had an image of himself surrounded by triumphant sound, yet somehow the sound seemed to issue from him. He was always at the centre. In his fantasies and ambitions he was always striving ever higher. He sensed something within himself that would not let him rest.

So at school he was quick, nervous, eager. He never stayed still. One teacher compared him to a sparrow that darts its glance in every direction. Sparrow became his nickname. He was now spare and lean. At a younger age he had been slightly plump. He used to slap his cheeks to see if he could diminish them. As soon as he entered the grammar school, however, he grew thin with tension and concentration.

He had two especial friends by the time he had reached the sixth form. Richardson was a boy of quiet and humorous cynicism. He could impersonate everyone, and took great delight in doing so. Palmer was strict, methodical and reticent. They were both attracted by Daniel's wild energy. They never discussed girls. They discussed ideas. "It's all so Kafka-esque," Daniel might say. Or "hell is other people, according to Jean-Paul Sartre." He described the school itself as "Orwellian."

He had an hysterical laugh. A word would set him off. One

day, in a history lesson, the teacher spoke of "some old cobblers" reading Tom Paine's *Rights of Man*. Daniel looked at Richardson, and Richardson looked at Daniel. Richardson snorted, and Daniel was obliged to stuff a dirty handkerchief in his mouth.

Palmer looked at them severely. "You behave," he said afterwards, "like a couple of schoolgirls." This set them off again choking with laughter.

When they rode home on the bus Daniel had the habit of getting off three stops before his neighbourhood. He did not want the others to know where he lived. In his early days at the school he had lied about everything. "My dad," he said, "has a Buick." He pronounced the name of the car as "Brick." Or he might say, "My dad was one of the Dambusters." One of his first assignments in the geography class had been to draw a scale-plan of his house. He exaggerated the size and the number of rooms, so that the small council house in Camden was transformed into a large suburban villa.

He had other secrets. He never mentioned to his friends the fact that he was attracted to boys rather than to girls. They would not have welcomed the information. They would not have known how to respond to it.

He saw Harry, one Saturday afternoon, walking slowly along Camden High Street. He was arm in arm with a young woman, who was laughing at something he had said.

"Oh there you are," Harry said airily, as if they had parted company an hour or so before. "Have you finished school yet?"

"Another year." He detected a slight note of sarcasm in his brother's voice. "Are you still at the *Bugle*?"

"No fear. I'm going up in the world. I'm on the *Chronicle* now." Daniel tried not to show that he was impressed by this news. "In Fleet Street."

It was only now that Harry introduced Hilda to his younger brother. She put her head to one side and remarked, "You *look* like each other. Oh Hilda. What a very silly thing to say. Anyway, you do." She had noticed something else. She had noticed some communion between them. It was not of character, or of temperament. It was something harder and deeper, something almost impersonal.

"And what about you?" Harry asked him.

"What about me?"

"What are you going to do?"

"I sit my exams. And then I intend to go to Cambridge."

Hilda recalled how Harry had used the same phrase, "I intend to," with the same directness. "That will be nice," she said.

"Rewarding," Daniel replied.

"How's Dad?" Harry asked him.

Two evenings before, when Daniel was lying on his bed reading, he had heard his father opening the front door. He must have returned from another long journey. He always entered the house quietly, not letting the door slam. Daniel resumed his reading. Then he heard a crash, and a yell. He got up from his bed, and walked slowly down the stairs to find his father standing in the living room with an old cloth armchair upturned on the floral-patterned carpet. There was a smell of dust in the air. "It just fell over," Philip said. "I never touched it."

At that moment Sam came into the house; without greeting them he went straight to his room.

"A leg must have been loose." Daniel settled the armchair upright.

Philip promptly sat down in it, and asked his son to pour him a whisky. "How does Sam seem to you, Danny?"

He hated being called Danny. Danny was the young child on the council estate. His name was Daniel. "I don't know how Sam seems, Father. I know not 'seems.'"

"What?"

"Hamlet. Shakespeare."

Philip was immediately impatient with his son. He had come to the conclusion that Daniel was prim and affected. He did not understand how this had happened. Once he had been so likeable and cheerful. Perhaps he also realised that his son now disliked him. Or, rather, that Daniel felt disdain for him.

In truth Daniel blamed his father for life in a shabby house in a shabby street. He resented the lack of ambition that had consigned the family to this council estate. He disliked Philip's weary look, and detested his air of defeat and resignation.

"I suppose," Philip said, after a pause, "that you are doing well at school."

"I think so."

"Whatever you do, Danny, you must . . ." He trailed off.

"What did you want to tell me, Father?" There was some malice in his voice, which he did not believe he had intended.

"You have brains. You are quick. Don't let it go to your head."

"My head is fine. So are my brains."

"Don't be clever."

"That's exactly what I intend to be."

They were not looking at one another; they were staring into infinite space.

Philip began again. "So you want to go to university?"

"To Cambridge."

"That's a big step."

Daniel seemed to consider this truism for a moment. He disliked his father's faint cockney accent, especially since he had gone to some trouble in removing all traces of his own.

He had managed to hypnotise himself. He had drawn a large black dot on the ceiling of his narrow bedroom, and stared at it with concentration until he felt his ordinary awareness slip away. Then he repeated certain words out loud—cornflake, lunar, rain—without any London intonation. Much to his surprise, the method worked. "It *is* a big step," he said. "That's why I'm making it."

"Are you ready for it?"

"Ready?"

"There will be people there with a lot of money. There will be a few snobs, too."

"So?" How dare his father assume that he would be the victim of snobbery?

"There won't be many of you."

"Many what?"

"Working-class boys."

Daniel was too angry to speak for a moment. "I don't think these divisions mean anything."

"Wait and see." It occurred to Daniel that his father was jealous of his success. He had no knowledge of Philip Hanway's early ambitions, but he sensed his father's envy. "I'm only a lorry driver, Danny. I never expected to be a lorry driver. I don't want to be a lorry driver. So I don't amount to much." Daniel did not reply. "When I was your age I had ambitions. I know. The same old story. But you get beaten down. You get distracted. You get betrayed. That's when some people become sick. That's when some people die."

"The horror of life." Daniel had recently come across the phrase.

"Is it? That says it. The horror of life."

Daniel knew that he ought to feel pity for his father, but instead he was still filled with anger and resentment. "Why did Mother disappear?"

"She ran away with another man. That's all I know."

"Did you try and find her?"

"What was the point? She didn't want us."

"You could have tried."

"When you drive long distances, you can dream. Dream of the past. Dream of what might have been. I spend my time dreaming." Daniel noticed that his father had changed the subject, but he did not interrupt him. "My life is over. I know that. That's why I worry about Sam. I wouldn't want to see him—" Philip put his hand up to his face, and started to weep. Daniel was horrified by this display of feeling. He should, perhaps, have gone over to his father and tried to comfort him. Instead he sat solemnly in his chair, staring at him but not daring to speak. "That wasn't meant to happen," Philip said after a few seconds.

"No," Daniel replied. "I don't suppose it was. I still have some homework to finish." He rose and left the room.

"How's Dad?" Harry repeated the question.

"He is—he is—fine. As far as I know."

Daniel replied to his brother's question in as easy and non-chalant a manner as he could muster. He wondered whether he should mention their father's explanation for their mother's disappearance. He looked up at Harry, and Harry's eyes told him to stay quiet. He thought that he had seen, within them, the image of a woman with her finger to her lips.

"Got a girl yet, Dan?"

"He's only a child," Hilda replied for him. "Fancy asking that."

Daniel resented being called a child. "I do have a friend," he said. "She works in a flower shop near my school."

Harry knew, from the way that Daniel put his hand up to his neck, that he was lying.

"Let's have a walk in the park," Hilda suggested. "It's ever such a nice day." Daniel winced.

He joined them reluctantly. He did not care to be seen in their company. He started walking a few paces behind Harry when Hilda noticed another similarity between the two brothers. Their pace was equal. Their posture was alike. The direction they were taking, without appearing to notice one another, was identical. They were advancing towards the same destination without being aware of the fact. They stopped beside a fountain and small pool. A short distance away was a stone folly, wooden benches set up inside, its roof ornamented with stone doves and weeping angels. It was a secluded spot from which to sit and stare at the rising and falling water.

"I used to come here," Harry said, "when I had finished at the *Bugle*. It was quiet, in the evening. I used to watch the ducks getting ready to sleep."

"I used to come here," Daniel said, "on a Sunday afternoon. It was so cheerful and peaceful then. I used to watch the children feeding the ducks."

"I used to lose track of time."

"I used to fall asleep."

The sparkling of the sun on the water of the fountain cast a strange light over them, and they seemed to Hilda to have grown taller. Harry put his arm around her shoulder. "Cup of tea?"

There was a café in the park, the haunt of solitary people, pensioners and pigeons. The mild light of early spring shone upon the paper cups and plates. "It all comes down to this, Dan," Harry was saying. "You've got to take your chances where you find them. No one gives you help in this world." He seemed to have forgotten George Bradwell. "Every man for himself."

Hilda burst out laughing. "Oh look. Isn't it funny?" She was watching as a terrier chased a squirrel across the grass. The squirrel then scampered up a tree, leaving the dog staring upwards and barking furiously. "They never catch them, do they?" she said. The little dog was trembling with purpose and desire, his body shaking with fierce energy. The squirrel, clasping the bark, remained quite still. He gazed down at his pursuer, while the dog directed his bright and eager glance upwards. Their eyes met, and darkness called to darkness.

"As I was saying, Dan, life is a struggle. A battle."

"I don't want to fight."

"Then you'll do nothing. You'll go down." He jerked his thumb towards the ground.

"I won't go down. But I don't have to fight."

"You two." Hilda was laughing again. "You would think there was a war on."

Harry felt contempt for Daniel's passivity, but he took care not to show it. Nevertheless Daniel felt it. The little dog was still barking. "I saw Sam recently," Harry said.

"Where?"

"He was walking along the Embankment. Chelsea. He didn't seem to notice me."

"He doesn't see anything. Not really. He sees what he wants to see. What he intends to see. Sometimes he stares and stares into space. But he's happy enough, I think. He sees something I don't see."

"Nutter?"

At that moment Sam cried out in his sleep. He was still in his bed, having walked through London for most of the night.

"I don't know," Daniel replied. "I hope not."

"Does he have a job?"

"Dad—Father—gives him money. I don't think he wants to work."

Daniel walked home sensing that he had made a bad impression on his brother. Harry had looked at him strangely when he had said that he had no wish to fight. But it was the truth.

He disliked confrontation of any kind, and could not bear disagreements or disputes.

"I hate sports," he wrote in his diary. "I hate team games. Wednesday afternoon is my black afternoon. Everything about it repels me. Packing up the kit. Walking to the playing fields. Undressing in the changing room. It is all so *undignified*. And unnecessary. What is the point of running around in the mud with a ball on a winter's day? Everything is cold and wet and dismal. Cricket is worse. I went to the public library to find out the rules, and I still don't know them. I hate that hard little ball coming anywhere near me. I always duck it. That's why no one ever chooses me. I'm always the last one standing. It's embarrassing. Anyway I can't stand the team spirit. Savages in a pack. I don't know how they can get so worked up over *nothing*. And the communal bathing is misery. It is all so grotesque."

He had a horror of being late for the first class of the morning, and was often the first to arrive in the schoolyard. This schoolyard sloped down towards a wooden fence that separated it from the road. That road had once been a river, and the sloping yard a grassy bank. There had been a river here for hundreds of thousands of years, a remnant of the vast ocean that had once covered the site. Where Daniel stood and dreamed, there had swum the plesiosaur and the coelacanth. But the ocean had gone, leaving behind the river. This river created fertile ground. To its banks came hippopotami and elephants the size of small dogs. Some early settlers had encamped just where Daniel was standing. There had been a fight here. A man had been struck in the face with a rock, and had died. He had fallen at Daniel's feet.

Battles had also been fought in this favoured region of the river. And Daniel watched as slowly the yard was filled with the noise and dispute of schoolchildren. Something glinted at his feet. He stooped down to pick it up, when suddenly he felt an overwhelming desire to throw himself upon the ground; he steadied himself, by putting his hands on the tarmac, and remained crouched for several seconds. The sound of winds and waters was in his head. Then it passed. "Ready, steady, go," someone shouted at him. He had looked as if he were about to start a race.

He worked hard, throughout the last autumn and winter of his school years, preparing for his final examinations. "Exams are three days away," he wrote. "I must not panic. I must revise everything one more time. I hope it's Cicero or someone else easy. I hope it's not Tacitus or Ovid. Now I feel sick. I don't suppose I'll get an hour's sleep between now and exam day. I must concentrate. I have to be steady. Otherwise I will become like that tramp."

He had seen the tramp a week before. "I saw a beggar by the road today. I didn't feel pity. I felt fear. Fear that I could become like him. One little slip and I could go down. It's all so hopeless. I don't think anyone understands me. Hell is other people."

Yet his fears were unwarranted. He received high grades in his examinations and at once, through the agency of his school, he applied to both Oxford and Cambridge.

He had visited Cambridge in a day of gentle sunlight and shadow, iridescent in the watery atmosphere of the neighbourhood. He had gone up in the train with his schoolfriend, Palmer, who had also applied. His memory, ever afterwards, was of undergraduates sitting and laughing by the side of water, of empty courtyards, of great establishments of enduring stone, all unimaginable and unattainable. "It is very civilised," Palmer said as they travelled back. "I can see us there." Daniel, who thought nothing of Palmer's chances, merely nodded. As he returned to London he felt mournful, as if he were leaving all his hopes behind.

"What college did you like most?" Palmer asked him.

"I don't know—I don't want to think about it. Not yet."

"I liked Clare. I liked the little bridge and the gardens."

"There's more to life than gardens."

Philip Hanway insisted on driving him to Cambridge, on the day before the beginning of the university term. This horrified Daniel, who had a vision of arriving at his new college in his father's lorry. He tried to persuade him that he was perfectly happy to travel by train, alone; but, no, his father insisted that he would hire a car for the day. He wanted to make sure that Daniel was "settled in."

"Do you think," he asked Daniel as they drove together along the A11, "do you think that you will ever write?"

"Write?"

"Novels. Plays."

"I don't know. I don't think so."

"Oh."

"Why do you ask?"

"No reason. Curious."

There was something happening on the right-hand side of the road. Daniel thought he could see people running—running at the speed of the Morris Minor in which he and his father were driving—running figures even then overtaking them. And then they vanished into the distance. It had been a trick of the light reflected in the window.

"And now," he said to himself, "my life begins."

IV

Are you hungry?

S AM HANWAY had not prospered at school. He had made
no friends. He did not antagonise anyone; he simply preferred his own company. He was absorbed in some private
world, of rage and affection, which did not encircle other
people. He did not excel in his studies; he was wayward and
inconsistent. He would approach a subject with interest and
great excitement for a week or two, and then would lose concentration.

Outside school he wandered around the estate, picking
up a stone or examining a brick; he would study them with
wonder and concentration, absorbing them within his being,
before discarding them. He was a large boy, with a round face
and powerful limbs; he had grey eyes and wore spectacles.
When he took off his spectacles, his face seemed to flinch; he
had the slightly blank look of someone running through mist.

"When I leave here," he told one of his teachers, "I want to
go to a circus school. I want to learn how to do tricks with
animals. Zebras, most likely." This was not considered to be
very practical and, as soon as he reached school-leaving age,
he enrolled at the labour exchange.

Sam found work in the local supermarket. Here he was
employed to stack goods upon the shelves, and to pack the

shopping bags of customers. He had to look tidy, and to act smartly. With uncharacteristic energy, on the first day, he rose early and washed himself in the bathroom sink; he put on a shirt and tie, and took from his wardrobe the cheap grey suit that his father had purchased for him. It did not fit him well, and under a leaden sky he hastened to the supermarket on this first morning.

He took off the jacket and put on a striped apron and white hat. The changing room was beside the ventilation system for the dairy counter. It smelled faintly of cheese or curdled milk, a disquieting and even depressing smell. "Sam? Is that your name?" He nodded. He was being addressed by a young woman with pale prominent eyes; her flaxen hair was tied back, and Sam tried not to notice the pimples on her face. She looked vulnerable, as if a layer of skin had been stripped from her. "I've got to get you started," she said. He felt uncomfortable in the presence of females, and had not mastered the art of talking to them. "There's nothing to it, really." She put out her hand, as if it belonged to someone else, and placed it limply in his. "This is cheese. This is milk. This is butter." He could see what they were. "You don't have much to say for yourself, do you? Well. Keep smiling. It won't be as bad as all that."

He learned how to unpack the goods, and arrange them on the shelves. He sized and sorted the various bottles, tins, packets and boxes; he carried in the fruit and vegetables; he replaced the cheese, the milk and the butter. The girl with the flaxen hair sometimes watched him. "Worse things happen at sea," she said.

His ordeal started when he was asked to stand by the till and pack the bags of the customers. Each face became a terror. He was being judged. When he was slow, or clumsy, he blushed. He realised that people were cruel because they were unhappy. He thought he saw lines of suffering humanity, shuffling towards him with their wire baskets or trolleys. He detested the children looking up at him with blank incurious eyes. If somebody complained, he insisted on explaining himself. He would look at them quietly and attentively before answering them in a low voice. He outlined in detail the proper way of filling a shopping bag, with bulky dry goods at the bottom and perishable goods at the top. So the days passed, one like another. It was as if he were living in a cave. If nothing mattered, then he could exist like this.

He did not eat in the canteen. He disliked the smell of beef and custard and tomato sauce. He bought a chocolate bar, instead, and sat in a bus shelter on the high street. So he remained apart from the rest of the staff. They were not malicious, but they were not particularly friendly. They would grow impatient with his long explanations. They greeted him hurriedly, and walked on. He knew all these things; but he never took offence.

One Saturday morning he was standing by the till, as usual, packing the bags. He glanced down the waiting line of customers. There was a middle-aged woman standing at the end of the queue. He looked at her a second time. She was wearing a blue cardigan and white blouse. He knew that face. It was her. It was his mother. She became aware of him in the instant that he recognised her. They gazed at each other. In his consternation he bowed over the counter and, when he looked up again, she was gone.

"What's the matter with you?" A man, harsh and impatient, was standing in front of him. "You don't know how to do this, do you?" Without any thought, Sam lashed out at him. The woman on the till moaned, with a sort of pleasure, when the man fell to the floor. There was general uproar and Sam was hauled away by the manager before being dismissed from the staff. It happened within an hour. And in that hour Sam's life changed.

He vowed that he would never work again. He had no plan of action, no goal, but the very act of working seemed to him to be a form of death. He could live off the food in the house, purchased by his father; his father had a habit of leaving his wallet on the mantelpiece, when he returned from his long hours of driving, and Sam took small sums. He did not tell anyone that he had been fired. He left the house at the same time each morning, and returned at the same time each evening. He wore the same grey suit. He wandered.

One late afternoon he was walking along one of the paths in the local park, not far from the café where Harry and Hilda and Daniel had drunk tea beneath the trees. There was a young man sitting, slumped, upon a wooden bench. His clothes were old and soiled; he looked weary, his face hollowed by exhaustion or want. He was sighing, or groaning, it was hard to say which; he was trembling, slightly, as if he were trying to ward off pain. His eyes were closed, and there was spittle at the corners of his mouth. Sam sat down quietly beside him. He stared straight ahead, frowning slightly, and from time to time he would glance at this fellow on the bench. The young man opened his eyes and stared at him. Sam said nothing, and looked ahead once more. He could have sat there indefinitely. He had no reason to move on. One place was as good as another. But a sudden thought struck him. "Are you hungry?" he asked him. The young man did not reply. "Hang on," he said. "I'll be back in a minute." After a few minutes he returned with two packets of crisps and a bottle of Tizer. The young man took them without a word. From that day forward, at the same time, Sam always brought two packets of crisps and a bottle of Tizer to the bench where the young man was waiting for him.

Now that he had lost his job, Sam also seemed to become part of a floating world. There was, for example, the matter of the stone post. It stood at the corner of Lowin Street and the high street. Its function was obscure, and Sam had no idea of its age. It was a weather-beaten piece of old stone that may have been on that spot since the building of Camden Town; it may even have stood there in an earlier period. Who could tell? Now, from across the street, Sam had the time to observe it. A young boy came up to it, placed his hands upon it, and began to beat it like a drum; he seemed to derive enormous pleasure from this. Someone called him, and he ran off. Sam continued to stand and watch. He noticed a curious fact or coincidence—most of those who passed the post put out a hand and touched it. It was an unwitting, and perhaps even an unconscious, gesture. Yet the stone post was being endlessly patted and felt.

As he continued watching the stone, it seemed to become aware of his presence. Sam was astonished when the stone rose several feet into the air; as it hovered there several ribs and pillars of stone, several arches and mouldings, began to exfoliate from it, creating an intricate shrine or shelter of stone. He thought he could hear the sound of hammering, of banging, of the labour of construction. Then it began to fade into the air. The stone post, once more a solitary presence, hovered above the ground before descending and resuming its original position. All this may have been the work of a moment. Or it may have taken many centuries.

If he had shouted aloud, he would have drawn attention to himself. He wanted to find somewhere in seclusion, somewhere he might sit and think. There was such a place. The church of Our Lady of Sorrows, the church where Harry had thwarted the arsonist, was only a few hundred yards away from this corner of the high street. Sam had passed it many times.

He bowed his head as he went into the porch, struck suddenly by the coolness of the air. The church itself was empty.

He walked down the aisle, and then hesitated. Above the altar was a cross on which hung the figure of the suffering Jesus—this was not what he had come for. But then he saw the lady, smiling, with her right hand raised in greeting or in blessing. She was dressed in blue and white. Sam crossed the aisle and walked over to the Lady Chapel.

He sat down on the narrow wooden pew and bowed his head. Then, after a long silence, he began to speak to her. "Do you mind if I talk to you? I have no friends, you see. I have no one to tell. I could have gone home, and forgotten all about it, but that would have been wrong. That would mean nothing had happened. But everything has happened." He spoke in a slow, soft voice. "But now I have been chosen. I have been chosen to experience—well, you can call it a miracle if you like. I think it was a miracle. What do you think?" He looked up at her, wondering, enquiring, reflecting. She regarded him with pity, and put her finger to her lips.

He sat in silence once more. He felt secure here, as safe as if he were in his own room at home—no, safer, because he was under the protection of the lady. He was suffused with warmth, although he could not tell whether it came from within or without. Who was that standing a short distance away? An old nun had come up to the altar with lilies in her hands; she crossed herself before the statue, and then changed the flowers in the silver vases to either side of it. She had noticed Sam but she seemed to pay him no attention. She crossed herself again, and left the chapel as quietly as she had entered it.

After she had gone Sam looked up again at the lady. "She has offered you something," he said. "I have nothing to give you. Do you need anything from me?" She did not reply. "Probably not. But I promise you this. When I see a person in trouble, I will try to help." He thought of the young vagrant on the park bench. "That will be helping you, I hope." He stayed there a little longer, until with a sigh he got up from the pew and left the church.

He came back to the chapel on the following morning. He sat in the same place, and gazed impassively at the statue of the lady. He noticed now that she had blue eyes, and that three tears ran down her right cheek. Perhaps she had wept last night. He wondered what had caused this. Did she know already of the young man? "Don't worry," he said. "Everything will be all right."

He came each day, and soon realised that three or four different nuns in turn changed the flowers and the altar cloth. He knew them all by sight, but they had not broken their silence. Then one of them surprised him. It was the oldest of them, the one he had seen on his first visit to the chapel. She was about to withdraw, having completed her ministrations, when she turned and walked over to him. It seemed to be a sudden decision.

"Are you troubled, son?"

"No. I'm happy. I think I'm happy."

"You pray to Our Lady?"

"I speak to her."

"Do you?"

"On the first day she put her finger to her lips."

She made the sign of the cross, and walked away.

The nuns began to pay more attention to Sam. They smiled at him as they dusted the altar and polished the rails; they would walk down the aisle and nod as they passed him. One of them left a missal in his accustomed seat and then, a week later, he found a rosary there. He did not know what to do with it. He put it in the pocket of his trousers, and would sometimes slide his fingers through the hard wooden beads.

He washed his clothes in the kitchen sink at home, and dried them in the garden, but of course he became more shabby. There came a morning when one of the nuns approached him. "Do you know anything about gardening?" she asked him. He shook his head. "Well, you can learn. You're strong, aren't you?"

"Yes."

"We need a handyman. Mother Placentia thought of you."

Of Mother Placentia, he knew nothing. He had vowed never to work again, but he was drawn to the company of these women. "I can do that," he said.

"Good. Come into the sacristy."

He had not known that there was a convent attached to the church of Our Lady of Sorrows. This small establishment lay behind the church, surrounded by a high red-brick wall. If you had asked any of the local residents about the nuns, they would not have known how to answer. No one knew when, or from where, they had come. They had always seemed to be part of the neighbourhood. But they were rarely seen. They stayed behind the high walls.

Sam entered through the gate of the convent in the company of Sister Eugenia, the nun who had come up to him in the church. They crossed a courtyard, with the basin of a dried fountain in the middle where fallen leaves rustled in the dust. There was a sundial in the corner of the lawn, its gnomon broken. A bird was perched on the stone rim of the basin of the fountain, singing its eternal song; yet it seemed to Sam that it sang more slowly than any bird he had ever heard.

Sister Eugenia led him down a corridor, on the walls of which were hanging woodcuts and engravings of sacred scenes. The sister approached a door at the end of the corridor, and knocked upon it gently. "Who is knocking?" asked someone within.

"Eugenia, Mother."

"Enter in God's name, Eugenia."

She opened the door, and asked Sam to go in before her. "It is the young man," she said.

"Is it you? You are younger than I expected." Mother Placentia was a small, plump woman with an expression of brutal amiability; her head was shaken by a slight but continual tremor. On the wall above her was a portrait of the Virgin, hands clasped in prayer or pity, her outline traced in blue and gold. "How old are you?"

"Seventeen."

"So you are the young man who sees visions in the heart of London." He said nothing but continued to look steadily at her. "You are as still as a lamb. That is good. Do you know the saying, 'rise up west wind and refresh my garden'?" He shook his head. "You must be our wind. You must refresh our garden. Can you do that?"

"I hope so."

"What is your name, young man?"

"Sam. Sam Hanway."

"Hanway?" She seemed momentarily distracted. "A good name. An old name."

"We may be old without being good," he said.

She burst into laughter which ended with a fit of coughing. "The Lord has given you wit," she said.

The garden smelled sweetly of several herbs, but there was little for Sam to do. One of the nuns, Sister Idonea, tended the sage and the thyme and the rue. He was there to remove the weeds, water the lawns and beds, and burn the dead leaves of autumn. He also performed the tasks that the nuns could not; he built shelves, he painted doors and fences, he restored the stone paths that crossed the courtyard. Yet it seemed that the nuns simply wanted him to be part of their community; he had been given a sign by the Virgin, and they wanted to see what might happen to him.

He came to know the sisters very well. Mother Placentia

ruled over them with the same forceful amiability she had displayed to him. She was massively calm, she was dispassionate, she was obdurate. Sister Delecta and Sister Prudentia, for example, had been involved in an argument over the number of wax candles needed for the vigil of the Assumption of Our Lady. Their quarrel had been loud, and had reached the ears of Sister Idonea. She had stopped shelling peas and listened to them with great eagerness, registering the use of such words as "pitiful" and "ridiculous." She repeated the conversation, with some exaggeration, to Sister Clarice who was known to be a particular favourite of Mother. The abbess called in the two offending sisters. As soon as they had entered her office she rose up from her chair and slapped them both on the right cheek.

Sister Idonea was listening at the door, and later gave an exultant report to anyone who cared to listen. "*Ave genetrix*," Mother Placentia had said. "You give birth to quarrels and dissensions, do you? You fight like sows in a sty?"

"No, *madame*," Sister Delecta replied. She was the youngest, and supposedly the demurest, of the nuns. "We had a difference of opinion."

"There will be no differences in this place. All are one. On your knees."

They fell to their knees as Mother Placentia, standing before the portrait of the Virgin, began to pray in a loud voice. "Hail Mary, full of grace, the Lord is with thee. Blessed art thou among women." The two nuns joined in the prayer, murmuring in low voices. When it was complete she turned to them. "Leave this place on your knees and creep to the cross in the chapel. There you will prostrate yourselves for an hour, before rising and resuming your duties in a cheerful spirit." So the nuns painfully and slowly made their way towards the chapel in another part of the building. Sam had seen them. He had entered the chapel in order to mend a broken transom light, when he glimpsed them lying on the chilly tiled floor. He backed out of the door. He gathered later that there had been much recrimination between Sister Idonea and Sister Prudentia, conducted in frowns and grimaces rather than words. The whole convent had taken sides. Salt and pepper were not being passed down the table; bread was in short supply for one or two nuns; there was much coughing and clearing of throats whenever certain nuns sang the divine office.

Yet the days passed tranquilly for Sam. He would arrive at the convent early in the morning, and would begin work at once; he hardly spoke to anyone in the course of the day, and would eat whatever food Sister Idonea had left him for lunch. In the evening he visited the young man in the park; he rarely spoke to him but gave him the crisps and sweet drink, which he could afford from the small wage the convent paid him.

It came to the attention of Mother Placentia that there were what she called "poor men and women" in the vicinity of the convent; she said that they were drawn to the place as to a shelter. If she could not accommodate them, she could at least nourish them. So she instituted an afternoon meal to be distributed at the gate of the convent. Sam volunteered to hand out the bread and soup or stew. He felt at ease in the company of tramps and wanderers. He was even comforted by their presence. He was not shy, or awkward, with them. They had looked with mild curiosity at this young man among the nuns, but soon he was expected. That is what he had always wanted—acceptance. He did not want to be singled out, to be looked on with pity or condescension.

He soon learned that no one vagrant was like another. They were all in one sense touched by misery, but it manifested itself in different ways. In some of them it was not manifest at all. These were the cheerful ones who, in the extremity of failure or distress, still laughed at the absurdity of the world. One of them wore an old and heavy coat, in the pockets of which he kept a surprising variety of objects. He would pull out a trowel, or a chipped cup, with all the delight of a conjuror successfully performing a trick. One old woman, the creases of her hands and face lined with dirt, would sometimes dance in the middle of the road. She called Sam "sweetheart." Yet others remained gloomy and silent. These were the ones who most interested Sam. He tried to speak to one middle-aged man, whose head was always covered by a hood, but the man had merely sighed and walked off.

Some kept themselves apart. Where the others would form groups, or pairs, they would sit by themselves on the pavement—their backs against the convent wall—or stand alone a little way off. The reason for this solitariness was clear to Sam. He had experienced it himself. It was the fruit of pride and introspection. Pride is possible even in misery. In his own misery, Sam had not wanted anyone to come too close. So he respected those who stayed aloof. He glanced at them quickly, when he handed them the food, and then looked away.

There were those who engaged him in conversation. Some of them spoke quickly and eagerly, like children, while others spoke softly and slowly. Yet it seemed to Sam, strangely enough, that they spoke with one voice; or, rather, that one voice spoke through all of them—the way that a hundred birds seem to sing the same song. That, at least, was how he put it to himself.

"Do you think you'll be joining us?" one middle-aged man asked him. He had a bald spot on the top of his head, with long black hair cascading from its rim.

"Joining?"

"Coming along with us. When this place goes."

"It won't go."

"Oh yes it will. I see it all the time. I'm used to it."

"I don't know whether I'll go with you or not."

"I think you will."

Nothing disturbed the even tenor of the days. Sam still lived at home, but he rarely saw his father. He had not told him that he worked in the convent; it was a secret thing, belonging to a secluded part of himself. He kept the rosary on a little wooden table in his bedroom; it reminded him of his life with the nuns; it reassured him, in its plainness and simplicity. He knew now that each bead was a prayer, a prayer perfectly formed, a sphere of grace. So he would hold the rosary, grip it tightly, and close his eyes—then he saw images, images of flame and ruined walls, of sunlit fields and hills, of innumerable faces gazing upwards. He did not know what these images meant, but he was touched by them. He still sometimes visited the Lady Chapel, too, where he sat in front of the statue of the lady. "Thank you," he said one day, "for letting me stay. I feel safe here."

Yet, on a day after one of these visits, everything changed. He set off from his house early that morning, making his familiar way to the convent. But he could not find it. The gate and the walls were not there. The convent had disappeared. He ran through the streets, returning by different routes to the same place. The convent was gone. He looked for signs of the tramps and beggars who had wandered through the neighbourhood; they, too, had vanished. He asked several people if they had seen the nuns, but they looked at him curiously and shook their heads. Nuns? What nuns? He was distraught. He cried out—to what, or to whom, he did not know. Weeping, he beat his fists against a stone wall. Eventually he went back to the church. There was no chapel. There was no lady. The nave was dark. He sat down in a pew and began to beat his head against the wooden rail in front of him. That was the day when the young tramp in the park also disappeared.

V

A marmoset

H ARRY HANWAY was bent over his typewriter, smoking
as he read the page still in the machine. He was writing a story—he used the word casually and naturally now—
concerning the resignation of a middle-ranking minister from
the Wilson government. It was not the stuff of headlines, but
with careful nurturing it could grow. Harry knew that the
minister had been hastened from office as a result of his affair
with his secretary, already a married woman. So Harry chose
his words carefully, hinting rather than stating impropriety,
lending an air of ambiguity to all his phrases, making it clear
that the minister was a married man with three small children.
He enjoyed this process. It gave him power.

His career at the *Morning Chronicle* had so far been a success.
He had begun work as one of the reporters filing copy for the
gossip column, purportedly written by "Peregrine Porcupine."
Harry found himself at parties and at first nights, at society
weddings and at political conferences, on the chance that he
would see and talk to a "famous name" or would pick up
some gossip that could be repeated to the newspaper's reader-
ship. His ready charm, his affability, and his London accent
distinguished him from the mass of ex-public-school boys
who staffed other gossip columns. He looked, and sounded, as

if he could be trusted. He soon impressed his superiors with his ability to deliver "scoops" over his rivals.

It was Harry, for example, who broke the news that Joey Hanover had been lured by ATV from BBC Television with the offer of five thousand pounds for each half-hour programme. He had seen Hanover sitting alone at a table in a pub close to Portland Place, and had sat beside him. He did not look, or behave, like a journalist. He was an ordinary Londoner. So Hanover, slightly the worse for drink, had confided in him. "You and I, chum," he said, "are idiots. Sitting here and drinking in the middle of the afternoon." He stared balefully at Harry for a moment. "What do you do?"

"I work in a shop. A shoe shop. It's my day off."

"Is it now? What kind of shoes?"

"All types."

Hanover was silent for a moment. "Do you know who I am?"

"You're Joey Hanover. Everyone knows you."

"Oh do they?" Once more he lapsed into a morose silence. "What if I were to tell you that Joey Hanover is a chump? A right disaster?" Harry sensed, with growing excitement, the approach of a good story. But he took care to remain calm, and even unimpressed. "I am about to walk away from my closest mates. And for what? Lucre. Filthy lucre."

"There's nothing wrong with money."

"You're right. There is nothing wrong with money. Where would we be without it? But bang goes the old team. Whoosh." He threw up his hands. "Excuse me." He came back from the bar with what looked like a large gin and tonic. The other customers were still pretending to ignore him. "And what's it all for? Five thousand per show."

"That's a lot of money."

"Anyway, it's too late now. It's done. Hello ATV."

Eventually Harry rose from his seat, on the grounds that he had to meet his girlfriend, and made his escape. He hailed a taxi and within half an hour he was at his desk. He opened *Spotlight*, and found the telephone numbers of Hanover's manager and press agent. The story was on the front page of the first edition.

On the following morning the editor asked to see him. This was an unexpected summons, since Andrew Havers-Williams did not generally mingle with the junior staff. Harry considered him to be something of a "toff," a man of impeccable and even dandified dress; he wore silk waistcoats and silk ties; he swept his luxuriant white hair back in bouffant fashion; his enunciation was clipped and precise; his voice had the timbre of an expensive education. "Well, Hanway," he said as Harry entered his office. "Well done. Very well done. The proprietor likes this sort of thing." His tone suggested that the proprietor, Sir Martin Flaxman, was a man of comparatively simple tastes. "Personally I know nothing about this Hanover chap. Comedian, is he? Where did you find him?"

"In a pub, sir."

"A pub? I see. Well done." He had an air of forced cheerfulness, as if he were aware of a disparity between them that could only be negotiated by a show of bonhomie. "How long have you been with the paper?"

"Two years."

"Two years on Porcupine is long enough, don't you think?" Harry nodded. "I'm going to hand you over to the news desk."

That had been Harry's aim from the beginning. "I would welcome that," he said.

"Talk to James White."

James White was the news editor. He was middle-aged, tall, balding. He had been an officer during the War, and had retained the manner ever since. He owed his post solely to the fact that he had attended the same school as the editor, and he was widely disliked by the staff of the news desk. He was something of a martinet, something of a bully. "Don't just stand there," he said on the first day. "Do something. Make yourself useful. Wait. I want you to go to the Old Bailey. See if anything's happening." That was how he always addressed Harry—"I want you to . . ." He was generally stiff and condescending; he was always irritable, as if he was chafed by some inward discontent.

Yet Harry soon learned how to deal with him, as he learned how to deal with his other colleagues. They were immensely susceptible to flattery. "Good piece," he would say. "Good piece." Or he would pat someone on the back. "Terrific story. Terrific." He realised that many of them lacked self-confidence. They had wanted to be barristers, or politicians, or writers; but they had ended up as journalists. They gathered at the end of the day in the Duke of Granby, a long and narrow pub near the corner of Chancery Lane and Fleet Street. Here in an atmosphere of forced joviality they discussed the day's stories and events at the newspaper itself; they gossiped mercilessly about their contemporaries; they mocked the journalists on rival newspapers; they were sarcastic about the politicians of the day; they drank great quantities of beer or lager to keep themselves in good humour. They prided themselves on knowing the ways of the world, as a little tap on the side of the nose would signify. They were generally red-faced, with wary eyes.

Three political journalists were employed on the *Chronicle*, the most senior of them being an excessively neat and fastidious man. George Hunter was always rearranging the objects in front of him. It was said that he could not enter a room without emptying the ashtrays. He had a gentle and unemphatic voice, sometimes trailing off into silence. It was said by his colleagues that this was a ruse—that his silences were a way of extracting confidences from otherwise reticent politicians. No one likes silence in a conversation.

"Well, George," Harry might say in the Duke of Granby, "have you had a good day?"

"Yes. A good day."

"It's warm in here."

"It *is* warm in here. Yes. What are you drinking?"

"A pint of Courage. The very best."

"A pint of the very best, Suzanne."

He was a perpetual echo. This was another secret of his success. He never seemed to have any opinions of his own. He was cautious and circumspect. He spoke respectfully of Mr. Harold Wilson and Mr. Edward Heath. He alluded to various political events and arguments in a low voice, as if they were still decidedly confidential. Yet he was observant. He missed nothing.

His two younger colleagues did not share his inhibitions. They talked of politicians in terms of personal intimacy, called them "Willie" or "Jim." They professed cynicism but, as Harry noticed, they were thrilled to be addressed or recognised by these apparent worthless ministers. Yet Harry enjoyed their company. They were high-spirited and facetious, causing each other to laugh helplessly at some absurd or improbable fiasco. Nick Salmond was a good mimic; he could impersonate Wilson's flickering eyes and snake-like tongue, and Heath's convulsive shuddering laugh. They knew all the gossip, too, about the sex lives of prominent politicians. They luxuriated in speculation and innuendo. James Thorn was plump and pale; he always wore a flower in his buttonhole, and always dressed in a pinstriped suit. He had a voice, as Harry once said to Hilda, like an organ pipe. Both Salmond and Thorn were longing for George Hunter to retire, although uneasily aware of the rivalry that would then rise between them. They sat on opposite sides of the same desk in the newsroom, beating out stories on their typewriters as the deadline drew ever closer. Harry had come to realise that words were cheap, and that they could be manufactured by the yard. The journalists would write something, and then write it again. Then they repeated it as if it were a new thought, and then recapitulated it in a slightly different way. They would conclude the paragraph with the same sentiment. And so it went on.

There was no subtlety or profundity in what they wrote. Neither of them pretended that there was. They repeated the conventional wisdom—the wisdom, if that is the word, shared by the majority of other political journalists at any one time. They both wrote editorials on political matters, in which they attempted to be authoritative. They relied upon portentous cliché masquerading as strong opinion. They were stern and, in the guise of anonymity, they were self-righteous.

Harry began to understand the way in which the political world worked. It was driven by ambition, and anger, and jealousy, concealed beneath the pretence of honesty and good intention. Nick and James realised the subterfuge well enough, and their conversation was filled with gossip about the weaknesses and vices of the politicians; but they wrote only about policies and issues, helping to sustain the deceit. George Hunter seemed genuinely to believe in the virtues of public office. He was considered to be old-fashioned. Nick and James merely gave credence to the lies they saw through. Over a drink, Harry felt at ease with them. He felt that they understood the world in which he, too, wanted to play a part.

He and Hilda Nugent had, on the strength of his new income, moved to a basement flat in Notting Hill. It was a part of London that neither of them knew, and at first they had been alarmed by its air of decay and general dilapidation. The large terraced houses and stucco mansions had been divided into small flats and rooms for a population of beatniks, immigrants from the West Indies and transient workers. It was called "bed-sit land." It suited them. They were still unmarried. Harry did not want to marry. He had told Hilda that he feared the expense and responsibility of a child. She might have suspected that there were other reasons but, if she did, she hid that thought from herself. She supposed that she was content with her present life. In turn Harry did not choose to enquire about his future with her. He did not reflect upon it. He did not believe that reflection was necessary.

So, as an unmarried couple, they found a place among the transient or louche population of Notting Hill. They felt at home with the peeling stucco and the untidy balconies, the unswept basement areas and the faded paintwork. They had not chosen the area deliberately. Perhaps the area had chosen them.

Hilda had found work as the manager of a coffee shop in Bayswater, called "The Wait And See." When she had first told Harry the name she had become helpless with laughter. "Wait and see?" he asked her. "What is the hidden meaning in it?"

"There isn't one." And then she added, "Wait and see." She rearranged three small china bowls on the mantelpiece. "Haven't you got anything else to ask me?"

"Anything else? As in?"

"Well, how do I *like* it?"

"Like it?"

"Yes. Enjoy. Take pleasure in. Derive comfort from."

"How do you like it?"

"The job is just fine. Thanks for asking. There are times, Harry, when I feel that you don't care for me at all."

"That isn't true."

"Well, now I've said it."

Sometimes she described to him the events of the day. "An

old man came into the café today. He was perfectly dressed, bowler hat and all. He was tall and stout and wore a three-piece suit. 'Hello,' he says. 'I am Arthur Effles.' That's a *funny* name, isn't it? 'May I just order a cup of tea?' Then he sits down, very deferentially I thought, and lights a fag. 'You see, young lady, I am here with a purpose. I have rented a room in the neighbourhood. Just a plain, simple room. I have rented rooms in other parts of London. Then I fan out, so to speak, from street to street. At present I am on your street, which is Coppice Street. I visit every establishment—just like this one—and make myself thoroughly familiar with it.' He kept on making little bows and blowing little kisses. He had a beautiful smile, like a *patriarch*. Do you know what I mean?"

"I suppose so."

"Do you *suppose* or do you know? Oh forget it. It doesn't matter. So anyway he smiles this lovely smile. 'I talk to a person such as yourself, and I find out all about the neighbourhood. When I have walked down all the streets, and discovered all its secrets, I leave my lodging and rent somewhere else.' Then he gets up and sits by the window. For the rest of the morning he just looks into the street. I could tell from the way he sat that he loved windows."

"He sounds like a daft old bastard."

"I wouldn't describe him as *daft*. Perhaps a little bit *cracked*." She sensed that she had bored him with this story. So she said no more.

Late one afternoon, as she stood behind the counter, a young man entered the coffee shop. He lingered over the menu, asking her carefully and specifically about every item. Even as he did so it seemed to Hilda that he was troubled by some inward thought or inward distress. Without knowing anything about him, she pitied him. Eventually he ordered a ham sandwich and a cup of tea. She watched him surreptitiously as he chewed the food, and drank the tea; he was staring far away.

She presented him with the bill.

"I'm afraid I can't pay this," he told her. "I have no job. No money." He looked at her without expression.

She was so surprised that she did not know how to reply. "No money?" He shook his head. She stood there for a moment, and then impulsively went back to the counter and put three pastries into a paper bag. He took them and, without a word, left the coffee shop. She sat down at one of the tables, and burst into tears. Hilda told Harry the story that evening, omitting the detail of her tears.

He sighed, and looked away for a moment. Somehow he knew that she had encountered Sam.

She followed Harry's career with more interest than her own, questioning him about his work and colleagues. "How is the balding bully?" she asked him. She was referring to James White, the news editor.

"Getting more beastly every day. Whenever I think of him, I feel an inexpressible sensation of weariness. Or boredom. One or the other. What is the point of these people? He's so damned superior. But he has nothing to be superior about. He has a companion. A comrade in arms who has a pudgy face and smokes all the time. That's all I know about him. All I want to know."

One evening, she said to him, "I saw that man you interviewed. Cormac something."

"Cormac Webb?"

"That's it. Webb." Cormac Webb was a junior minister in the Department of Housing. He had been interviewed by Harry because he was the youngest member of the Labour government. Webb had struck him as being brash, exuberant and opportunistic—all the qualities that Harry admired. He had told Harry, off the record, that he preferred champagne to beer and that his favourite restaurant was Simpson's in the Strand. He exuded a sort of charmless bonhomie. "Where did you see him?" he asked her.

"He was going into that Ruppta's building." These offices were immediately across the street from The Wait And See. Asher Ruppta was a businessman, of ambiguous nationality, who had become the subject of hostile controversy and bitter complaint in Notting Hill Gate. He was known as a brutal and rapacious landlord, buying up old houses and subdividing them into smaller and smaller flats that were then rented to immigrants from the West Indies. It was reported that he terrorised the older residents until they were forced to move out or to sell their properties to him. Then he would bring in new tenants and charge them exorbitant rents. His "agents" always had bull terriers with them. "Then I saw them walking towards the park. Later, that is."

What would Webb have to do with Ruppta? The fact that Webb was in the housing department occurred to Harry as soon as he asked himself the question. But why would he visit Ruppta's offices? Why did not Ruppta go to Whitehall? "Did you tell me once," he asked her, "that Ruppta's staff use the coffee shop?"

"That's right. Lunchtime. She eats *so* much. She orders *three* sandwiches."

"Who does?"

"The secretary. And then there's a typist, who looks a little bit like a mongoose. No. A marmoset."

"What does a marmoset look like?"

"Like *her*. Anyway she's leaving. I don't think she likes it there."

"You remember how to type, don't you?"

"Of course I do. Have you forgotten how to breathe?"

"Are you any good?"

"Any *good?*"

In his excitement it did not occur to him that Hilda might want to stay at the coffee shop.

It did not take him very long to devise a scheme whereby Hilda would enter the office of Asher Ruppta. She took the secretary and typist into her confidence. "You know," she told them, "I am *sick* of making sandwiches." Later she added, "I used to be a typist, like you. I *loved* it."

"Well, you can go back to it," the typist said on the following day. "I'm off. I've had enough."

So Hilda entered the employment of Asher Ruppta. He was a short thickset man, in middle age, of olive complexion. He had gold rings on the second and third fingers of his right hand; he wore an expensive silk suit, and a pair of horn-rimmed spectacles hung from a silver chain around his neck. He could have been a banker, or a heart surgeon. Hilda later described him as "very *sleek.*"

"So you know my ladies," he said to Hilda on the morning she had come for an interview. "My ladies are very special. They are very good ladies." He could not have been more polite, more gallant. Could this have been the man who threatened old women with bull terriers? He looked at her with a certain amount of merriment, as if he had divined her question. "Julie says that you are an excellent typist."

"I hope so. I think so."

"How many fingers?"

"Excuse me?"

"How many fingers do you use?"

She held up her hands. "All of them."

"Excellent. You have a pianist's hands."

"I can't play a note." She was laughing.

"You can make music on the typewriter. Please to sit there." She sat down in front of a large Remington. "Now, Miss Hilda, you can begin." He started to dictate to her a letter concerning the freehold of a property in Lancaster Gate. He seemed to Hilda to be making up the figures as he went along.

She and Julie Armitage, the secretary, now shared an office. Julie was thin, but she rarely stopped eating. She kept a pocket knife and a jar of Colman's mustard in the drawer of her desk. She cut up a Scotch egg, or a pork pie, into several very small pieces; then she spread mustard on each one of them evenly before placing them in her mouth in a rapid but somehow absent-minded fashion.

Julie was not happy with the world as she found it. Her face looked as if it were incapable of smiling, and the sides of her mouth were sure proof of the theory of gravity. She complained about the weather, about the bus service, about the previous night's television programmes—and of course about her own job. "I've got too much on my plate," she said one afternoon. That was true, Hilda thought, in another sense. "Mr. Ruppta doesn't understand." She pronounced his name in a deliberately formal way. "I am that busy. I hardly have time to take a wee. And my back is giving me gyp." Hilda could not help laughing. Julie looked at her in a pained fashion. "It's all right for some."

"Let me help." Hilda tried to sound apologetic. "Give me some of your paperwork."

"Would you?"

So Hilda became better acquainted with all aspects of Ruppta's business. "He's claiming for payments he never made," she reported to Harry. "That's thieving, isn't it? He makes up lists of works that were never done. He lies about the number of tenants in a property. I know that for a fact. I have the real numbers in my desk. Sometimes I hear him talking on the 'phone. He is ever so smooth and polite. A real *charmer*. He talks very carefully and precisely. Like a walking dictionary. He never loses his temper. Not *him*. I should think he would stay calm in an avalanche. Yes, he *would*. He is never even *annoyed*. Which is annoying. But I don't think he's a gentleman at all. I think he is a bit of a villain. I have to pass on messages to him. 'Flat 38 is done.' Or 'number ten is vacant.' That kind of thing. Very suspicious. But he just smiles and puts a finger up to one of his eyebrows. He likes to smooth them down. 'Thank you, Miss Hilda,' he says." Harry had been taking notes.

There had as yet been no further sign of Cormac Webb. Then, one evening, he walked into the office. Asher Ruppta had been to the bank earlier in the day, and had drawn out a large sum in cash. Hilda knew this because he had taken with him a black attaché case equipped with a safety lock. He always used this to carry money.

Webb did not identify himself to Julie or to Hilda but went over to Ruppta's door and gave it a sharp double rap. "Ah," Ruppta said as he opened the door, "my very good friend!" The two men shook hands, and entered Ruppta's private office. Hilda pretended to be checking her pages of typing, but in fact she was listening as carefully as she could without arousing Julie's suspicion. She heard stray phrases, such as "the provision" and "the regulator," but the rest was murmured conversation. After a few minutes Webb left the office, carrying the attaché case. He still did not seem to notice the presence of the two women. But he was smiling.

Harry was delighted with the news. "This is it," he said. "We've bagged him."

He cleared the story with James White. "That little cripple," White said with some satisfaction. Cormac Webb had a slight limp.

The news editor then took the story to Andrew Havers-Williams who remarked that "Webb is not one of nature's gentlemen." It only remained, he said, for "that chap, Hanway, to catch him at it."

Julie volunteered the next piece of information. "That per-

67

son," she said to Hilda on the following morning, "comes here every month. On the dot. I don't know who he is and I don't want to know. He has ever such a cruel mouth. What does he do with all them attaché cases?"

Hilda observed that, on the day after Webb's visit, Asher Ruppta purchased a property in Queensway that had previously been subject to a "building order." It seemed that this order had been lifted only a week before. A "building order" gave tenants certain rights of appeal and of rehousing.

Looking back over the files, Hilda noticed that other "building orders" had been allowed to expire or had been lifted. In one file she noticed a letter, dated 31 October 1968, with the heading of the Department of Housing. It was signed by Webb himself. It was couched in formal style, but the gist was clear enough. Asher Ruppta's property holdings were due to be investigated by an official from the department, but the government had decided that such action was neither necessary nor desirable. It seemed that Webb had intervened and stopped an investigation into Ruppta's business.

"I'll tell you what he's doing," Harry said to Hilda that evening. "He is giving Ruppta inside information. That's what he's doing. I wonder how much he's being paid."

"*Hundreds.*" She opened her eyes wide.

"Heck." He had a habit of scratching his face that Hilda still found endearing. "When is he coming next?"

"The first of next month. Around five."

On that day, Harry and a photographer from the *Chronicle* were sitting in The Wait And See. They were drinking coffee and watching the street from the window. There was a new girl behind the counter, Millicent, who had been handed a pound note for allowing them to stay there. "Here he is," Harry said. He had become very excited. The photographer swiftly picked up his camera from the Formica table, and took several photographs of Cormac Webb walking down the street and entering the building. Thirty minutes later, he photographed him coming out of the premises with an attaché case.

Webb had seen them. He seemed to Harry to have some difficulty in mastering his expression as he walked across the road towards them. The photographer kept on snapping him.

"You can put that fucking thing down," Webb said as he came into the coffee shop. "Can we speak outside?"

"Sure," Harry replied. "We can speak anywhere."

"I know you. You're from the *Chronicle*. You interviewed me."

"That's right. Can I ask you about your relationship with Asher Ruppta?"

"I don't have one. And that's that."

"What's in the case?"

"That's none of your business. I warn you. I don't remember your name."

"Harry Hanway."

"I warn you, Hanway, that if you publish any of this you will be out of business."

"Out of business? That's a curious phrase."

"You will be finished. Do you understand that?"

"That really depends on whether you have done anything wrong or not."

Webb glared at him, and limped away.

Harry spent the next two days preparing the story. He consulted the Land Register. He found out the leases attached to various properties. He found the title deeds and records of "building orders." There was a significant pattern of Ruppta buying up properties within a few days of the "building order" being lifted. Harry was not able to prove directly that Webb had sold Ruppta information, but he knew how to surmise and suggest within the bounds of libel.

He was about to give the story to James White when he

was called to the office of the editor. To his surprise he was greeted there by the proprietor of the *Chronicle*, Sir Martin Flaxman. He was a small man and seemed frail; but he had a full head of sleek black hair which was, perhaps, a little too long at the back. He had a forceful manner, with a bluffness that might have been mistaken for geniality. Harry wondered how such a small man could make so much money. In fact Flaxman had made his fortune from selling medical supplies in Asia and Africa.

"Well, Harry," he said, "I've been hearing all about you. You know when to go for the balls, don't you?" He squeezed Harry's arm. "Fuck it. I'm frightened of you already. Look at me. I'm shaking." Andrew Havers-Williams, strangely divorced from the conversation, was looking out of the window towards the steeple of St. Bride's Church. "Do you know what I tell Andy here? Spread enough shit around and something will grow." He was still holding onto Harry's arm. "There's good shit and there's bad shit. I'm looking out for you, Harry. You're my boy." And with that he abruptly left the room.

"Very colourful." The editor cleared his throat. "That story about Webb and Ruppta."

"Yes?"

"How far has it got?"

"As far as it can. I was about to pass it over to White."

"That won't be necessary."

"I don't—"

"We won't be going on with it." Harry remained silent. "Sir Martin doesn't want to publish it."

"Why ever not?"

"I'll tell you something in confidence. I shouldn't, but I will. I owe you an explanation. In the past Sir Martin has been in business with Ruppta. As a good reporter, you will be angry. I understand that. But as an employee of the *Chronicle*, you have to accept it. For the sake of your career."

Harry did indeed think of himself as a "good" reporter, whatever that meant, but he did not want to jeopardise his future at the *Chronicle*. That was more important. Sir Martin Flaxman had, after all, expressed an interest in him. The abandonment of the Webb story was exasperating, but he might be able to use it to his advantage in the weeks and months to come.

VI

Squeeze in

A CTUALLY, I don't much care for the place. It isn't exactly what I expected." Daniel Hanway was confiding in his former schoolfriend, Peter Palmer, who had come to see him in the middle of the second term. Palmer had been given a place at the University of Liverpool.

"Have you made many friends?"

"Friends? No. Not really." He did not want to admit loneliness or the fact that he looked warily upon his contemporaries.

"I bet," Palmer said, "that you don't feel as clever as you used to."

"What do you expect? My director of studies isn't interested in anything I have to say. He just sits there smoking his pipe. He has the most boring opinions I have ever heard. He's in love with Ben Jonson, for Christ's sake. You're right. I don't feel so clever any more. I think there are people here who are cleverer than me. I hate that. I might as well be invisible."

They were sitting in two black leather armchairs before a small gas fire. It was the biggest room Daniel had ever possessed, and a small bedroom lay off it. He had refused to put posters on the walls, so that his surroundings had a quality of bleakness that secretly he enjoyed. It suited his mood.

"I feel," he said, "that I'm on the sidelines of everything. There's something really great going on somewhere, but I have nothing to do with it." They could hear from the room upstairs the sound of music and laughter. "Come on," he said, "let's walk to Grantchester." It was a walk he had already done many times, along the path and the fields beside the river Cam, where he could brood on his unhappiness. "I can't stand the lectures," he was saying to Palmer as they crossed the first bridge on the outskirts of Cambridge. "Total waste of time. I have come up with a plan to avoid those wankers. Do you want to know what it is?" He savoured a few seconds of silence. "This is what you do. Say that you are studying the poetry of Browning. If you've got a strong enough stomach, you don't have to *read* him. Not as such. You read nine or ten books about him. They will be so boring that you can sort of skim them. Then you take their main arguments, mix them up, blend them together and press them into shape. Hey, you've got yourself a great piece of cookery. A great essay. Then you memorise it for the exam."

"Isn't that, well, a bit mechanical?"

"The syllabus is mechanical. Exams are mechanical."

They walked on a little way until they came to a small stone chapel standing five or six feet back from the bank of the river. "This is the place," Daniel said, "where the Virgin Mary was supposed to have appeared before a female hermit. Thirteenth century. So they built this little shrine."

"You don't believe that stuff?"

"I wouldn't rule it out. Do you smell that lovely scent?"

"Water lilies."

They were silent for a while. "What's with the moustache and long hair?" Palmer asked him. He had been waiting to ask the question all day.

"I just woke up one morning and decided to grow them."

"You and a thousand other hippies."

"What's that supposed to mean?"

"The spirit of the age. The new youth."

"That's all romantic shit. I just wanted to grow a moustache. Isn't that a good enough explanation?"

"A band of brothers."

"Listen to yourself. You're as bad as those cunts who go on *sit-ins* and organise poetry *workshops*."

"You can't just dismiss them."

"Yes I can. They're pathetic. What does it matter to me that I'm living in the 1960s? Does that make anything so different?"

They had come to the fields outside Grantchester. "Sunday is the worst day," Daniel said. "Don't you feel it? It is so empty. So melancholy."

"Now who's the romantic?"

When the bell rang for dinner in Hall that evening, Daniel put on his black gown and walked down his staircase. The bell might have signalled a funeral.

"Squeeze in, dear." Ernest Hughes was a plump young man who believed that he bore a resemblance to Oscar Wilde, whom he called "Oscar." "There's always room for one more. If there is semolina again, I shall scream."

This prompted a snigger from Stanley Askisson, a young man from the north who had a great affection for the novels of D. H. Lawrence. Ernest looked at his soup with a placid expression. "Don't you think, Stanley—"

"I do think." He sniggered again. "Don't I think I should be more polite?"

"Don't you think that we should bring back the sedan chair?"

"Don't talk shite."

"I happen to believe it is the perfect form of transport."

"You're an idiot."

"Oh dear."

"There's a difference between me and you, Ernest. Not in money. Not in class. Not in brains. I have my gods. You have your gods."

"Oscar said that gods are vulgar."

"Oscar Wilde was a great fat insect. A spider."

Ernest blinked and breathed hard. "You don't know what you're talking about."

"I know a fake when I see one. He was false. False to himself, and false to others. Each man kills the thing he loves. I don't think so." He was very fierce. "Not unless that love is unnatural and obscene."

Ernest now seemed close to tears. He put his spoon in the soup and said nothing. Daniel enjoyed sitting beside Stanley. He savoured his presence, and would from time to time lean over so that their bodies briefly touched.

The conversation, formal and hesitant, turned to a new album by a rock group of whom Daniel had never heard. "I hate that capitalist shit," Stanley said.

"Capitalist? What's so capitalist about entertaining the people?"

"The people? The people are fuckers."

Daniel and Stanley went together to the college bar. "Hughes is a slug," Stanley said. "He leaves a trail of slime. He uses words without knowing their meaning. He is all pretence."

"I don't mind him," Daniel replied.

"Oh you don't mind anything. You don't mind the world. You want to get on in it."

"What's wrong with that?" Daniel experienced a sudden sharp surge of anger. No one had ever made him angry before.

"What's wrong with it? Wherever you look, there's hypocrisy. There's sham. No one ever dares speak the truth. Say what they really think."

Daniel felt that Stanley was accusing him of some crime

that he was not aware he had committed. "Why do you think I want to get on?"

"Because you're weak."

"Like Hughes?"

"No. Not like that. He is weak in the soul, in the life force. You are weak in the mind."

"I don't think so."

"You don't know yourself. So you don't trust yourself."

Again Daniel felt the anger rising within him. He felt threatened. He felt that he was being goaded. "I don't know how you can say that."

"I am not attacking you. I am attacking the false you. The false Daniel Hanway who works too hard and is nervous all the time."

"That's very kind of you."

"Cruel to be kind. That's the phrase, isn't it?" Stanley went over to the bar, and brought back two more pints of lager. "Sup up," he said. "Where I come from, we can drink that down in two minutes." He had a cheerful grin that Daniel had not noticed before. "You mustn't take me too seriously."

Another student came up to them. "Have either of you got a copy of *Troilus and Criseyde*?" They shook their heads. "Oh well. Thought I'd ask." When he walked away, they sat in silence for a few moments.

"Why is it," Stanley asked him, "that we are all so uneasy with each other?"

"Lack of confidence?"

"Something like that."

"I've been looking for some ideal friend. Some companion." Daniel had been hoping to say this for some time. "But I've found no one."

"I don't think," Stanley said, "that I'll make it to thirty. I won't survive that long. I'll burn the years away. I'm always going to be poor. I know it. But I don't mind that. Poverty sings." His eyes were very bright; he was looking away, over Daniel's shoulder, with an expression of eagerness upon his face. "I don't think I could stand to live for very long. It just gets harder all the time."

"I know what you mean," Daniel said. "Everything is difficult. I can't look forward at all without shuddering."

"Shudder. That's a good word. Like slither."

"Or mother."

Stanley looked perplexed. "Now that's a strange association. What have you got against your mother?"

"Nothing. I haven't seen her for ten years." Then he told him the story of his mother's disappearance. He had never discussed it with anyone before. But in the company of Stanley he wanted to make an emotional impression; he wanted to convince him that in some way he had been deprived of love. In the telling of the story he feigned more hurt and surprise than he believed he felt. But his words were more truthful than he realised.

They were sitting in a corner of the bar, within an alcove on the walls of which were various *film noir* posters. Daniel had fallen silent after explaining how his father had never mentioned his mother again. Stanley then bent forward and kissed him on the lips. There was no one else near them. Daniel's eyes widened, and he looked at Stanley in astonishment. Then he returned the kiss with such passion that he bit Stan's lip. "Be careful," Stanley said curtly. And then he added, "I don't want this thing to happen. But it will happen."

Daniel was still breathless. He was shaking with nervous excitement. "Do you want us to?" Stanley nodded. "I never thought—I never knew—"

"That I was queer? Well, I am. Sort of. And I am not. I knew you were. As soon as I saw you." Daniel blushed.

They determined to keep their liaison a secret. It was not difficult. Their contemporaries would never have recognised or understood a relationship of this kind—it was beyond any possible range of their experience. Ernest Hughes may have sensed something—in a look, or in a gesture—but he said nothing. Sometimes he pursed his lips and looked superciliously at Daniel; but Daniel looked back at him with as innocent an expression as he could muster.

Daniel had hoped that in Stanley Askisson he had found his ideal companion, but he was soon disenchanted. There were many times when Stanley was curt and angry with him; Daniel came to dread his harangues. Their lovemaking was often awkward and unsatisfactory. Stanley would lie on his back, looking up at the ceiling, while Daniel would try to arouse him; when he did not succeed, he felt humiliated. Stanley would pick arguments with him, and even insult him.

"This is your life," he said one day. He picked up a sheet of paper, and drew a series of squares with a pencil. "You are in a box every hour of every day. Work. Work." He stabbed each square with the pencil. "I feel sorry for you. I pity you."

"You want me to be more like you, I suppose."

"You arrange your hours as if you were in some sort of military campaign. But who precisely is the enemy?" Daniel was silent. "Come on. Get out of your box. Let's go for a walk."

They competed with each other in their studies. One afternoon Daniel entered Stan's room in order to see what books he was reading and what essay he was preparing. He wanted to look at his notes. "What are you doing here?" Stanley had come in unexpectedly.

"I was waiting for you."

"So why are you going through my papers?" Daniel had disordered them on the desk.

"I was curious."

"You were spying on me."

"Why?" The word stuck somewhere in his throat.

"So that's it. *I* am your enemy."

"No. Of course not." He did not sound convincing.

Their supervisor, Eric Hamilton, was an academic who had spent his career in the college. Despite all the appurtenances of middle age, including a brown tweed jacket and a pipe, he looked oddly boyish. His clothes were always crumpled. The bottoms of his fawn trousers were spattered with mud, after his bicycle ride to the college from his small terraced house in Trumpington Street. He had a habit of tilting his head to one side, listening with a slight smile to his students' remarks.

"It seems to me," he said in one morning supervision, "that *Volpone* comes from a city vernacular tradition." It seemed to Daniel that half of his sentences began with "it seems to me that." "What is the phrase Jonson employs? 'Language that men do use.' That is the vibrant thing. I would like to say that this has the sheer edge of actuality. Felt life. Do you see?"

Daniel had no idea what he was trying to say, and simply continued reading his essay in which Hamilton took no particular interest. Hamilton seemed more ready to listen to Stanley Askisson, however, who could talk about felt life and the vibrant thing for as long as was necessary. Daniel sensed the favouritism, and resented it.

So he retreated to the safety and the silence of the university library. He became known to the staff, and was told that there would be summer work in the understaffed accessions department. "You are very familiar with books," the sub-librarian said. "Not to mention keen on them. We can do with you."

Daniel put his name forward, for work in the vacation, and was accepted. He was also allowed to keep his room in college during the summer months. He wrote a short letter to his father, announcing the good news, and prepared himself joyfully for a summer of toil. Stanley Askisson was going back to his mother's house in Hartlepool.

And so the summer passed. He hardly noticed it. After finishing work in the library he drank alone, most evenings, in a small pub close to the college which was used by a local population of shopkeepers, workmen and retired couples. No one from the college or the wider university frequented it. He sat in the back parlour, drinking pints of bitter.

One evening, late that summer, a stranger walked into the pub and ordered a pint of cider. "Is anyone sitting here?" he asked Daniel, pointing to the bench beside him. Daniel shook his head. "Ta." He had thick dark hair, swept back and rendered glossy with brilliantine; he seemed to Daniel to have a coarse but pleasing face, with a day or two's growth of stubble. "Your very good 'ealth," he said, raising his glass.

"Thanks."

"Don't mention it. I won't." He drank down some cider, and sighed. "That's sweet. That's the ticket. What do you do then?"

"I'm an undergraduate."

"Ah. An under*graduate*."

"What do you do?"

"This and that. Sometimes this, and sometimes that. Sometimes both together." He tapped the side of his nose. "You're queer, aren't you?"

Daniel was alarmed and embarrassed. "What makes you think that?"

"The way you looked at me. Don't get me wrong. I don't mind queers. I like them. What do you study?"

"English literature."

"*Lit*erature? Is that a fact? What's your name?"

"Daniel."

"Pleased to meet you, Dan." He held out his hand. "I'm Sparkler."

"That's a strange name."

"You can call me Spark or Sparkie or Sparkle. I'm quick, you see." The young man now held up Daniel's watch. "Never shake hands with a stranger, Dan."

"How did you do that?"

"It's a gift, isn't it. Can you keep a secret?" Daniel nodded. "Let's go to another pub." When they got outside Sparkler turned the corner and led him into the back yard. "Look," he said. He plunged his hands into his pockets, and brought out watches and wallets.

Daniel was astonished. "Are you a thief?"

"That's right. A tea-leaf. I came down here because the coppers don't know me." He stuffed the objects back into his pockets. "Let's move."

Daniel walked with him in a state of some bewilderment. He found himself enjoying the company of this good-looking young man, and was in fact exhilarated at the thought of his being a petty criminal. "How long," he asked him, "have you been doing—"

"The thieving? Ever since I was that high. I'm a natural, aren't I? It's my calling. I get to travel. I'm my own boss. I don't pay no tax."

"Have you ever been caught?"

"Caught? *Caught?* Can you catch a firefly? You can catch fleas, I know, but not with your hands you can't. No more can they catch me. You ask too many questions, under*graduate*." He laughed, and put his arm around Daniel's shoulders, causing him a shock of pleasure. "You've got to be hard. Hard and smart. And *quick*. These mods aren't hard. They're all flannel. You're a Londoner, aren't you?"

"Camden."

"Why is a London boy doing literature, then?"

"I just like it."

"Can you write good English?"

"I hope so."

"Let's go in here." Sparkler took his arm from Daniel's shoulders, and led him into another pub. "Two of your very finest pints, landlord," he said as he went up to the bar. "I feel a terrible thirst coming on me. Makes me see red."

"Pints of what exactly?"

"Two pints of Bulmer's best. My young friend here insists on the best. Now then, gentlemen. I have a pack of cards about me somewhere."

"No betting allowed," the landlord said.

"No bets. No bets. Just a bit of harmless fun." Then he performed a card trick, to the delight of the locals, before retiring with the two glasses to a corner of the pub where Daniel was sitting. "Keep them happy," he said. "And then they don't ask questions. They accept you. So you can write good English, can you?"

"Yes. I can."

"I have a load of stories to tell, don't I? You can write them down for me. How many pockets can a pickpocket pick before he pips Sparkler? I'll give you something in return." He winked at him, and then stretched his legs beneath the table. Daniel's mouth went dry, and with trembling hand he raised his glass and drank from it. "This is what we'll call it. The Sparkler Papers."

"It has a ring to it." Daniel was still thoroughly bewildered by the events of the evening. Why had this good-looking stranger taken such an interest in him? Had they really met by accident or coincidence?

"I'll tell you about the time when I met a very kind lady. She took care of me when I was broke. She looked after me. One day you may meet her. When you come up to London.

Have you got a pen on you?" Then he wrote down a telephone number. "Ring me the week before. Then I can give you my address." He leaned forward and whispered in his ear. "You can suck my cock." So began Daniel's "transcription" of The Sparkler Papers.

Whenever Daniel went up to London, he told Stanley Askisson that he was visiting his father. In truth he had forgotten all about his family. It was something from which he had escaped. So in the vacations, instead of returning to Camden, he resumed his job at the university library. He was allowed to stay in his college rooms, too. Except for his one day a month in London with Sparkler, he devoted his time to work among books.

Daniel and Stanley stood outside the examination schools, where their finals were to be held. Daniel had not been able to sleep the previous night. He was filled with such alarm that he was sick that morning, retching violently into the hand basin in his bedroom. The world spun about him. Only when he had washed and dressed did he regain some semblance of ordinary life. Outside the building he dug his hands deep into his pockets to keep them from shaking. Stanley was smoking a Players cigarette, and was making nervous jokes about running out of ink.

Three months later the results were published. Daniel had obtained a first-class, and Stanley a second-class, degree.

"Now I see things from the point of view of failure," Stanley said. Then he burst into tears.

Daniel put his arm around him. "It will be all right," he said.

"No. It won't be all right. It will never be right again."

"You're taking it too seriously."

"And you're not?"

There was an immediate change in their relationship. They were no longer intimate. In fact they tried to avoid one another as much as possible. Daniel had performed so well that he was offered a research fellowship by the college, a post that he accepted with enthusiasm. This was the place in which he now wished to settle and to prosper. Stanley Askisson drifted to London where, after taking a civil-service examination, he found himself a junior clerk in the Ministry of Housing. Soon enough he was working directly for Cormac Webb. Daniel Hanway, meanwhile, had begun work on his dissertation on "The Criminal Element in Eighteenth Century Literature." He continued to see Sparkler in London.

VII

Red red robin

I T WAS raining, a mild and gentle rain that shrouded the city
in a pearl-grey light. Sam was walking through what was
for him still an unfamiliar part of London, south of the river.
He sensed a difference of atmosphere; there was no urgency,
no energy, in the air. The rain billowed around the houses like
a bland mist. He pushed open a gate and walked up a small
front path between patches of grass; he rang the bell, and the
door opened a fraction before he was admitted.

Fifteen minutes later he came out across the threshold.
It was still raining. He was accompanied by a middle-aged
woman, who stopped and put her hand up to a pocket in her
jacket. "I almost forgot," she said. "Take it."

"I don't want this, you know."

"Still, I like to give it to you."

He took the envelope and, without looking back, went
into the street. He did not look up until he passed St. George's
Church in Borough High Street. An old woman was sitting on
its worn steps, her hair tied together with rags. Sam reached
into the pocket of his jacket, and gave the envelope to her. He
knew that it contained a five-pound note. He was given the
same amount every week, and always handed the money to
the first vagrant he saw. And who was the woman in the house

from whom he had received the money? Sam had found his mother at last.

Three months earlier he had entered the church of Our Lady of Sorrows in Camden, where he had first seen the statue of the Virgin. He had been hoping, ever since, that the chapel and the statue would somehow reappear and that the nuns would also return. What had come and gone might come again.

He sat at the back of the church, his hands clasped in front of him; he repeated some words that the nuns had recited to him. "*Ave maris stella, virgo et puella.*" The door leading from the porch was suddenly opened, and there stepped a woman into the nave wearing a white raincoat and a blue scarf. She entered one of the pews, and Sam saw her for a moment in profile. Hurriedly he left the church and stood on the gravel path outside the porch. What should he do? Should he talk to her? Would she recognise him? He feared another rejection—that was how he put it to himself—and so he decided to wait in the street where she would not notice him. A few minutes later she left the church and came out, taking off her scarf as she swung open the wooden gate in front of her. She turned left and walked quickly away. Sam decided to follow her, at a careful distance.

She entered the underground station at the top of Camden High Street, and stood in line for a ticket. Sam hated this station. It had an acrid smell of old machinery, and the booming sound of trains echoed from the depths; the dank atmosphere was filled with foreboding. He did not appreciate the world under the ground. Yet he waited in the queue, unwilling to let his mother out of his sight, and then followed her down the escalator to the southward-bound platform of the Northern Line.

He sat at the other end of the carriage, from where he kept on glancing at his mother. He had known her at once, in the supermarket and in the church, but he had not recognised her by sight; he had recognised her by feeling. He had been drawn to her by some bond of sympathy or perception that was instinctive and unassailable. She was staring straight ahead, immersed in her own thoughts. She seemed to Sam to be troubled; he wanted to approach her, and to comfort her, but he could not do anything so bold.

She left the train at Borough and Sam followed her through the wind-haunted passages, past the peeling advertisements and the grubby white tiles, past the piss-stained corners and the rusted metal grilles, until she came out into the hall of the escalators. He watched her rise slowly, and then himself stepped on the moving stairs so that he would not lose her. She came out onto Borough High Street and began walking south, taking the old pilgrim trail from Southwark. Sam felt curiously light-hearted as he followed her. Eventually she turned up the path of a small terraced house.

There was a low wall on the other side of the road, bordering a wild waste of garden in front of an untenanted house. Sam sat there, and waited. At regular intervals cars drew up to the parking spaces in the road outside. Individual men would then enter the house, leaving after an hour or so. Two young women came up, arm in arm, and were admitted. They did not leave.

Sam came again the next day, and then the next. He did not know what he was waiting for. He knew only that this was what he was supposed to do. He noticed that all the curtains of the house were drawn, and that he could hear no noise. Then on the third day he walked up the narrow path and rang the bell. A young woman, holding a plastic cup in her hand, came to the door. "Can I help you?"

"I've come to see Mrs. Hanway."

"Who? There's no one of that name here."

"I know her."

"Let him in." It was his mother's voice.

The young woman moved aside, and Sam crossed the threshold into a hall decorated with crimson flock wallpaper and a number of watercolours of pastoral scenes in heavy gilt frames. He went towards his mother standing at the end, at the foot of a staircase.

"Well, Sam, you have found me."

"I saw you in the church. In Allington Street."

"I go back there sometimes. I like it."

"So do I."

He looked away from her for a moment, but she did not look away from him. "I would know you anywhere, Sam. Your hair is not as light as it used to be. Come in here. Mary, will you make us a pot of tea?" She led him into a small room with a window overlooking an empty yard and a brick wall. A blue vase of tulips had been placed on the table at which they sat. "I haven't seen you for a long time," she said.

"I was seven."

"You're nineteen now, aren't you?"

"Eighteen."

They were silent for a moment as Mary brought in the tea.

"So you've left school."

"Yes."

"What are you doing now?"

"Nothing." She stared at him for a moment, with a fixed attention. "What do *you* do?"

She threw her hands up in the air. "This." Then she questioned him about Harry, and about Daniel, listening eagerly as he tried to remember all the details of the immediate past. She never once mentioned Philip Hanway.

"Why did you go away?"

"Why does anyone do anything? No. That's unfair on you. I was in trouble. That's all I want to say."

"Where did you go?"

"I went away. It doesn't matter where." He remembered now the paleness of her pale blue eyes. "I didn't want to leave you. I didn't mean to leave you. Your father wanted it. He didn't want to see me again. It wasn't easy." She paused for a moment. "It was the hardest thing in my life."

"You thought it was for our own good."

"Yes. That's it. Your own good."

"We knew that something was wrong."

"What did your father tell you?"

"He didn't. He never said a word."

"Didn't you ask?"

"We talked about it to each other. But we never wanted to mention it to anyone. I think we felt guilty for something, but I don't know . . . "

"*You* felt guilty? How do you think I felt? I have never felt anything else." She reached over and touched the vase of tulips. "You never spoke to your father?" Sam shook his head. "You boys were always very private. You never gave anything away. You were the strangest boys in the world. Nothing will stop Harry. Nothing will trouble Harry. Danny is more fragile. And you were always the dreamer. I was always most concerned for you. Do you remember the time when—No. Let's not talk about the past. You're grown-up now. You're an adult."

"So what should we talk about, as *adults*?"

"How do you get by?"

"Get by?"

"If you have no job, what do you do for money?"

"Dad helps me. I live at home. I don't cost much." He laughed. "I've nothing to spend it on."

"Don't you have a girlfriend?" He looked at her, and said nothing. "Don't you have *any* friends?"

"Who would want to be friends with me?"

"Don't say that."

"I just did." He looked at the vase of flowers. "There are lots of people in the world who have no friends. Sometimes I see something interesting. Or I feel something. But I know that I have no one to tell."

"And the red red robin comes bob bob bobbing along."

"What?"

"Nothing. It was a song I knew as a kid." They stared at one another. "Now that I've found you," she said, "I'll never let you go."

"Is that another song?"

"No. It's the truth." She stood up and left the room, returning a few moments later with a five-pound note in her hand. "Here. Take it."

"I don't want it."

"Take it. I need to give it to you."

"To buy myself a friend?"

"Buy whatever you want, Sam."

So began the series of their strange meetings. On the same day each week, at the same time, he would ring the doorbell and would be admitted. He looked forward to the pot of tea brought in by Mary; he looked forward to the fresh flowers in the blue vase. He looked forward to hearing his mother's voice. It was nothing she said in particular, but the soothing syllables of her conversation induced in him a feeling of repose.

"I see faces before I go to sleep," she said to him one afternoon. "I don't know them, but I think somehow I recognise them."

"Ancestors?"

"Do you think so? That *is* a nice idea. One of them did look a bit like you. He had your smile."

"Sometimes," she said on another occasion, "I smell the strangest things. The smell of burning rags, where there is nothing burning. Sometimes I smell the perfume of roses on a busy street."

A fortnight later Sam said to her, "I've got a job."

"Oh yes?"

"As a nightwatchman. I'll still be able to come around in the afternoon."

"That's what your father used to do."

"He was the one who found it for me."

In fact Philip Hanway had become more and more concerned about his youngest son. When he eventually discovered that Sam had no work, it occurred to him to contact his old employer: there was no qualification needed to be a nightwatchman. So, on Philip's recommendation, Sam was hired.

"You may get lonely," his mother said to him.

"Me?"

"Your father used to complain."

"I'll get used to it, I expect. I get used to everything else."

"Have you mentioned me to your father?" she asked him a week later.

"Do you want me to?"

"No. Some things are better left unsaid, don't you think? What about your brothers?"

"What *about* them?"

"Have you seen them?"

"I don't think so."

"And what does that mean?"

"Sometimes I think I see their reflections. Sometimes I think I see them across the street. I see them in my dreams all the time."

"You know, Sam, you baffle me."

"Just begin at the beginning. You'll find your way." He looked at the blue vase. "How do you pronounce it? Vase as in stars? Or vase as in maze?"

On another visit he spoke to his mother about his work as a nightwatchman. "I like it. I like to sit and think. Why do I prefer blue to red? If colours were words, what would they say? Why do eyes get tired?"

"Some questions, Sam, have no answers."

"Do you know who you remind me of? The unknown soldier. You don't have much expression, do you?" It was Julie Armitage. Sam had been given work at a newly built office block along Kingsway; just before his arrival, the property business of Asher Ruppta had taken premises in the same building. Julie immediately felt sympathy for one whom she considered to be a fellow sufferer in the world. "Here. I've made you a nice sandwich. Do you like Spam? I *love* it."

He picked up a neatly quartered piece. "You have some, too."

"Oh no. It's for you. Oh well, all right then. If you insist." She bit into it while all the time keeping her eyes upon Sam. "What do you think of corned beef?"

"Take it or leave it."

"I like it with pickle. Not that piccalilli muck. I can't abide it. Just regular Branston. Next time I'll bring you a pickled egg."

"I've never seen a pickled egg."

"It's just an egg, really. They sell them in pubs."

So began the friendship between Julie and Sam. He came on duty at five in the evening, and she finished work at six. She would come down with a "snack," as she called it, and sit down beside him as he ate it. She began to confide in him. "He's planning something." "He" was Asher Ruppta. "He sits very still and smells his fingers. I know the signs. Sometimes he whispers a word or two. As if he was praying."

"What does he do?" Sam asked her on another evening, between mouthfuls of cold sausage sandwich.

"Now there's a question. What doesn't he do? He does this and he does that. Am I making myself clear? As clear as mud?"

"Perhaps it is mud."

"You are a sharp one, aren't you?" She was silent for a moment. "I think you're right, actually. It is mud. Deep and dark. But you would never know it. It all looks good on paper."

"I think there's something going on," she announced two weeks later. "He has been meeting people out of the office. He never does that. I've had to book him tables in restaurants." She seemed excited by these events.

Sam now visited his mother two or three times a week, before setting off for his work. He mentioned Julie Armitage, and Sally laughed. "*That's* a coincidence. I knew—" But when he spoke of Asher Ruppta, her eyes widened and she looked away. From that time forward she sometimes asked about Julie and her employer, in an indirect and only slightly curious way.

Sam saw Ruppta often enough. He would walk out of the lift at approximately the same time every evening, and pass the young nightwatchman on his way to the street. He was courteous, politely nodding to Sam before putting on the black Homburg hat that he always wore. Yet he rarely looked directly at him; whenever he did so, his hooded eyes seemed to flash with some inward fire. Sam then saw the spirit of Ruppta as a hawk or some other bird of prey. He thought that he had seen such a bird, perched on the roof of the building, its wings unfurled, but in a moment it was gone.

One evening a young man rang to enter the lobby. "I'm here to see Mr. Ruppta's secretary," he said. He looked at Sam curiously, as if trying to recall where he had met him.

"I'll call her," he said. "Can I give her your name?"

"Stanley Askisson."

Julie came down with a small package wrapped in brown paper. She gave it to Stanley Askisson, who thanked her and walked out. Before he left the building, he stared once more at Sam.

"There's something going on," she said. It was her favourite phrase. "Do you fancy some pork scratchings? I'll bring them down. There was money in that packet. Banknotes."

"Who is he?"

"I don't know. Ruppy just told me—"

"Who?"

"That's my secret name for you know who. Ruppy told me to give the money to someone called Askisson."

"He seemed to know me. But then he didn't know me."

Stanley Askisson came back two weeks later, and waited in the lobby until he was given a package by Julie. "Do you know what?" she said to Sam as soon as Askisson had gone out into the street. "There's no reference to him in any of the letters or papers. This is the problem. There is no mention of the money anywhere. It might as well be fairy gold."

"Fairy gold?"

"It fades away."

"But he won't fade away, will he?"

"He could be a blackmailer. Is that what you're thinking, Sam?" Julie put a great deal of faith in Sam's sagacity; she interpreted his periods of silence and withdrawal as wisdom.

"Wait and see," he replied.

"Next time I'm going to follow him. There's something going on."

"Won't he mind?"

"Who?"

"Ruppta."

"He won't know anything about it."

★　★　★

Stanley Askisson returned a fortnight later, by which time Sam and Julie had formulated a plan.

She left the package with Sam before slipping out into the street wearing a scarf and a nondescript beige coat. On Askisson's arrival Sam gave him the package, with the excuse that Julie had left early for a dentist's appointment. Askisson seemed surprised, but made no comment. Once more he looked at Sam curiously, as though he had known him in some other circumstance. He left the building and, as usual, turned right. Julie followed a short distance behind. She did not want to be seen, of course, but she need not have taken any great precaution. Askisson would not have known her. He never recognised the faces of young women.

Everyone became anonymous on Kingsway, a barren valley carved through the teeming alleys and lanes of nineteenth-century London. All the life of the neighbourhood had been laid waste by the clearance for this site, and none of it had returned. Stanley Askisson walked south towards Bush House before walking around the curve of Aldwych towards a bus stop on the south side of the Strand. The sky was blood-red with a fiery setting sun. Julie kept him in sight. When he boarded the 173 bus she followed him, sitting on the long seat close to the conductor's platform.

Askisson left the bus at the stop halfway down Whitehall, where Julie also alighted. She followed him down White-hall until he turned into the portal of one of the govern-ment departments. When Julie passed it, she saw that it was the Ministry of Housing. The next morning, before Ruppta arrived in the office, she telephoned the ministry and asked to speak to Stanley Askisson. He answered the 'phone in his customary manner. "Office of Cormac Webb."

"Sorry. Wrong number." Now she knew. Webb was a name familiar to her. Ever since she had shared an office with Hilda

Nugent, she had been aware of his connection with Ruppta. It seemed that the payments were still being made, indirectly through Askisson, and of course she suspected the nature of the bargain. What had happened to Hilda, by the way? She had telephoned one morning to say that she was ill, and had never returned to work. Ruppta had seemed preoccupied at the time, and so Julie never raised the matter with him.

She told Sam about her pursuit of Askisson. "Ruppy is giving money to Cormac Webb," she said. "He wants something. Information."

"Planning permission," Sam replied. "He's a property developer, isn't he?"

"Don't you think it's *exciting*? I do."

He had not considered it in that light. He had not really considered it in any light at all. But now he took more interest in Asher Ruppta. And Ruppta began to take more interest in him. He would stop at Sam's desk, before leaving the building, and engage him in brief conversation. "How are you, Mr. Sam?" he would say. "Has Julie brought you anything nice today?" He was always watchful, somehow looking all around Sam as if searching for his shadow. Ruppta believed in the spirit world. He had been brought up by his mother on a small island of an archipelago in the Celebes Sea. And now he sensed something about Sam. He was not sure what it was, as yet, but there was a quality associated with the mystery that Ruppta had experienced as a child.

"He's been asking after you," Julie said to Sam one evening. She had just presented him with a sausage sandwich. "Tuck in. He thinks you've got promise. Potential."

"Potential for what?"

"Fire bombing. No. I'm joking."

On the following day Ruppta came up to Sam in the lobby. "You are a young man," he said. "Do you want to sit behind a desk like this for ever? Is it right?" Sam shook his head. "I need a smart young man. On my island, Sam, there were conjurors. *Aslohi*. They had assistants. *Mekini*. These assistants would help them with their tricks. They would climb up poles and disappear. They would rise into the air. They would fall into a trance. You can be one of my *mekini*."

"How do I fall into a trance?"

"This will not be necessary. You can deliver little items from me. You can receive letters for me. Perhaps you will follow people. Who knows?" He was about to walk away, when he turned back to Sam. "On my island there were creatures you could not see and you could not hear. They hid in the green tapestry of the forest, in the humid air, in the great old rocks. Do you have such creatures in London, Sam?"

"Not to my knowledge."

"It is not a question of knowledge."

So Sam became a courier, and messenger, for Asher Ruppta.

VIII

What is it?

HARRY HANWAY began to rise among the journalists of the *Chronicle*. He had become chief news reporter, and his byline now appeared on the front page almost daily. He had not forgotten about Cormac Webb; indeed he had kept all the material for possible use at a later date, but he had been willing to suppress the story at the request of Sir Martin Flaxman. This prompt and willing acquiescence recommended Harry to the proprietor of the *Chronicle*, who started to invite him to parties at his house in Cheyne Walk.

For the first time in his life Harry was being introduced to the powerful and to the merely famous. Most of them were cordial and self-deprecating, although Harry realised that success had made them so. It was extraordinary that they all knew, or professed to know, each other; a television presenter was on first-name terms with a businessman or a bishop. It seemed to Harry that, for them, the rest of the world did not really exist.

He began to understand, too, how alliances and affinities might be formed. Here was an admiral talking to a leading businessman; there was a politician talking to a pop star. Despite the air of bonhomie, what brought them all together was self-interest.

"They call me a muck-raker." Sir Martin was talking to a

small group of people. "What's wrong with raking muck? If you spread enough shit, something may begin to grow." He laughed very loudly. "But you have to get the best journalists. Like Harry here. Most of them are arse-lickers. Tame poodles pretending to be guard dogs. But not Harry. He knows what he is. And he likes it." The little group broke apart, aimlessly colliding with other little groups.

Harry stepped back, and found himself standing beside Cormac Webb. Webb looked at him without betraying any feeling. There had been a flash of recognition, and resentment, but this had been followed by an impassive expression; he was pretending not to remember him. "How are you, sir?" Harry asked him.

"Tremendous." He smiled. "Nose to the grindstone." He was oddly chastened. Harry noticed that there were white specks of dandruff on his dark pinstriped suit. He seemed shorter, and slighter, than Harry had remembered; he was more vulnerable, as if he had suffered some loss of power.

Sir Martin took Harry aside, put his arm around his shoulders, and whispered to him. "I've been told that Webb is about to retire. For personal reasons. No more use to me now. He won't be coming here again." Then he added, under his breath, "And here's another cunt." Harry looked up and saw a Conservative front-bench spokesman holding an animated conversation with an actress. "He wants to get into her knickers." Sir Martin took Harry over to him. "Robin," he said, "let me introduce you to Harry Hanway." The actress walked away.

Robin Green concealed his annoyance very well. He had a smooth and well-oiled manner, with a delicate persuasive voice. "Delighted," he said. When he smiled he showed his teeth.

"Harry's my boy. He can sniff out secrets like a pig can scent truffles. Secrets smell. Do you have any secrets, Robin?"

"Alas no." He did not look at Harry, but glanced in his direction. "Sorry to disappoint you."

"I don't believe you, Robin." Sir Martin was as always very emphatic. "Every man has a secret."

"And every woman, too," Harry added.

"Is that so?" Sir Martin looked at him with amusement. "You must tell me about her some time."

"Her?"

"I'm sure you had someone in mind." Harry had been thinking of his mother. "You must meet my daughter, Harry. Guinevere! Guinevere! Come over here."

A girl of nineteen or twenty reluctantly crossed the room. "I sent her to finishing school," he told the two men. "I wanted her to become a toffee-nosed bitch and marry a millionaire."

"Dad!"

"Now she wants to be a social worker. I told her to get a proper job."

Harry was drawn to Guinevere. She had long dark hair, and large brown eyes; her lips were slightly parted, as if she were about to speak. For some reason Harry saw her swimming in the ocean. She was suspended in the bright blue water.

"Are you one of Dad's attack dogs?" She was smiling.

"I'm probably a poodle."

"But poodles can bite."

"I am tame." They looked at one other for a moment, held by the mutual gaze. "So you want to be a social worker?"

"Don't laugh."

"I am not laughing. It's a very good thing."

"Now you're making fun of me."

"I'm not. I promise you. I would hate to make fun of you."

"Would you?" She looked at him with genuine gratitude. "That's all Dad ever does. I don't think he likes women."

"I don't think he likes anybody."

"I don't know why I'm telling you this. What was your name again?"

"Harry."

"The trouble with Harry."

"What?"

"It's a novel."

"I never read novels."

"Good for you."

"I don't see much point in them."

"But you journalists write novels, don't you? You call them stories. Dad is always going on about 'good stories.'"

"It's just a term," he said.

"God, I hate these parties." She looked quickly around the room. "Mum always stays in the country. She can't stand his friends. She says that it's a dance of death."

"I can see why."

"Do you know why I want to be a social worker? I want to get away from all this. Do you know how people are forced to live? One family in a room. No hot water."

"I know."

"But do you know? *Really* know? Come with me one day. I'll take you to Limehouse, where I'm being trained."

"Of course." He did not want to disappoint her.

They met three days later, on a Saturday morning, outside Limehouse Underground Station. He did not know how to greet her, but she put out her hand. "It's quiet around here," she said. They were at the end of a long narrow street dominated on both sides by warehouses of dark brown brick, derelict and empty. "The local people want them torn down. They need council flats. Come on. I'll show you."

They walked away from the immediate environs of the river and turned down a side street of dilapidated terrace houses.

These were all multiple dwellings—the front doors were open and there were sounds of babies crying, of voices being raised in small rooms. A group of children was playing in the street, while two or three disconsolate men in tattered suits sat on the front steps and watched them. "Irish," Guinevere said. "Or Jamaican. Whoever has the least money."

A settlement of round huts, created out of mud and straw, had once been raised here by the river. Their roofs had been made of thatch, and they had been built in two parallel lines just like these nineteenth-century tenements. The same sounds, and the same voices, had come from these frail huts; children had played in the space between them, and men had watched them as they sat upon the ground by the threshold of their dwellings. Now someone called out, "Peter! Peter!"

Guinevere led him into one of the houses. A powerful smell of damp in the hallway mingled with the stale air. "I visit the family on the first floor," she said. She walked up the stairs that were covered in chipped and broken linoleum, and knocked on the door at the next level. "Mrs. Byrne," she called out. "It's Guinevere."

A middle-aged woman came to the door. "I've just finished feeding them," she said. "You'd better come in." Three children were sitting around a Formica table; they were all holding slices of bread, their white faces slightly smeared with jam. They looked up at Guinevere and Harry without expression.

"This gentleman is a journalist," Guinevere said. "I wanted him to meet you. To see how you were getting on."

"Oh we get on. We're not complaining." Harry observed another room, to which the door was closed. "My husband's still sleeping. He has the fits."

"Tell the gentleman how much you live on."

"Twelve pounds a week. He draws it from the social security." She looked at the closed door. "Twelve pounds doesn't go far these days. Not with five of us." Harry went over to a window that overlooked the grimy street. As his eyes grew accustomed to the dirty brick and the dust upon the windows, he was astonished to see his brother leaving one of the tenements. There was no doubt about it. It was Sam. He walked down some steps into the street, paused for a moment, and then turned left. Harry took a pace backward when he thought that Sam had stared up at him. Then Sam walked off and was gone.

"That Ruppta," the woman was saying. "He is a tartar."

"What was that?"

"We're talking about her landlord," Guinevere told him. "Asher Ruppta. Have you heard of him?"

"Yes."

"He comes down terrible hard on people such as us," the woman said.

"If they can't pay one week's rent, he threatens them with eviction."

"Out in the street, sir. With three little ones and him with the fits."

"He owns most of the houses in this street," Guinevere said. "They were going to be torn down, but then the decision was reversed."

"Is that so?"

"There are a lot of blacks," Mrs. Byrne said. "I've nothing against them personally."

Harry experienced a strong desire to leave this small room, and get out into the air. He went over to the window, and looked impatiently down into the street. Guinevere sensed his mood, and reacted accordingly. "We should go now, Mrs. Byrne," she said. "I just wanted to say hello."

Harry put out his hand, and then surreptitiously left a ten-pound note on the Formica table. Mrs. Byrne saw it, but she said nothing. Like her children, she stared at him without noticeable expression.

"Thank you for coming," Guinevere told him as they walked back into the street.

"Thank you for inviting me."

"I hope you weren't too bored."

"Bored? Never."

"How can it happen?"

"What?"

"This." She gestured at the mean houses. From one of them came the sound of "Old Man River."

"That is something to ask Asher Ruppta."

"How much do you know about that man?"

"Enough."

"Why don't you write about him? Expose him?"

"You know," he said, "you have the loveliest hair." He felt as if he were poised on a bank beside clear water, about to jump in.

Hilda Nugent's instinct and secret wish was to marry. On her occasional visits to Southend, her foster-mother constantly brought up the subject. "It's not right," she said. "Living in sin."

"Don't be so old-fashioned, Mum. Everyone does it nowadays."

"That doesn't make it right."

"We are as good as married."

"I wouldn't say that without a ring on your finger. Mark my words."

And, secretly, Hilda agreed with her. She would allude to the subject, with Harry, from time to time. "Are we putting down roots in Notting Hill?" she might ask him.

"Roots?"

"Are we going to stay for a long time?"

"I really don't know. What do you think?" He was irritated by her constant use of "we."

"We have a good routine, don't we?"

"I suppose so."

"We are comfortable."

Yes. You are as comfortable as an old armchair. He did not say it but he considered saying it.

The result of such conversations was always inconclusive. "Sometimes," she said, "I think I'm living with a stranger. I don't really understand you."

"There isn't very much to understand."

"There you go again. You're keeping me away. You don't want to be touched. *Disturbed*. Sometimes I think I should just get up and walk away." She had in fact never thought that.

He looked at her and said nothing.

"You just like to use people. You don't give a damn for any of them. All you really care about is you. Y. O. U."

"I can spell, Hilda."

Whenever she considered the possibility of Harry leaving her, she panicked. She expressed her doubt and fear in oblique ways. "It really is terrifying," she said to him one evening.

"What is?"

"One single little day might change everything. I could be run over. Extinguished."

He laughed. "I don't think it's a question of extinction."

"How do you know?"

Harry stayed on the track of Asher Ruppta, not knowing where it might lead. He decided to approach him directly, and to seek an interview with him. He telephoned Julie Armitage; he knew all about her from Hilda's descriptions but, fortunately, he had never met her. That would have been a complication. He told her that he was writing a profile of her employer; she seemed strangely excited, and promised to phone him. He believed that he could hear the rustle of a crisps packet as she spoke to him.

On the following day he received a telephone call from Ruppta himself. "I do not give interviews," he told Harry. "I keep silent. If I am silent, then I am not disturbed. Good day to you, sir."

"I just had a few questions."

"Alas, I do not know any answers."

"There were some planning permissions—"

"It would be better if you did not come too close, Mr. Hanway. You have an interesting name, by the way."

He found out that Ruppta owned a large mansion on the corner of a quiet avenue in Highgate, and he drove there one evening, curious to see if he entertained any visitors. The property was protected by iron railings above a brick wall, and there was a large security gate in front of a gravel drive. He parked close by, and waited. It was a quiet late-summer evening in the leafy street, and Harry wound down the window to enjoy the perfume of the luxuriant trees and hedges. On an evening such as this, all London seemed to be still. Then he heard the unmistakable clicking of high heels. A woman was walking quickly along the street. She stopped by the security gate, and looked up nervously at the house. Then she pressed a bell. Harry realised, after a moment's incomprehension, that it was his mother.

"Hello?" Harry recognised Ruppta's voice.

"It's Sally."

A buzzer sounded, and the gate swung open.

Harry sat in the car, staring straight ahead but seeing nothing. He could not move, or think. He knew that he should drive away, but he had not the strength to turn the key. What was she doing there? Was she still in her own old business? What had Ruppta said to him? You have an interesting name. Ruppta had not threatened him, but he had laid down a warning. Harry now realised that there would be an unspoken pact between them. He would no longer pursue his investigation of Asher Ruppta.

Harry and Guinevere met for the third time in Fountain Court, part of the gardens of the Inner Temple where a small fountain played into a pond fringed with trees.

"I don't know anything about you," she said.

"What is there to know? I'm twenty-one and I'm single."

"What? Harry Hanway? No girlfriend?"

"I do know a girl, but we're not really close." The light of the water gleamed in his eyes. "Actually I don't see her that often."

"You never mention your parents."

"I don't have any."

"Oh."

"They were killed. In a car crash."

"That's a terrible thing."

"I don't really like to talk about it."

"Do you have any brothers or sisters?"

"No. Just me. Only me." Then he leaned over and kissed her.

They continued to meet at Fountain Court. "I think you're very ambitious," she said to him one afternoon.

"How can you tell?"

"The way you carry yourself. The way you dress. When you took me to that restaurant last night, you looked at the menu for a moment and then made up your mind. You're impatient, too."

"I'm sorry."

"No. I like it. You know what you want."

"I know what I like." He kissed her on the cheek.

"You talk quickly, too."

"Perhaps I have a lot to say. How is Mrs. Byrne, by the way?"

"She says she is very poorly. My boss is thinking of taking the children into care."

"Care? Is that the right word? Oh look. There's a squirrel."

"There's a change in the air about you," Hilda told him.

"What on earth does that mean?"

"I don't know. But I feel it. I see it."

"Why are you trembling?"

"I just am."

"Are you not hungry?"

"I wouldn't mind if I never ate another thing."

"What is the matter with you, Hilda?"

"You are the matter, Harry. I think that everything is going to be different." He looked away from her briefly, as if something had caught his eye in the corner of the room.

"What if I were to get sick?" she asked him on another occasion. "Would you look after me?"

"Of course."

"No, you wouldn't. You would tell me, ever so nicely, that it was *my* problem and that you had other things on your mind. Then you would creep away, but not before blowing me a great big kiss from the door."

"Honestly, Hilda, I just can't *win* with you."

"Oh but you have won. And you know it."

As she hugged him one evening she smelled some other perfume on the lapel of his jacket. She held onto him, clinging for life. "Now what is it?" he asked her. She broke down in tears. "What *is* it?"

"You know what it is."

Gently he disengaged himself from her, and left the flat.

Hilda sat down, trying to steady herself with the arm of the chair. Some music started playing in the flat next door, and the refrain of the song rang through her head after the music had stopped. "It's all about your eyes. They hypnotise." Slowly she got to her feet, put on her coat, and opened the door of the flat. As she left she heard a child crying in another room, and she realised that she was still crying too. It had been raining, and the pavement shone with the reflected light of the street lamps. The autumn had arrived two or three days before, with a sudden chill in the air. "The Americans," she said to herself, "call it fall." As she walked towards Portobello it began to rain again, a slow and fitful shower, but she went on bare-headed without noticing it. Two days later she knocked on the door of the ice-cream van by the beach at Southend. "I missed the Raspberry Wriggle," she said.

IX

A cat may look

SEVENTEEN HOURS of supervision?"

"*Mea culpa*. But I *do* have to admit that I am a trifle *squashed* by the end of term."

Daniel Hanway, in the middle of dinner, was listening to a conversation between History and Biology at the high table. After completing his doctorate, he had been elected a junior fellow and deputy supervisor in English at his college.

Classics now joined the conversation. "I trust that you acknowledge that it is your job."

"I would like to say that it is part of my *job*, as you put it."

"But I put it so well."

History was short, with a slightly hooked nose, and a mass of fuzzy hair. He looked as if he had experienced an electric shock. Biology was bushy-haired, bushy-bearded and bushy-eyebrowed; he chortled rather than laughed. Classics was more saturnine; he wore a brown corduroy jacket, brown corduroy trousers, a green tie and white shirt. He had several other ties, jackets and trousers of the same colours so that he could remain in costume for his students.

Mathematics and Philosophy were arguing about the depth of nuclear bunkers. Philosophy "hazarded a guess" at seventy feet, at which Mathematics smiled politely, if mockingly. "Fifty feet?"

"Oh no."

"Thirty feet?"

"No, no. The figures are quite wrong. Absurdly so, if I may say so."

"But wouldn't I be *dead* otherwise?"

"No, not dead at all. Far from it. Very much alive. You need only dig thirty-six inches. The radiation is blown away."

History and Biology had moved on. "Oh these skinheads are absolutely ancient. They resemble the Mohocks of the eighteenth century. As Professor Leavis said—"

"*Dr.* Leavis."

"The *mobile vulgus* are always with us. What does our colleague from wildest London think of the *vulgus*?" History addressed the question to Daniel, whose origins in Camden Town were already well known.

"*Odi profanum vulgus,*" he replied, "*et arceo.*"

"Oh really? Where did you pick up your Horace?"

"He has been a good friend of mine for years."

"Is that so? But do you really despise the crowd?"

"I despise anyone who cannot think for himself."

"So you admire Oswald Mosley?"

"I know," Classics said, "let's look up Mosley in *Who's Who.*"

On returning to his rooms after dinner, Daniel continued his letter to his old schoolfriend Peter Palmer. Palmer had been appointed a junior lecturer in history at Durham University, and they corresponded now on their respective roles. Long-distance telephone calls were so expensive.

"Yesterday," Daniel wrote, "the English faculty met for the first time this term. When I say met I mean *collided*. Someone is teaching structuralism. Someone else is teaching Marxism. And then someone else is teaching old-fashioned lit crit. Did you ever hear of Lionel Manning? He wrote a book years ago on George Eliot. Rubbish, actually. But he's supposed to be an authority. Whatever *that* means. He considers himself to be a wit, but he just says absurd things in a high-pitched voice. 'The French don't think,' he said to me, apropos of some existentialist nonsense he had been discussing. 'The English *can't* think. That is why they produce very good novelists.' You get the general idea. He also has bad breath.

"You must have heard of Reginald Pearsall. He of the polonecked sweater and black leather jacket. He has a face like a skull and when he smiles it is positively revolting. Very rigorous. Very low church. He goes on about moral belief and moral certitude. His favourite phrase is 'what, precisely, do you mean by . . . ?' He adores George Orwell. A great bore, in other words.

"I have some younger colleagues. Dominic Tennyson likes to be called Dave. His surname is suspect, too. Could he have changed it by deed poll? He has just published, in *The Journal of English Literary Studies*, an article entitled 'The State of Jacobean Coinage with Relation to the Plays of Philip Massinger.' I'm not making it up. He has a deadly rival in Jeremy Jones. Now Jones has published an essay in some other journal. 'The Use of the Term "Almighty" in Eighteenth-Century Sermons.' What is the *matter* with these people?

"And then there's the poet. Paul Wilkin. Remember him?"

Paul Wilkin had enjoyed a modest success several years before. He had published his first book while in his twenties, where it had been acclaimed by the usual poetry reviewers as "a startlingly original voice" and "an impressive debut." On the publication of the second volume, Wilkin was described as "one of the leaders of his generation." But then of course there came along other young poets, who were reviewed in equally trite and effusive terms. There was never any shortage of praise for first or even second books of poetry. Now in his forties, Wilkin was an envious and distrustful man.

He had been published once by the famous firm of Connaught & Douglas, before, as he put it, "moving on" to a smaller publisher; yet he had remained a guest at their annual parties for the last fifteen years. So he spoke fondly of "Jack" Priestley, of "Willie" Maugham and of "Wystan." Of his contemporaries, however, he was scathing and dismissive. He scanned the literary pages of the newspapers and magazines for any mention of his name, and realised soon enough that these references were becoming more and more infrequent. He had a long thin face, and long untidy hair; his mouth was thin and small; his chin was weak, and was emphasised by a narrow moustache.

At their first meeting Daniel Hanway had professed admiration for Wilkin's poetry. In truth he regarded it as no more than adequate, and on occasions old-fashioned and mediocre. But Wilkin had been delighted by Daniel's enthusiasm. Immediately he saw in him a young academic of great promise; in the future, perhaps, he might become influential. He might even be persuaded to write a book about the poetry of Paul Wilkin.

So Wilkin became very friendly with Daniel. He invited the young man to tea in his rooms, and then eventually to dinner at his house. Wilkin lived with his wife Phyllis, a middle-aged philologist, in a semi-detached house close to the railway station. They had two Persian cats, and the house smelled of damp and pet food. Mrs. Wilkin was a timid and bedraggled woman who hardly spoke at all, but who seemed to look reproachfully at Daniel as she served him small portions of unappetising food.

Wilkin himself hardly stopped talking. He had a flat expressionless voice, but it had a rasping note when he became angry.

He was in turn boastful and querulous, complaining about a certain "bastard" of a reviewer or "prick" of a poet. His conversation settled on his own triumphs and tribulations, with reference to the prizes he had won or the magazines in which he had been published. The literary world, in his conversation, seemed to Daniel to be a vast boxing ring in which "contenders" and "young pretenders" vied for mastery. There were "heavyweights" and "lightweights"; it was a world in which intense rivalries, and enmities, could develop. Somebody had been given a "thrashing" in the *Observer*, while someone else had been "put down" by *The Listener*.

"I settled my account with Hunt," Wilkin had said to him. He almost spat out the name. "He went for me in the Staggers—" This was the name, among the literati, for the *New Statesman*. "He tried to demolish me. But I was still standing. Then lo and behold, a book of his essays was published last month. Can you imagine the conceit of it? Collecting your own articles? Anyway as a critic he is complete crap. Complete. So I just pointed out his mistakes. Just left it at that. Did you see the piece in the *Journal*?" Daniel nodded, although in fact he never read that newspaper. "I made short work of him, I must say. He can't write. He simply can't write. I saw him off."

"When did he review your book?" Daniel asked him.

"Oh, three or four years ago."

"Graham Maland?" he said to Daniel on another evening. "I wouldn't trust him as far as I can spit." Graham Maland was a young novelist who had published three novels within the space of five years, all of them widely praised and admired. Wilkin did not reserve his animosity only for his fellow poets. "Have you ever seen him?" Daniel shook his head. "He's a fat little pudding. Full of suet. And what a shit. I happen to know that he got a ten-thousand-pound advance for his next novel. Ten thousand pounds! It's ridiculous. Anyway, there's a rumour going around that he's a plagiarist. Someone sent the manuscript of a novel to him, and he just copied the plot. That's what people are saying. And I tell you what. I'm sure he's queer."

Daniel still went to see Sparkler in London, where he lived in a small flat on the same terraced street that Harry and Guinevere Flaxman had once visited. "Would you like to go to a queer pub, Dan?" he asked him one evening.

"In Limehouse?"

"No. Across the water. We'll swim."

It was crowded and noisy. They went up to the bar where two middle-aged men were standing, identically dressed in dark slacks and scarlet blouses; both had a small scarf tied around the neck. "I'm Pooky," one of them said, "and she's Spooky." They were heavily made-up, but no amount of powder or mascara could conceal the years of humiliation and panic.

Daniel looked down the other side of the bar. A young man, wearing a black leather jacket, was talking over his shoulder to someone whom Daniel could not see. "If you come near me one more time, you bastard," the young man was saying in an off-hand manner, "I'm going to break all of your fingers."

"That one over there?" Spooky was talking to Sparkler. "Oh she's been around for *years*. Her trousers are so tight you can see her piles."

"He's got a boner."

"Everyone gets a boner in here. You should go into the gents."

"Who's your thin friend?" Pooky asked Sparkler.

"Dan."

"Danny Boy. Oh Danny Boy, the pipes, the pipes are calling." Pooky had a pleasant baritone voice. "Can I hold up your umbrella, Danny?" Daniel looked perplexed. "It's just a *camp*. What do you do, Danny Boy?"

"I'm a teacher."

"Ooh, Miss Comprehensive. Do you fancy chicken?"

"Under-age boys," Sparkler told him.

"No. I don't."

"No harm in asking. A *cat* may look at a *queen*. And I know what you do, Sparkie. I've heard all about you. From a certain older gentleman."

"Oh yes? Who?"

"He is known to us as the bony queen of nowhere."

"I know exactly who you mean."

"Oh my gawd." Spooky raised a glass to his lips. "Here she is." An old man, wearing a tweed suit and red jumper, was approaching them. "Good evening, cunt face."

"Hello, pussies." He had a distinguished, if slightly fruity, voice. "Good evening, Sparkie boy."

"Evening, major."

The major's rheumy eyes travelled in Daniel's direction. "Who is this one?"

"A friend."

"A friend? Oh well done, Sparkler. Have a banana." It was clear that the major believed Daniel to be more a customer than a friend. "Anyone seen Tony Cointreau?"

"Over there." Spooky nodded in the general direction of the dance floor. "Looking for trade."

Tony Cointreau was wearing a square pork-pie hat made out of leather, a loose-fitting shirt and torn jeans embroidered with stars. He never stopped moving, swivelling his hips, tapping his feet, half-turning. "That young man," the major said, "gave me crabs."

"You shouldn't be sleeping with rent, you old cunt. Apologies, Sparkler."

"No offence. No offence."

"But at my age—"

"At your age you should be dead."

Tony Cointreau came over to them. "More old queens than in Westminster Abbey." The remark was ignored. It had been made before. "Whose round is it?"

"Yours, you silly slut."

"Do you know what I fancy?" Pooky asked no one in particular. "A nice bit of black cock."

The major turned round from the bar. "Yum yum. Sloppy seconds for me, please."

Two men were kissing in a corner, inviting looks of disapproval or envy. The whole darkly lit space was filled with looks, glimpses, sneaks, peeps, glances, winks, nudges, touches, strokes, nods interspersed with grins and smiles. The air was filled with the smell of beer and leather and cigarettes. Daniel enjoyed his time with Sparkler.

"Why not come to a party in London?" Wilkin was sitting with Daniel in the cafeteria of the English Faculty. "I can't promise you'll enjoy it. But you may meet some interesting people. It's the annual bash of Connaught & Douglas." Daniel accepted the invitation readily enough. He was intrigued by the prospect of seeing what Wilkin called "the literary mob." "I'll tell you what," Wilkin told him the following morning. "We'll have lunch with some chums first. They always meet on Fridays." Daniel then learned that there was a lunch club of young writers and journalists known as the Ancient Druids after the public house in which they met.

They travelled together on the train to London. "Did you know," Wilkin said, slapping his leg with his hand, "that Jemimah Slater is in trouble for plagiarism? She wrote an article for *Eighteenth Century Studies* on a possible source for *The Rape of the Lock*. It turns out that she got it all from a post-graduate thesis she was supervising. It couldn't happen to a nicer girl, could it?"

"Will she be suspended?"

"Oh no. She'll get away with it. It will be hushed up. It always is. That's the way they operate."

"*They?*"

"Did you see that piece on Tom Eliot by Gardiner? Gardiner gave me a good review once. Fine critic."

By the time they arrived at Liverpool Street Daniel was exhausted.

They took the underground to Tottenham Court Road; from there it was a short walk to the Ancient Druids in Poland Street. They entered the pub and walked up a steep staircase to a small dining room on the first floor. Already sitting at the table was a burly young man introduced to Daniel as Denis Davis. He was an American or Canadian (Daniel did not know which) who had come to London to earn his living as a poet and literary journalist. He greeted Wilkin warily, and looked with suspicion on Daniel. "You Cambridge types scare the shit out of me," he said cheerfully. "You are so moral. So analytical. Frank Leavis still rules. Is that right?"

"I am not a Cambridge type," Wilkin replied. "I happen to teach there. That's all. And Dr. Leavis has retired."

Then there entered the room a young man with round spectacles, and a diminutive moustache. Wilkin introduced him to Daniel as Clive Rentoul, who specialised in interviews for the arts and books sections of the *Globe*. Both Davis and Rentoul were wearing turtle-necked sweaters. Daniel began to regret his suit, white shirt and tie.

The next arrival was Virginia Crossley, a young novelist who had been at Oxford with Clive Rentoul. She seemed to Daniel to be shy but not at all ill at ease; she observed intently everyone around her. The last to arrive was Damian Etheridge, announced to Daniel as the literary editor of the

Chronicle. He sat next to Daniel at the table. "Daniel Hanway," he said. "I've heard of you."

"You have?" Daniel was flattered.

"And I know another Hanway. I wonder if you are related."

"Who is it?"

"Harry Hanway. Our deputy editor."

"He's my brother."

"Oh is he? Your brother is doing very well. He is about to marry the proprietor's daughter."

It was Daniel's turn to be surprised. "Is that so?" He had not forgotten meeting Hilda Nugent with Harry in the Camden park, four or five years before.

"And she's the only child. If you know what I mean." He rubbed his thumb and forefinger together.

"Graham Maland?" Clive Rentoul was saying in an incredulous tone. "A marginal figure. A Little Englander. He's not a serious writer."

"The serious writers," Denis Davis said, "are Joe Heller and Saul Bellow. Maybe Mailer. They're the heavyweights. Saul is superb. And Jerry of course."

"Jerry Lewis?" Crossley asked him in what she thought was an ironic manner.

"Jerry Salinger. Raise high the roofbeam, carpenters. Great steal from Sappho." Daniel had no idea what he was talking about; he suspected that Denis Davis had none, either. "The Americans are the future. I want to say—"

"Oh," Rentoul said. "What do you *want* to say?"

"Have you ever thought of reviewing?" Damian Etheridge asked Daniel. "I'm always looking for new talent for the book pages."

"I would be happy to try. I don't know if I would be any good at it—"

"Nothing to it. I'll send you some new novels. Have a go at them."

"You're very pleased with yourself, aren't you?" Virginia Crossley was leaning towards Damian Etheridge.

"I don't think so, Virginia."

"Why are you giving novels to someone you have just met? Excuse me, I think you should show a little more respect for fiction."

"Respect?"

The others sensed the beginning of an argument, and looked uneasily towards Virginia and Damian. "And you review five or six at a time. As if they were tins of baked beans."

"There are just so many of them."

"I waved a flag," Denis Davis said to her, "when I read your piece in the *Standard*."

This seemed to mollify her. "The one about new fiction?"

"When you said that in history you can make things up, but in fiction you have to tell the truth."

She laughed at her own remark, as if she were hearing it for the first time. "Well, that is the case." It occurred to Daniel that her apparent shyness was actually slyness—and that she had a high opinion of herself. Her voice had a slight rasp, a metallic quality that was oddly intimidating. "At least," she added, "I take fiction seriously." She looked at Damian Etheridge.

"I bet you take everything seriously," he said.

"And what is wrong with that?"

"Nothing. Nothing at all." A few minutes later he whispered to Daniel, "That's what's wrong with her books."

"Wrong?"

"They're very heavy. Teenage suicides. Back-street abortions." She heard the word "abortions" and glared at him. "As I was saying," he added in a louder voice. "The French nouveau roman is doing very well here. In critical circles."

Daniel could hear Rentoul's voice in conversation with someone else. "You *must* have come across totalism. It comes out of situationism. Have you read Derrida, by the way? You simply *must*."

"I've tried. I don't understand a word of it. I prefer Heidegger."

"Oh that's very old hat. All that *Dasein* business. A real German bore."

"I've just turned in," Davis was saying, "a piece on Jimmy Baldwin." Daniel had never heard the phrase "turned in" before, but he assumed it was of common currency.

They carried on drinking into the late afternoon, their voices getting louder and their conversation more animated. They were arguing about the books pages of the various newspapers and periodicals—which had the best contributors, which chose the most interesting books. Clive Rentoul was complaining about the favourable treatment given by the *Observer* to the poetry of Sylvia Plath, Thom Gunn and Ted Hughes whom he denounced as the "Cambridge versifiers." Wilkin had nothing to say in their defence, of course, but he objected to Rentoul's description.

It was time to attend the party at Connaught & Douglas. The offices of the publishing house were in New Bond Street. So they crammed into a taxi, excited by their sudden physical proximity, and made their way through central London. In this company it seemed to Daniel to become an unfamiliar city, brighter and more colourful than the one he had known as a youth. It had become a place of promise as well as of pleasure. When they arrived at their destination they all clambered out of the cab, leaving Daniel to pay the fare.

The party was held in the board room and chairman's office of the company, taking up the first floor of a late-eighteenth-century house. Wilkin immediately went up to a tall, doleful man who did not seem particularly friendly towards him. Wilkin beckoned Daniel over. "This is Max Sitwell," he said. "Max works on the *Sunday Times*."

"Daniel Hanway."

"Are you a poet, too?"

"Far from it. I teach."

"At Cambridge?" Daniel nodded. "I was at Cambridge. Caius. A million years ago. I hated it."

"I don't think," Daniel replied, "that it has changed much."

"Oh look," Wilkin said, "there's Graham." He went over to a portly young man, wearing large horn-rimmed spectacles, whom Daniel recognised to be Graham Maland. With a nod to the doleful man Daniel joined the two of them. Clive Rentoul came over, too. "I loved the last novel," Wilkin was saying to Maland. "Superb."

"My favourite character," Rentoul said, apparently laughing at the memory, "was the taxidermist. Hilarious."

Daniel noticed that their appreciation of Maland's work had risen very quickly. Maland seemed embarrassed by their compliments, as if he suspected them of not being quite real. "That's very kind of you," he said. "How about you, Paul? Are you publishing another volume?"

"Not yet. Not yet. I'm waiting for the right time."

Maland quickly turned away and introduced himself to Daniel Hanway. Daniel was now quite drunk, and he was amused at the self-composure with which he greeted the famous young novelist. In other circumstances he might have searched for something to talk about. "I wouldn't necessarily believe," he confided in Maland, "everything that they say." Later he would not remember using those words.

"I don't." Maland smiled. "I don't believe any of it."

Daniel felt relieved and reassured by this answer, as if a whole complex of problems had been resolved. He joined another group that included Damian Etheridge. "I do think that Benny Hill is the true successor to Puck," someone was saying.

"Do you? What an interesting point. But surely he is Falstaff? And Hancock is Hamlet."

"Perfect."

He then found himself in a group around a television journalist who had just published his memoirs. He was a man in late middle age but he was glossy, perfectly preserved, with a shine on his skin and a shine on his suit. Daniel noticed that the others gazed towards him, as if some source of enchantment was to be found in the glowing cheeks and forehead. He did not appear on television. Television appeared on him. Despite his modest stature he was larger and more capacious than those around him. But then it seemed to Daniel that some kind of bright liquid was flowing down his face and falling onto the ground. He was beginning to dissolve.

Daniel overheard conversations. "Oh the *Spectator*. Terrible circulation. Shadow of its former self under Lawson. Gale has just appointed some teenage literary editor. Ridiculous. Think of all the perfectly good literary journalists there are."

"The opera was so—so Shakespearean."

"Tremendous fun."

"There was a dog in it."

"I thought the dog was *marvellous*."

Then Daniel dropped his glass.

He found himself leaning against a wall on the pavement outside; he was smoking a cigarette which (had he known it) he had begged from a passer-by. He was swaying, with half-opened eyes, and was in danger of toppling forward into the street. Then someone put an arm around his shoulder. "Are you all right, Danny boy?" It was Sparkler.

X

That's the way to do it

S AM HANWAY had become Asher Ruppta's "odd-job boy," as Ruppta called him, expected to perform various tasks from visiting the bank to sorting out the diverse files created by the business. He spent much of the time with Julie Armitage in a small back office, where every morning he would find an offering of food on his desk—a ginger biscuit, a packet of nuts, a sausage roll, a pork pie, a bar of Bounty. He felt like a pet rabbit. Soon Julie would be stroking him.

He was often asked to collect the rent from Asher Ruppta's various properties. Julie Armitage used to commiserate with him, for what she considered to be an unenviable task, but in fact Sam felt no awkwardness or embarrassment as he went from door to door with his rent book. He looked forward to the opportunity of talking to people, of learning about their problems, of hearing their complaints. He took an almost aesthetic interest in speculating about the truthfulness of those whom he interviewed. He would speak to them in a slow and steady voice; he was infinitely patient with them, but he was determined. He could wear down the most spirited or most volatile of the tenants with his politeness. He had an air of remoteness about him, also, as if he were not quite sure what he was doing in any particular place. He looked as if he might ascend into the sky at any moment. His eyes were pale, lending his face an air of placidity and calmness.

He also liked talking to Asher Ruppta: Ruppta would sometimes break off from business and, stretched out in his chair with his hands behind his head, he would tell Sam about his childhood on the island of the Celebes Sea. He would tell him stories of creatures of shifting shape that lived in swamps or marshes, of ghost birds that could be heard but never seen, of spirits that waited for the living in the shadow of barns or old buildings. His face then seemed to Sam to be set in a more cruel and ferocious look than the pliancy and passivity of his customary expression. On Ruppta's island each dwelling had its own familiar soul, to whom offerings were made at dawn.

One evening Ruppta told Sam the story of the boy who became a tree. It began when his palms started to itch; he scratched and scratched, but the itching would not stop. Then the tips of his fingers began to tingle, and he began to tap them relentlessly on the crude wooden table in his small house. He woke one morning to find two fingers of his right hand covered in warts or growths, so strong and tough that they looked as if they were made of horn. He could not cut them with a knife, and when he tried to tear them away from his flesh the pain stopped him. After two or three weeks, the fingers of both hands were covered with these strange growths. The local doctor was baffled by the symptoms; he gave the boy some ointment, made from hyena fat, but it had no effect. Then the boy's mother took him to the wise woman of the district. She took one look at his warts, and then turned away. Already the woody warts had covered the skin up to his wrists; they were of mottled texture, and dark brown in hue. They resembled the bark of a tree. The wise woman told the boy's mother that there was nothing to be done, but that he would not die. It was a disease, she said, that came from the forest. There had been stories of it over many generations. It had no name.

It was at this time that the boy began to sense a heaviness in his legs. There were small bulbous lumps swelling on the soles of his feet, and his toes were beginning to sprout the same dark wart-like growths. The layers of wood had also become thicker and harder upon his hands, and soon began to move upwards along his arms. One morning he saw some ants crawling among the layers; it seems that they had found something sweet to eat.

The growths had soon covered his feet, and were moving up his legs; he noticed that twigs and small branches were growing where his toes had once been. When he tried to walk, there was a soft scraping across the floor. Patches of green mould formed on the bark along his arms and, if he scraped them, pieces of the wood would become detached and fall away. He called out, day and night, "*Pahintuin! Pahintuin!*" Make it stop! Make it stop!

By now the bark had come up to his chest, and wooden growths had reached the back of his neck. He felt them moving onto his scalp and into his hair. Then he felt flecks of wood within his eyelashes. He sensed that there were little pieces of wood underneath the skin of his face. He was now helpless. He lay upon the ground outside his little house, where his mother fed him. He could no longer move, since the tendrils coming from his body had fastened themselves into the earth.

Eventually the people of the village could bear it no longer. He was an abomination. Against the protestations of his mother, and of his younger brother, they dragged the boy into the forest and left him there among the trees. He did not die. He seemed to find some nourishment within himself, and the frequent rains quenched his thirst. Eventually the bark covered his eyes, and his limbs were entirely engulfed in its mantle. It is also possible that certain roots slowly penetrated his skull and somehow changed the nature of his brain. His mouth was the last human trace of him, but that turned into what looked like a knot of wood. The boy now resembled a fallen tree of gnarled or rotting bark, a haven for small insects. The birds alighted upon it, and pecked at grubs or larvae.

The boy's mother visited the forest every day, and sat beside what was now no more than a fallen log. She stroked the green moss that had grown across its bark, and passed her hands slowly over the rotting wood. It smelled now of vegetable decay. She was sure, sometimes, that she felt a sensation of warmth. How did Asher Ruppta know this? He was the boy's younger brother.

"The Byrnes are very troubling to me," Ruppta said to Sam one morning. "They are never paying their rents. They must be taught a lesson."

Sam visited Mrs. Byrne on the following day. "I need the housing benefit for *him*." She nodded towards the closed door of the bedroom. She offered two or three pound notes. "For the sake of the children, sir. Look at them. Can't you see their poor pale faces?"

Reluctantly Sam accepted the money, and noted down the amount still owed.

"God bless you, sir. I'll pay it all back to you. I'm expecting a parcel from Belfast." She stared at the closed door. "He had one of his fits last night. I had to sit on him. My own health is terrible poor." The three children were eating bread with Marmite, their lips and cheeks smeared with the brown paste.

After the unsatisfactory interview with Mrs. Byrne, Sam walked up the next flight of stairs and knocked on the door of the flat immediately above. The tenant knew Sam's touch, and the door was flung open. "Come on in, Sammy boy. Time for daylight robbery, is it? Smash and grab? You should wear a hood and mask." It was Sparkler.

Sparkler had been a tenant in Britannia Street for four years. He had always lived in this part of London, and he relished the anonymity associated with it. But he enjoyed the weekly visits of Sam with his rent book. "Now then, Sammy boy," he said, "cup of char? Soak your powerful mind in tea."

As they sat together Sam told Sparkler stories about the other tenants whom he visited. He called him Spark. "Well, Spark," he said on this afternoon, "the Robertsons have vanished. Everything has gone. Bed. All the furniture."

"As clean as a whistle, is it?"

"A bone picked clean," Sam replied. "Nothing left at all."

"That is a very remarkable thing, Sammy. How did they manage to get away without making any noise at all?"

"The area is strange like that. Nothing ever seems to stick. Everything just fades away."

"I know exactly what you mean, Sammy boy. The streets will swallow you up. They're misty. Like the Thames next door. It was tough in 1944."

"What made you say that, Spark?"

"I was thinking of mist. And smoke. I was six at the time. There was this shelter. I hated it. Mum hated it, too. So we stopped going."

"Wasn't that dangerous?"

"Oh yes. Of course. It was a big oblong room, with a wooden bench along each wall. There was a tin tacked to one corner, with a candle stuck in it. It smelled terrible of piss and vomit. It's gone now. At least I think it's gone. What if it were still there? Still smelling? It don't bear thinking about, do it?

"Boys like to explore, don't they?" Sam was silent for a moment. "I used to go down into the ground."

"Yes. Boys go where they are told not to go. I'm still that way. I *won't* do what I'm told. There was an underground bomb shelter on the common. A big one. Still there, I think. Its entrance was boarded up after the War, but I knew a way of wriggling through. There is always a way, you know. You just have to know how to look for it. There was rooms on either side. Do you believe in ghosts?" Sam nodded. "Do you? Do you *really*?"

"I do."

"This was the curious thing. I was lagging behind a friend of mine. His name will come to me in a minute. Keith Watson. I was creeping past one of them rooms, when I saw something out the corner of my eye. It was like a flickering light coming from inside. I went back and there—you'll never believe it, I know you won't—there was a garden. A lovely garden full of flowers. And in the middle was an old gentleman tending to it. It was only there for a moment. And then it faded away. I wasn't scared or anything. I was happy. But I never told Keith Watson." Sam now smiled at the memory.

Sparkler and Daniel Hanway were sleeping in the same bed when they were woken by shrieks coming from the flat below. "Smoke!" Sparkler shouted in alarm. He threw on a robe and rushed out into the hall. "Call 999!" He rushed downstairs, where a fire was eating Mrs. Byrne's front door. He kicked out at it, and one of the panels fell apart. "Open it," he shouted, "open it!" Mrs. Byrne had the presence of mind to unlatch it, and Sparkler rushed in. "Get me some water," he said. "Let me get to the sink." The flat was full of smoke, and he could not see the children. He soaked his robe and then draped it across the door. Some of the flames were extinguished. He performed the same manoeuvre three or four times until the door was merely smouldering. Sparkler flung open the windows to disperse the smoke hanging in the air. The children, in their pyjamas, were huddled in the kitchen; they did not cry, or speak, but stared solemnly at Sparkler. He went into the adjacent bedroom to check on Mr. Byrne but, to his surprise, found no one. It looked as if Mrs. Byrne was accustomed to sleep alone in the bed.

By the time the firemen had arrived, there was little to do except to secure the damaged door. They were intent, however, on finding out the cause of the sudden blaze. "Do you have any idea what happened?" one of them asked Mrs. Byrne. She shook her head, but then looked towards Sparkler. She knew better than to speak, and he understood her. Another fireman then discovered some burnt rags, smelling of paraffin. "Do you have any enemies?"

"The poor Irish always have enemies."

"Anyone in particular?"

"I don't think so. No."

"Hooligans," the fireman said. "Yobs. There are some nasty gangs in this part of the world."

Mrs. Byrne went into the kitchen. "All of you get dressed now. We're going to your Aunty Theresa." Sparkler had followed her, and now she whispered to him. "Lend me five pounds for a taxi?"

He went back upstairs, and borrowed the money from Daniel. He came back into bed a few minutes later, and embraced him. "At least you're still nice and warm," he said. "Why didn't you come downstairs?"

"I was scared."

"You're always scared." Sparkler kissed him again. But he could not sleep. He lay in bed with his head propped up on a pillow. "I wonder," he said.

"Wonder what?"

"I wonder if Ruppta was trying to frighten them away."

"Your landlord? That would be a dangerous thing to do."

"He may be a dangerous man. I will have a word with Sam."

"Sam?"

"He is Ruppta's collector. I don't know his last name. Everyone just calls him Sam." Daniel stared up at the ceiling, glimmering in the dark room from the light of the street lamps outside. "There was no Mr. Byrne." He told Daniel the story of Mrs. Byrne's husband and his fits. "But he wasn't there."

"I suspect," Daniel replied, "that he hasn't been there for some time."

"But she still picks up his social security."

"She tells them that he is too ill to collect it himself."

The next morning Mrs. Byrne returned by herself, with two large shopping bags and a suitcase. Slowly, and with great care, she packed all the food stored in the kitchen cupboard; she folded the sheets and towels, putting the plates and cups between them. There was nothing else that belonged to her.

Sparkler came down to help her. "I'll be all right," she said. She seemed to him to be meek and uncomplaining, as if she had been expecting misfortune all along. "I'll just be on my way," she said. "I won't keep you."

"Is there anything I can do for you, Mrs. Byrne?"

"Keep an eye out for Ruppta."

Sam was surprised and shocked when he arrived to collect the rent on the following morning. He stared at the charred front door of Mrs. Byrne's flat, knocked, rattled the handle, and, realising that there was no one inside, hurried up the stairs to Sparkler. Daniel was still staying with Sparkler in the little flat. Alarmed by Sam's knocking, he rushed into the bathroom and closed the door. He did not at first recognise Sam's voice.

"What's going on?" Sam asked Sparkler. "What's happened?"

"Someone set fire to Mrs. Byrne's door."

"Whoever could have done such a thing?"

"I don't know, Sam." He turned and looked out of the window. "I have no idea. What do you think?"

"She never paid all of her rent."

"You told me."

"I explained this to Mr. Ruppta. I explained that her husband was unemployed, and that she had three small children."

"There is no husband."

"What?"

"He didn't live there. But she's still collecting his social security."

"Oh." There was no expression in his voice.

"Tell me this. It may be important. What did Ruppta say?"

"He never said anything."

"Is it possible, Sam—"

"That he wanted to scare them away? It is possible. Yes. And I will find out. I promise you."

Sam was now feeling uncomfortable in the small room; he was perspiring, clutching the notebook in which he kept account of the rents. "I can't believe that he would do such a thing."

To Sparkler's surprise he then crouched down on the floor, bent forward, and seemed to be attempting a handstand. "What are you doing, Sam?"

"I am going to stand on my head. It clears my brain. It helps me to think." This is what he proceeded to do. He managed to balance gracefully upon his head, his arms outstretched upon the carpet. After a minute he relaxed his stance and brought himself gently to the floor before standing up. "I know what to do now," he said.

Daniel was astonished. He recognised his younger brother's voice when he said "I know what to do now." He shrank away from the door.

★ ★ ★

Julie Armitage had prepared a plate of small sandwiches for Sam's return. "Spam or fish paste?" she asked him as soon as he came into the room.

"A bit of both."

"Ooh." She squealed in delight. "*Cheeky.*"

He knocked quietly on the door and entered Asher Ruppta's inner office. Ruppta was sitting in his chair, looking carefully at his hands. "Mrs. Byrne's front door has been set on fire," Sam said.

"Is that so? That is very unfortunate. Was anyone hurt?"

"No. But she left with the children straight after." He stared at Ruppta. "I don't know how it could have happened."

"Shall we call the police, Sam?"

Sam remembered the absent husband. "I don't think so. We need to find a new tenant."

"We should really call the police."

"They never do anything."

"But the police protect us, Sam."

"Too much trouble."

"Well, if you say so."

It seemed to Sam that his employer could not have instigated the arson. Why was he so eager to summon the police, if he had been the guilty party? No, there was another cause for the attack. He was reflecting on these things on his way to his mother's house.

She greeted him with a kiss, and then folded back the side of her hair with her hand. It was a gesture that he remembered from childhood. "And what have you been doing?" she asked him.

"There was a fire in Britannia Street."

"When?"

"A few nights ago."

"Bad?"

"Not really. But one of the families left. They didn't feel safe, I suppose." Then he told her about Mrs. Byrne and the three children.

"Poor cow," she said. "I know what it's like. What number?"

"Twelve."

"But that's where Sparkler—" She stopped, confused, and her face reddened.

"How do you know Sparkler?"

"Friend of a friend."

"Friend of whose friend?"

"I know a man who knows him. Would you like a pot of tea?" She went out of the room for a moment. "Mary will bring you one. Do you think Mr. Ruppta is responsible for the fire?"

"I hope not."

"He is a most unusual man. From what I have heard."

"What have you heard, Mum?"

"Nothing in particular." She seemed perplexed, almost worried. "Where *is* that tea?" She went out and came back with a full pot.

When he returned to Camden that evening he found his father lying on his side upon the worn carpet. "Thank God you're back," he said, "I can hardly breathe." His voice was high and quavering. "Someone crept up behind me and gave me a great thump. I can still see his shadow."

Sam telephoned for an ambulance. "Is it your heart, Dad?"

"I don't know. I don't think so. Your mother—"

They carried him on a stretcher into the ambulance, where they placed an oxygen mask over his mouth and nose; his forehead seemed to Sam to be suffused with a pale glow, or was it the brightness of the sweat against the skin? Philip Hanway looked up at the roof of the vehicle, his eyes flickering and darting as if he were deep in prayer. When they arrived at the hospital he was content to be lifted and handled, willingly giving up the burden of his body to others. He was no longer responsible for it.

He was taken to intensive care, and then wheeled on a trolley to the operating theatre. Sam remained behind in the small ward, where a male nurse was smoothing the bed in which his father had been placed. "The ambulance came within ten minutes," Sam said. "It was quick, considering the traffic."

"Oh they can drive, those boys. I'm surprised they never kill anybody. Still, it's all in a good cause."

"What are they doing to Dad?"

"I imagine that they are giving him an angiogram."

"Angelogram?"

"They insert a small cardiac catheter in the vein of the leg. Just by the groin. They proceed along the vein, right up into the chambers of the heart, through the pericardium and the atrium, into the pulmonary veins and semi-lunar valve." He recited this without much thought.

Sam grimaced. "Will he be in pain?"

"I am told that veins have no feeling."

Their conversation was interrupted by the arrival of another patient, a very large man perched on what in comparison seemed to be a very small trolley. He was followed by a young man and woman who seemed more distraught than he was. "What is his name?" the male nurse asked them.

"We call him Uncle," the young lady replied.

"We can't do that in a hospital, can we?"

"Benjamin. Rabbi Benjamin."

"Benjamin." The nurse leaned over him. "Can you hear me, Benjamin."

"He was so full of life. So full of words. Then he fell over, and was silent. He is a great man. A holy man."

"Can you hear me, Benjamin?"

"Let me be." His voice was low and powerful.

"I have to take some blood."

"Don't touch me."

"You need to be tested."

"I need nothing. I need no one."

"That's not strictly true, I'm afraid." The nurse placed the syringe in his arm. "That's good. That's lovely. Nice and smooth." He turned to the two young relatives, who were looking on anxiously. "Don't worry. I'm not going to drink it."

When he had removed the syringe, and sealed it, he walked over to Sam. He whispered to him confidentially, in the high voice of Punch, "That's the way to do it!" He went over to the relatives. "Does he have to pass water, do you think?" He approached the bed. "Do you need to spend a penny, Benjamin? Don't fret. We're used to it here. We would like you to use a bottle, Benjamin, if you can." Once more he addressed the relatives. "A lot of patients can't bring themselves to mention it. Not until it's too late. So I always raise the subject myself." There came a groan from the bed. "He's probably not urgent, though, is he?"

He left the ward with the syringe but returned a few minutes later and sat down beside Sam.

"How did you end up here?" Sam asked him.

"End up? That's a way of putting it, I suppose. Better than a prison or asylum, where a man of my talents might *end up*. But I'll tell you something. It's a horrible place at night. They say that suffering brings you wisdom. Understanding. Patience. Pain is supposed to purify the soul. It's all crap. Bollocks. I'm sick of hearing it. Suffering makes you weak. It makes you helpless. It leaves you at everyone's mercy. People you could spit on come to pity you. I've seen it. You are sick. They are healthy. They don't want to care for you. They want to triumph over you. Or they want something out of you. Gratitude. Love. A mention in the will."

"That's not a very nice thing to say."

"It's not a very nice world."

A doctor came in, looked at Sam with a mild expression, and shook his head.

The three brothers sat side by side in the chapel of the crematorium, looking straight ahead. "It's been a long time," Harry said. "You've put on weight, Sam. The way I see it is this. We can look back and weep, or we can look forward. When did you last see Dad, Daniel?"

"Six years ago, I think."

"Precisely. The same with me. You only saw him, Sam, because you still live in the house. We weren't a family any more."

They looked at the coffin as it slid slowly behind the curtain.

Their father looked back at them. He had no regrets now.

XI

Easily led

NOW THAT Hilda Nugent had gone, leaving a scrawled note about Southend, Harry Hanway began to see Guinevere more frequently. He moved out of Notting Hill Gate, considering it now to be a seedy area, and rented a small flat in Walpole Street, off the King's Road and conveniently close to the Flaxman mansion in Cheyne Walk.

He met Sir Martin, quite by chance, at the corner of Tite Street. "Hanway!" Flaxman yelled. He was wearing a dark overcoat and a black trilby, with a pair of brightly polished black shoes.

Harry was startled. He had been thinking of an appropriate present for Guinevere's twenty-fifth birthday, and had not come to a satisfactory conclusion. And there was her father waving and shouting at him from the other side of the street. Harry walked over to him. "I'm delighted to see you, sir."

"So you want to fuck my daughter, do you?"

"I wouldn't put it quite like that."

"How *would* you put it? Shag? Penetrate? Deflower? Or none of the above?"

Harry tried to laugh. "I'm very fond of Guinevere."

"Ditto."

"I respect her."

"Well, don't go near her cunt then." Sir Martin put his arm around Harry's shoulders. "You know she's a virgin, don't you?" Harry made no response. "And I insist that she remains that way until the day of her wedding. She isn't one of these London slags. Do you have a J. Arthur when you think about her?"

"Sorry?" He knew what Flaxman meant, but he wanted him to spell it out.

"J. Arthur Rank. Wank."

"No. I don't."

"I bet you don't think about her at all." Harry really did not know how to respond to this. "Come and walk with me back to the house. I like you well enough, Harry. You're a decent boy. And a good hack." He clasped his arm with a very strong grip. "I want you to do a favour for me. I want you to stick it to Pincher Solomon." Solomon was the owner of a string of betting shops in South London; he was known as "Pincher" because of his unorthodox ways of doing business. "I happen to know that he is defrauding the Revenue. I just can't prove it."

"So what—"

"Investigate him. Make him nervous. Get one of your financial people to drop a few hints."

Harry knew that Sir Martin was bidding for a franchise in racecourse gambling. Pincher Solomon was obviously a competitor, and Sir Martin was willing to employ the resources of the *Chronicle* to blackmail or intimidate him. It would not have occurred to Harry to refuse his proprietor's request. It was his newspaper, after all. So now as deputy editor, without consulting the editor, he began a dossier on Pincher Solomon and asked one of the financial journalists to consult the records of Solomon at Companies House.

He met Guinevere now two or three evenings each week;
they walked by the Thames in the direction of Lambeth, and
ate in an Italian or Indian restaurant at the upper end of the
King's Road. "Your father has told me to be careful with you."

"That's very good advice. For once."

"Am I allowed to kiss you?"

"On the cheek. When we meet or part."

"Can I hold your hand?"

"That is going too far."

So they talked of other things. "Why is English life so
unbearable?" she asked him.

"What do you mean?"

"One of my clients is dying in agony because she can't get
the right cancer treatment. And there's my mother going on
about pearl *necklaces*. It's all so wrong. So—"

"Unfair?" In his childhood Harry had been surrounded by
poor people, just a step away from destitution, and he had felt
no pity for them.

"Worse than unfair. It's evil."

"Have you told your father that?"

"He just smiles at me."

"He's good at that."

"You know," she said to him on another evening as they
sat in the Italian restaurant, "there are a lot of prostitutes in
Limehouse."

"Oh really?"

"All they drink is tea."

Harry shifted in his seat. "Extraordinary."

"Some of them go round to one of the flats in Britannia
Street."

"To a customer?"

"No. A friend. They call him Sparkler. I think he's queer.
Sorry. Homosexual. Sparkler has lots of stories."

"I bet."

"That reminds me. Do you remember Mrs. Byrne?"

"The one with the three children."

"Sparkler told me that she had been scared out of her flat. Someone set fire to the front door."

"Who?"

"That's what he wants to find out. He knows the neighbourhood very well. He suspects the landlord—"

"Asher Ruppta. I remember him."

"But it could just be a street gang." She had been picking at a seafood pizza. "Who can tell? Who can know?" He leaned forward and kissed her on the cheek. "That's not allowed. We are not meeting or parting."

"I'm a very lucky person. Having you."

"What do you mean—having me?"

"I mean, well—"

She really did not want her question to be answered. "There's no such thing as luck. I don't believe there is, anyway."

"You make your own?"

"Well, put it this way. You are charming."

"Thank you."

"You are confident. Yes. I think you have made your own luck. I don't know what drives you forward. Ambition, I suppose. I accept that."

"I am ambitious for both of us, Guinevere. I love you."

"I don't think you actually love me. I think you love the *idea* of me. I am the heiress. I am the only child."

"Of course. Everyone knows *that*. But I'm the best person to guide you. You said that I was ambitious. But I am also realistic, Guinevere. Maybe that's why your father introduced us."

Guinevere took him to a concert at the Albert Hall in the following week. "They say," she told him, "that music soothes the savage breast."

"I don't think so."

"Wait and see."

"I feel sorry," Harry said as they left the building after the performance, "for those musicians."

"What do you mean?"

"Once they wanted to stand out. I bet every single one of them wanted to be a famous violinist. Or whistler."

"Flautist."

"They all expected to be the best. What is the word?"

"Virtuoso."

"Exactly. They wanted to excel. But they ended up as part of a crowd. They must feel depressed when they wake up in the morning."

"I'm sure they enjoy making music together."

"You don't understand the world."

"I want a bit that's rare," Sir Martin Flaxman said to his butler, staring at a haunch of cold roast beef. "As if it's just been carved from the cow. Speaking of which, where is your mother?"

"She has a headache." Guinevere was sitting opposite him at the dining-room table.

"Headache? That's a woman's way of saying fuck you. Isn't that right, Harry?"

Harry was sitting beside Guinevere. "I wouldn't really know."

"Is that so? Hark the vestal virgin sing. Are you keeping your promise to me?"

"Of course."

"What promise?" Guinevere asked her father.

"None of your business."

"I promised," Harry told her, "to get him some details on a rival company."

"That's right. And I heard some good news yesterday. The old Jew has pulled out of the racing business." He was referring to Pincher Solomon. "That will teach him." He took a thick slice of roast beef, and covered it with a mound of horseradish sauce. "I like it hot, Harry," he said, drooling slightly at the mouth. "As hot as hell." Then he put a boiled potato in his mouth, and swallowed it. Suddenly he burped. There was a scent of horseradish in the air. "I'm going to get rid of Havers-Williams." He was talking about the editor of the *Morning Chronicle*. "He's a useless bastard. He mumbles." He took another bite out of the beef and horseradish. "I come from nothing, Harry. I'm a bastard. Did you know that?"

"I have heard."

Flaxman laughed very loudly. "No. A real bastard. Wrong side of the sheets. Do you know how that makes you feel? It makes you feel different. It makes you feel special. I made my first deal in the army. I sold military supplies to civilians. Does that shock you?" Harry shook his head. "Well, it should do." Flaxman swallowed another potato. "I am telling you this because you are almost part of the family. Almost. But not quite."

Guinevere suddenly spoke up. "Let's put an end to this nonsense. Do you want to marry me, Harry?"

"Yes."

"Daddy, will you sign on the dotted line?"

"You see what a romantic she is, Harry?"

Lady Flaxman entered the dining room. "I warn you in advance, Martin," she said to her husband, "that my nerves are bad today. Good afternoon, Mr. Hanway. What's all this about marriage?"

"I was telling Harry, Maud, that he is almost part of the family."

"Why he should ever want to be part of this family is beyond me. We are a frightful shower aren't we, Mr. Hanway? Simply frightful."

"He's after my money."

143

"Do you see what I mean, Mr. Hanway? There is no refinement here. No elegance." Lady Flaxman was a tall, thin woman with a voice of the purest diction and a black dress of the most elegant cut. She wore her jewels as if she had inherited them. In fact she came from a family of small traders in Enfield. "Are you sure you aren't making a most terrible mistake?"

"Oh no. I love Guinevere."

"Love is a very small word." Flaxman was sucking on a piece of fat. "For a very small thing."

"You see, Mr. Hanway, my husband has no finesse. He is nature, red in tooth and claw."

"I'm not the only one."

With a pained smile she sat beside her husband. "Is there any beef left?" Then she looked, slowly and sorrowfully, at Harry. "Like a lamb to the slaughter," she said.

"He is not being slaughtered, Mummy, he is getting married to me."

"The married state is like a butcher's shop, dear. Blood on the floor. Everything. The works." She toyed with a piece of potato. "If there is to be a marriage," she said, staring disapprovingly at her daughter, "it must be somewhere rural and delightful. A medieval churchyard. Graveyard. Yew trees. Bells. That sort of thing."

"As long as there is no confetti," Guinevere replied.

"Aren't you supposed to tie an old boot to the car?" her father asked her. He was looking at his wife.

"We don't want anything sexual," she said. "My mother will be there."

"The graveyard may come in handy."

"Oh I really can't bear it. I haven't got the strength to fight you any more, Martin. Where is the horseradish?" Harry handed her a cut-glass jar and its acccompanying silver spoon. She spread the contents delicately, and then began cutting up the meat in small squares. "I presume, Guinevere, that you will be wearing white?"

"If you say so, Mother."

"It is not what I say. It is what you may or may not have done." Sir Martin laughed. "It is not a laughing matter. A virgin bride is a wonderful thing. I should know. I was a virgin once. I was the cynosure of all eyes." She popped a morsel into her mouth. "I am very feminine, you see, Mr. Hanway. I am my own worst enemy. I am easily led." She glared at her husband. "Not that anyone considers my feelings any more. I might as well be deaf and dumb. I might as well be blind. Like those poor mice." Guinevere looked towards her father and raised her eyebrows. "Of course," Lady Flaxman announced to Harry, "there's no question of children."

"Mummy!"

"Guinevere is too frail. Too weak. It would kill her."

Harry looked at his intended wife without any expression.

The wedding took place on a grey and overcast day. The ceremony in the Guards Chapel was, at Guinevere's request, very simple. But she wore a white bridal dress, and Harry had bought a dark morning suit. They smiled pleasantly at one another when the union was pronounced by the priest. It was in fact Sir Martin who cried, sobbing quietly as he stood beside his daughter. As the newly wed couple walked down the aisle one of Harry's colleagues remarked that he seemed very pleased with himself—"As well he might," he added in a whisper. Guinevere, on the other hand, had an expression of faint bewilderment.

By the time of the reception, in the Ritz Hotel just across the park, Sir Martin had recovered his composure. He had already decided that he wished to make a speech, and so a microphone had been set up in a corner of the large room in which the party was being held. The walls glittered with long mirrors, and the thick scarlet carpet glowed in the light. The sun shone through the high windows so that the chandeliers, with thousands of pieces of intricate glass, seemed to swim in the general brightness. It had been noticed by some of Harry's colleagues that this was entirely a Flaxman affair; none of Harry's family had appeared, and it was presumed that none had been invited. Did he in fact have a family at all? One suggested that he was a Barnardo's boy, while another speculated that the Hanway relatives were too poor or too uncouth to be shown.

"I stand here a happy man," Sir Martin Flaxman was saying into the microphone. "Almost as happy as Harry. He is the cat who gets the cream, isn't he? I never thought Guinevere would marry. I thought she would become a nun. Seriously. I hope for Harry's sake that she doesn't behave like one." There were loud guffaws from some of the male guests. "I wish you luck, Harry. You'll need it."

"Really this is too much." Lady Flaxman had turned to her elderly mother. "He has no finesse. No style. No bearing." Her mother suffered from severe tremors in the lower part of her face, and could scarcely get the glass of champagne to her lips. When she felt the rim on her teeth, however, she gulped it down greedily. She was about to reply. "Shush!" her daughter told her. "I need to listen to this."

"I have an announcement to make," her husband was saying. "When I die—if I die—I intend to leave the business entirely in Guinevere's hands. I have watched her. I know her. She will make a good chairman of the board."

"Jesus H. Christ. This is an absolute insult." Lady Flaxman turned to her trembling mother. "I have a much better business brain. Guinevere is a mere girl. Do say something, Mother. Please."

★ ★ ★

146

In the middle of the night, one month later, Harry was lying awake beside Guinevere; she was sleeping, although she was as always restlessly dreaming. He could not sleep; he was making intricate plans for the future, visualising every scene and scheming every move. So he remained alert. But then he saw something. He saw what seemed to be a structure of light rising from Guinevere's body and taking her shape. This silver outline then seemed to sit upright. It was taller than Guinevere, by a few inches, but it bore the impress of her features. Then it bowed down, apparently in sorrow, before disappearing.

XII

The goddess of wind

I DON'T blame Harry for not inviting me to the wedding. I understand. I sympathise." Daniel Hanway was writing to Peter Palmer. "He wants to escape from his past. Including his family. I don't want to see him any more than he wants to see me. Other news. I have started writing fiction reviews for the *Chronicle*! The literary editor there is called Damian Etheridge. Very much a *journalist*. A bit stupid, actually, but friendly enough. He sends me notes with the books saying 'Don't hold back' and 'Lay down the law.'

"I know you are going to say that I have always despised novels. This is true. I stopped reading them when they reached the twentieth century. The funny thing is that this is the best possible preparation for reviewing contemporary fiction. Most of it is just embarrassing. *Excruciating*. You have never seen such garbage. Yet of course the regular reviewers treat these so-called writers as if they were Tolstoy or Proust. If I see the phrase 'an accomplished debut' or 'a return to form' or 'a magisterial performance' or 'voice of his generation,' I shall scream and scream until I'm sick.

"It actually makes me angry, although I admit that anger is an unworthy emotion. As you know I am the most mild-mannered person imaginable. But put me behind a typewriter and I become a *fiend*. I like to go for the established names. Braine. Golding. Greene. What a lot of charlatans they are! And I get paid thirty pounds a review!"

Still, he was getting noticed. At literary parties, for which he often travelled to London, his name was becoming recognised. "So you," one writer said to him, "are the *enfant terrible.*" He pronounced the French phrase exquisitely.

"I wouldn't say that." As usual, Daniel was very modest.

"Oh I would." There was a touch of contempt in his voice. "You like to pick a fight, don't you?"

"I don't think so."

"Why don't you do some serious reviewing?"

Daniel did not understand why he was so angry with him. Daniel discovered later that he had criticised a novel by one of his friends.

"You are making waves," another writer said. "Make sure that you don't go under."

At Cambridge of course he was ready to dismiss his journalism as a matter of no consequence—if anyone had asked him about it. But his colleagues did not mention it. He knew very well that it was considered vulgar and even indecent to appear in the "public prints." Yet he had an advantage over his contemporaries in the English Faculty. He had been commissioned to write a book.

One of the editors at Connaught & Douglas, Aubrey Rackham, had invited him to lunch at The Tramp in Air Street. "I have been keeping an eye on you," Rackham said as they sat down at their table. He had a low rasping voice, at once affable and conspiratorial. "You are terribly naughty in your reviews." He always wore a bright red handkerchief in the breast pocket of his suits, and was known to his acquaintances as "Hanky Panky." "Pure poison, dear. You are a wicked *witch*. I'll have a gin and It, please." He nodded to the waiter, and then winked at Daniel. "In this restaurant, they know what 'It' is." Daniel had no idea what he was talking about, but he laughed all the same. "Bottoms up," Rackham called out as the drink was placed in front of him. Daniel was then greeted with another expansive wink.

"Is there a book in you?" Rackham asked him after the first course was over.

"I beg your pardon?"

"Not literally, dear." Rackham squealed with delight. "You should be so lucky. I mean, do you think you could write a book?"

The idea had in fact often occurred to Daniel. There was, however, one obstacle to his ambition. He could never hit upon an appropriate subject.

"I admire your style, you see," Rackham was saying. "It just needs direction. Thrust." He settled comfortably into his seat. "A little bird told me that you are a cockney boy."

"I was born in Camden Town."

"Out of earshot of those silly bells. But you are a Londoner."

"Oh yes."

"I come from Devon originally. Home of old cows. Just up to lipstick level, darling." A waiter was refilling his wineglass. "There is a book I would like you to think about. Can you guess what it is?" Daniel shook his head. "The Writers of London."

He was perplexed and a little disappointed. He had been expecting Rackham to mention an academic topic, perhaps a book of literary criticism, or a new edition of a celebrated classic. The writers of London had never been part of the university curriculum. "London writers, or writers about London?"

"You can have it both ways, my dear. If you know what I mean." Another wink. "Look at that waiter. Straight out of Caravaggio."

So a few weeks later, after Daniel had prepared a synopsis, he was commissioned to write the book. He tried casually to mention the fact to Paul Wilkin.

"What?" He looked incredulous. "Who has commissioned you?"

"Rackham at Connaught & Douglas."

"Hanky Panky? That old queen?"

"Is he?"

"*Is* he? Is the pope Catholic?" It was quite like him, Daniel thought, to use a vulgar phrase.

"How much advance are they giving you?"

"A thousand pounds."

"A thousand pounds!" Wilkin tried unsuccessfully to conceal his envy and resentment. "So what's it about?"

"The writers of London."

"So it won't be a long book then." Now he was sneering at him.

Daniel decided that he had seen quite enough of Wilkin for the time being. He invented an urgent meeting and walked away.

He visited Sparkler on the following Sunday. They kissed amicably when he arrived at the little flat in Britannia Street. "I do believe," Sparkler said, "that you are looking well."

Daniel laughed. "How was I looking before?"

"You were looking like a piece of warm dripping. But now you look better. A few months ago—"

"Oh now you're going back to that drunken night at the party—"

"You was so drunk I could hardly see you."

"In—"

"New Bond Street. Next to the hatters. Opposite the jewellers."

"How do you know that?"

"Know? There is nothing about London I *don't* know. I'm

on first-name terms with the sparrows and very chummy with the pigeons. I'm like a black cab. I get about."

They went that evening to the Spit and Sawdust, a public house close beside the river. It was a few yards down from the local police station, and so was patronised by many officers. But it had also become a haunt for Sparkler, who enjoyed their company; they knew him to be a petty thief and a part-time prostitute, but this was no reflection on his character. Two of them were sitting in the saloon bar when Sparkler and Daniel entered.

"There you are," one of them said with a laugh.

"You are absolutely right," Sparkler replied. "Here I am. This is a friend of mine. He doesn't say much. What can I get you, Bill? And you, Ben?" He never did call them by their right names. He brought the drinks over, with the help of Daniel. "Bungho!" he said as he raised his pint of Guinness.

"Here's looking at you!"

"One in the eye!"

"That hit the spot."

Daniel said nothing. He did not feel at ease with these two policemen.

"What have you been up to, Sparkler?"

"Well, gentlemen, that is a leading question which I may not be at liberty to answer."

"Let me guess."

"Now don't embarrass me. I have feelings, don't I?"

"I'm weeping."

"Enlighten me on one thing, Bill. I came into your station about a month ago. To tell you about the arson attack on my block."

"Oh did you?"

"Yes I did. No one never gave me a ring about it."

"Did they not?" They looked at each other and smiled.

"You know that Asher Ruppta is the landlord."

"The wog? Of course we do. He is the big cheese around here." Ben was rubbing together his thumb and first finger. "He's got the lolly."

"If it was him what did it, and I only say if—if it *was* him, then he should be stopped."

"Where does your friend come from? Not around here."

"University."

The two policemen looked with suspicion at Daniel. "He ain't a student."

"I am a lecturer."

"Is that so?" He looked back at Sparkler. "You don't want to be worrying about Ruppta."

"I want to find him out."

"He has a lot of friends."

"I'm not scared of him. I'm not scared of anyone or nothing."

The other policeman had been watching Daniel. "What's a nice boy doing with a villain like this?"

It was not an easy question to answer. "Dry up," Sparkler answered for him. "None of your business."

"But it's yours, is it?" Both officers burst into laughter.

Daniel blushed, and looked away.

Sparkler changed the subject. "I might need a little bit of help."

"For what?"

"Finding them." It suddenly occurred to Daniel that this was the reason Sparkler frequented the Spit and Sawdust— "help" was offered and taken in both directions. Information was passed on.

"And what do you mean by them?"

"Them bastards that started the fire."

The policeman stared at Sparkler, his level gaze suggesting perhaps that this was not the best idea. But he said nothing. Then his colleague offered a diversion. Someone was sitting at a nearby table. He was a tall and emaciated figure, with long yellow hair. He must have been in his early twenties, but he was wearing the clothes of a middle-aged man—a black overcoat, black trousers, and a black cap. "Do you know who that is? That's the jackdaw."

"The jackdaw?" Sparkler looked up with surprise and interest. "What's he doing around here?"

"Sizing up the neighbourhood, I should think. You've got competition."

The young man with the black cap looked over towards them with what seemed to Daniel to be a contemptuous expression. The "jackdaw," as Daniel soon learned from Sparkler, was a notorious thief and receiver of stolen goods who operated south of the river in Southwark and Bermondsey. He had a reputation for viciousness. Although Sparkler had never met him, he was acquainted with several people who had been slashed or beaten by this emaciated young man.

Daniel noticed the thin creases upon his face, and the lines about his mouth; he noticed his slightly curled lip, and his insolent stare. The black coat and the black cap were old-fashioned. And there was something else. He was wearing brown shoes. Black trousers and brown shoes. The jackdaw was not someone who paid attention to his appearance or, rather, he was someone who advertised that fact.

"How long has he been here?" Sparkler asked them.

"A couple of days. No more. He's got nerve. He knows this is our pub."

"I wonder what he wants."

"What do you boys always want?"

"We don't normally cross the water."

"True."

"I'll be watching out for him."

"So will we."

★   ★   ★

Sparkler and Daniel walked back slowly to the flat, Sparkler looking behind from time to time. "What's the matter?" Daniel asked him.

"I want to see the man who isn't there."

They trod the dark streets in silence. There was fog in the street, spreading from the river; there was an acrid smell in the air, too, as if the fog were smoke from a bonfire. This was a damp and unwholesome place. The lights were burning in the downstairs rooms that they passed; where the curtains were not drawn Daniel could see plates on tables, cheap prints hanging from the walls, plain furniture, and people sitting or standing in silhouette.

Suddenly Daniel heard a most terrible scream: it crescendoed for some seconds and then abruptly stopped. It reminded him of an incident from his childhood. On Camden Common he had watched as a cat was seized by a fox. Daniel stood still, and stared about him.

"Why are you stopping?" Sparkler asked him.

"Somebody," Daniel replied, "has been killed."

"Well, blow me down."

"Seriously. You must have heard it."

"I didn't hear nothing."

"Are you deaf? It was so fierce."

"I never have heard that scream. Some people have. Some people haven't. My grandfather heard it once."

Daniel stayed for the rest of the weekend, eating with Sparkler in the now familiar cafés and cheap restaurants of Limehouse. He explored the territory for other reasons also. He had decided to write one chapter of his proposed book on the various novelists who had described the opium dens of the neighbourhood in the nineteenth century. There was one street in particular where the dens had been situated—Bluegate Fields—but it was now part of a park where blocks of council apartments rose. Yet still, in the lie of the territory, Daniel could see the image of the old street and its cobbled stones. He could glimpse it twisting its way among the small red gates and granite paths of the new estate; it would always be here, with its own burden of mystery. It was of the same order as the scream he had heard.

He and Sparkler came back on Sunday night from a meal in a local Indian restaurant, where Sparkler had insisted on ordering the hottest vindaloo on the menu. "That was a facer," he said, the sweat running down his forehead. "That will get the wind up me. Did you ever hear that song. 'I'm Doris, the goddess of wind. Tra-la.'"

"I am not familiar with it. No."

"Sung by Mrs. Shufflewick."

They had come up to the front door of the house in Britannia Street. When he put the key in the lock, Sparkler's expression changed. He took out the key and then placed it back in the lock. He opened the door very abruptly and ran up the stairs to the third floor on which he lived. Daniel followed him quickly, alarmed at Sparkler's reaction. The door of the flat was open, and he could hear Sparkler's voice raised in anger. "What the bloody hell is this?" he was saying. "For the love of Mike!"

"What is it?"

"I've been burgled. The burglar has been burgled. The thief has been out-thiefed. He's taken the watches. Can you believe it?" Daniel shook his head. "When one tea-leaf goes after another tea-leaf, what do you get? You don't get a cup of tea. Oh fuck." Sparkler went over to a small chest of drawers and opened one of its compartments. "Oh fuck." He intoned the word more solemnly. "He's taken my little red book."

The little red book was Sparkler's record of the visits of his male clients, Aubrey Rackham and Sir Martin Flaxman among them.

Sparkler pretended to strangle himself, writhing in such strange contortions that he alarmed Daniel. Then he lay down on the floor, and began banging his feet on the carpet. "I'm dead," he said. "I'm finished. I'm over."

"Don't talk like that." Daniel went over and stood above him. "Was my name in the book?"

Sparkler gave him a curiously impersonal look. "Of course not. You're a friend."

"Who was?"

"I can't tell you. What am I going to do, Danny? What am I going to do?" He rolled on to his front, and lay spread-eagled on the carpet. "I could go to the police." He started laughing, quietly at first; but he became louder and more hysterical.

"Calm down, or you'll burst."

"The jackdaw. That's the one. He must have followed us home the other night." He was silent for a moment. "Or those two coppers could have told him where I live."

"Why would they do that?"

"Did you notice how quiet they got when I mentioned the arson?"

"They were warning you to stay away. I noticed that."

"So now they have a little bit of insurance against me. The little red book is in their hands, courtesy of the jackdaw. Do you get it?"

Daniel did get it. It seemed likely to him that the two policemen, and some of their colleagues, were somehow collaborating with the arsonists who had driven the Byrne family from their flat.

"I'm going back to the Spit and Sawdust," Sparkler said. "I'm not going to be his candyass." He had an interest in American crime films, and on occasions borrowed his vocabulary from them. "Am I or am I not a flake?"

"You are not." Daniel said nothing else for a moment. "Is this really a good idea?"

"Don't worry. I just want to dance around him. I won't land a punch. I want him to know that I know."

The jackdaw was standing by the counter in the saloon bar when Sparkler and Daniel came in. "Well hello, my beauty," Sparkler said before greeting him with a brief but neatly executed soft-shoe shuffle. "Having fun?" The jackdaw looked at him warily, and said nothing. "Not so fragrant here as your side of the water, is it? They tell me that Bermondsey is pure heaven. Do you do a lot of business there?"

The jackdaw's expression was one of amused contempt. "This and that."

"More of this? Or more of that?"

The jackdaw sniffed. "Can it." He had a hoarse and rasping voice that was very like a growl.

"Now that is not nice. Not nice at all. Anyone would think you had a grudge against me. Next thing I know you will be breaking and entering." At that moment the landlord came behind the bar and asked them what they wanted to drink. Sparkler was distracted, momentarily, and ordered two pints of Guinness.

The jackdaw and Sparkler were both now standing at the counter of the bar, just a few feet apart.

"Breaking and entering," Sparkler said to Daniel in a loud voice. "That's a lovely phrase."

The jackdaw stared into the space immediately ahead of him. Then he began to whistle a tune that Daniel recognised. But he did not recall the words. The jackdaw whistled a few more notes, and then finished his drink with a flourish before wiping his mouth with a red and white spotted handkerchief. He tipped his hat over his eyes, strolled to the door and, on leaving, looked across at Sparkler. "Is your friend a nancy, too?" he asked him. Then he was gone.

Sparkler rushed to the door, but the jackdaw had already

slipped around a corner. "Push off," he shouted in his general direction. He came back into the bar. "I wonder," he asked Daniel, "if I will see him again?"

Daniel knew that he would. "That tune he was whistling," he said, "is called 'Sweet Mystery of Life.'"

XIII

Cheeky monkey

Is his nibs in?" the odd-looking young man asked Sam Hanway. "He's expecting me."

"Who shall I say—"

"The chancer from over the river. Pincher Solomon's friend. He'll know." He was carrying in his hand a small package that resembled a slim book.

Ruppta must have heard his voice—he was always very acute of hearing—because he opened the door at once. "Ah," he said, "the jackdaw is quick. He likes to chatter."

"I *am* quick. I told you so."

Ruppta ushered the young man into his office, from where Sam heard snatches of murmured conversation. He thought he heard the name of Sparkler mentioned, but he dismissed the possibility; there was no reason why his friend should be discussed by this stranger. There was the sound of laughter, and then Sam heard the familiar clicking of the lock to the safe in the corner of Ruppta's office.

They came out of the office, smiling, as if in memory of some shared joke. "Tell Mr. Solomon he has no need to worry now," Ruppta said. "I already had one. Now I have the other."

"Solomon will be very pleased. Hold onto them. Hold on tight."

"That is my intention. What is that English saying about birds in the hand? But you know all about birds, don't you?"

They shook hands, and Ruppta opened the door for him. "That young man is known as the jackdaw," he said after he had gone. "The jackdaw is considered to be an omen of death. Let us hope it is not the case here."

Sam left the office early that day, Ruppta permitting his departure on the grounds of what he called "this inclement weather."

He had decided to visit his mother at her home, and workplace, in Borough. One of "the girls," as they were called, came to the door. "Oh it's you," she said. "She's just popped out." She moved aside and, as Sam entered, she laughed. "You always bow your head when you come in. You would think this was a church."

He made his way to the room at the end of the corridor; the flowers were in a blue vase on the table, as usual, and the window had been left open despite the rain. He went over, and leaned against the sill. He liked to gaze at the rain. He did not hear his mother enter the room, and he was startled when she put her hand upon his shoulder.

"Lost in space?" she asked. "Your father used to like the rain."

"Yes," he said, "I was thinking. I never heard you come in."

"A penny."

"What?"

"For your thoughts."

"Oh nothing much. Nothing special."

"Your father used to think too much. That's probably what killed him. Is that an awful thing to say?" She leaned over the table and tidied the drooping stems of the flowers in the vase. "There. That's better."

"I'll tell you what I was thinking. Have you heard of Pincher Solomon?"

161

"Of course I have." His mother looked at him intently, almost fearfully. "He runs this area. Why do you want to know?" Then Sam told her the story of the strange young man with the long yellow hair who had come to Ruppta's office that morning. She stopped him after a moment. "That's the jackdaw," she said. "Watch out for him. Don't cross him. He can be dangerous. Everyone knows about him."

"Does he live around here?"

"He drinks in the Blue Elephant. Along with Solomon. Don't go near them, Sam. You will only come to harm."

"What do they want with Mr. Ruppta?"

"It doesn't matter. Stay away." Sally Hanway had dealings with Solomon. He took five per cent of her profits on the understanding that he would protect her from the attentions of the police or the threats of her rivals. "I wish," she said, "that you would find another job."

"Why? I like the one I have."

"You shouldn't be seeing these people. You shouldn't be dealing with them. They don't care what they do, Sam. They'll do *anything*."

He left his mother's house soon after, and began to wander through the streets of Borough. The air was full of noises—a football being kicked against a wall, the faint mosquito crackle of a transistor radio beside an open window, a car accelerating in the road, a child crying, all of them mingling together as the halo of the human world. Then Sam caught sight of the Blue Elephant public house. Instinctively he walked towards it and went in.

The interior resembled a large barn, with a circular bar in the centre of the open space and various chairs and tables scattered across the uneven floor. There were jars of pickled eggs on the counter of the bar, and the air was striated by cigarette smoke and the odour of stale beer. An Irish hound lay sprawled upon the floor, apparently asleep among the loud laughter and conversation of the clientele. A jukebox broadcast the voice of Johnny Mathis. No one paid Sam any attention but, as he went over to the bar, he noticed the jackdaw sitting on a wide deep sofa with three other men.

His companions had a distinctive, and almost shameless, air; each of them was dressed, like the jackdaw himself, in a variety of oddly assorted clothes. One of them wore a mustard-coloured waistcoat with white flared trousers; he had bright red hair that stuck out unevenly. Another had a pork-pie hat with a shiny grey suit; he was wearing white plimsolls. The third of them was older. He wore a blue cloth suit, and a black waistcoat with a watch chain draped across it; his shoes were patched with red and white leather. Sam surmised, rightly, that this was Pincher Solomon. The jackdaw, always quick and observant, recognised Sam at once and whispered to Solomon. "Over here," he called out. "Why don't you come over here?" Sam approached them slowly. "This is the gent I was telling you of," the jackdaw said to Solomon. "He works for old Ruppta."

"Oh does he?" Solomon had a soft voice with the slightest trace of a lisp. "Are you a good boy? Are you a slave to your master?"

"No. I am not a slave."

"You have more of an independent mind, do you?"

"I do my work. That's all."

"And what is that work?" Solomon seemed to look at him sideways, as if he were examining him secretly as he spoke.

"I collect the rents."

"That is very sensitive work. Very provoking. Very tiring."

"I don't find it so."

"Do you not? Most interesting. Most interesting indeed. Would you care for a drink? Benedict, will you bring our guest something?"

Benedict leapt to his feet. "What will it be?"

"Guinness."

"An excellent choice," Solomon said. "What shall we call you, sir?"

"Sam."

The jackdaw raised his head. "I knew a Sam once. He ended up in Pentonville."

"Past history, jackdaw." Solomon seemed to be concealing the fact that he was annoyed. "Past history." Then he turned back to Sam. "I don't suppose you would object to earning an extra spot of cash? I am not being indelicate, I hope."

"I don't suppose," the jackdaw said, imitating Solomon's soft and gentle delivery, "that you came in here by accident."

"It may have been a whim." Solomon replied for him. "A whim is a good thing. Did you come here on purpose, Sam?"

"I was interested."

"May I put it this way?" Solomon asked him. "Your lord and master asked the jackdaw here to help him in a delicate matter. Might Mr. Solomon one day ask the same of you?"

"That depends."

"Oh you are a clever boy."

"I would do nothing to harm Mr. Ruppta."

"And you are loyal, too. That is a great encouragement to me. That means everything." Benedict came back with Sam's drink. "This young man," he told Sam, "is as keen as the mustard. Are you not, Benedict?"

"Yes, sir, I am."

Pincher Solomon exchanged a look with the jackdaw. "You may be able to solve a little difficulty for me, Mr. Sam. We were just discussing it. Before you came in. Isn't that a coincidence? We need to get a certain letter delivered into the hands of a certain person. It is all very delicate." He placed the fingertips of both hands together. "Very sensitive. The jackdaw is too shy, you see. He hates to be recognised. As do all my boys. But you, well, you are anonymous. You look to me like a young man in an old photograph. One of the war dead, as it were."

"I can mention this to Mr. Ruppta?"

"He will be delighted. Overjoyed. Tell him that I am sending a little letter to Sir Martin Flaxman. Have you heard of him?" Sam shook his head. "Even better. Better and better."

As instructed, Sam returned to the Blue Elephant two days later. "Here is the famous letter," Pincher Solomon told him. "It is my epistle to the Romans. Fallen brethren, you see. This is what you must do. You must present yourself at the front door of this residence." He tapped the address on the envelope. "You must say that you have an important letter to deliver personally to Sir Martin. Personally. There will be the usual bustle and refusal. Then you will say this. 'Tell him it is about Tuesday evenings.' Repeat the sentence. He will see you then. Take my word for it. Give him the letter. Stay there if you can, while he reads it."

Asher Ruppta had borrowed the jackdaw from Solomon, so that the practised thief might steal Sparkler's diary; Ruppta knew that Sparkler had been asking questions about the arsonists in Britannia Street, and he wanted to prevent him from doing so. If he had evidence of Sparkler's illegal activities as a prostitute, he could at the very least evict him from his lodgings.

When Ruppta saw the contents of Sparkler's diary, however, he paused and reflected. Here was the name of Sir Martin Flaxman. Ruppta was also interested in another name. It was that of Stanley Askisson, who had carried the bribes from Ruppta to Cormac Webb at the Ministry of Housing.

Of course the jackdaw had first copied out the entries made by Sparkler, and then handed the paper with a flourish to Pincher Solomon. "The bum boy," he said, "has been careless."

When Solomon saw Flaxman's name, his eyes widened; then he smiled. In the letter conveyed by Sam, he suggested that Sir Martin might like to reconsider his plan to enter the business of racecourse betting.

When Sam knocked on the door at Cheyne Walk, it was opened by an elderly woman wearing an apron.

"I would like to see Sir Martin Flaxman."

"Well you can't. He's not available."

"Is he here?"

"It makes no difference whether he is here or isn't here. He is otherwise engaged."

"Engaged in what?"

"In *what*? How do I know? I'm only the cook."

"It's urgent."

"So is my steak pudding. Piss off."

"Tell him it's about Tuesday evenings."

"What was that, you cunt?" Flaxman stepped into view.

"Tuesday evenings."

"Let him in, Mrs. A. Come with me." He took him upstairs to a small office, and Sam took the envelope out of his pocket. "What is this?"

"It's a letter."

"I can see that it's a letter. What are these?" He pointed to his eyes. He opened the envelope quickly, and read the letter in an instant. His face flushed, and small beads of sweat formed on his forehead. He glanced briefly at Sam, with such a look of shame or embarrassment that Sam turned away. "Who do you work for?"

"Mr. Asher Ruppta." It was the truth. He saw no reason to hide it.

"There will be no reply," he said. And then he walked out of the room, leaving Sam to make his own way out.

As he left the house he heard another woman crying out, "I forbid steak pudding in this household!"

Sam was working in Ruppta's office on the following morn-ing, when Stanley Askisson came into the room. The door to the inner study opened at once.

"Ah, Mr. Askisson, you come at a good time."

Sam could hear their murmured voices, and put his ear against the door. "Our friend has gone," Ruppta was saying.

"You mean Cormac Webb? Yes. He is gone."

"And who has replaced him?"

"Alford of the bad breath." There was a pause, an inter-ruption that seemed to Sam to be full of meaning. He imag-ined Ruppta looking at Askisson, focusing his gaze upon him, imparting his thought without giving verbal expression to it.

"I have come across a diary," Ruppta said. "Your name is mentioned. It is all very discreet."

"My name?"

At that moment Sam heard someone beginning to open the door from the corridor; he took three paces back, and simulated a yawn.

"You should never let a lady see you yawn," Julie Armitage said. "It is not polite. Not unless you put your hand over your mouth." She brought out a large packet of nuts from her bag. "Do you want a peanut, cheeky monkey? Who's in there with him?"

"That one you followed."

Her eyes opened widely. "The one Ruppy gave money to?" Sam nodded. "Oh my giddy aunt." They looked at one another with mounting excitement, sharing the same recent inheritance of silence and secrecy. They were whispering. "What's Ruppy up to?"

"I don't know."

"Have some more peanuts. They help you think."

When Stanley Askisson came out of Ruppta's office, he walked to the door without glancing at Sam or Julie—perhaps even without noticing them. They both looked at him carefully, almost greedily, as he opened the door and left the room.

Ruppta came out of his office, whispering or singing softly to himself. "I am rehearsing a *limbay*," he said to them. "It is one of our songs. It brings down a guiding spirit. And then I offer it a sacrifice." Julie looked at Sam with an expression of irrepressible humour. "You may laugh, Julie. Laughter is good."

She swallowed her laughter, and looked around at Sam. "We were talking about Terry Thomas," she said.

Another layer of dust had settled in the Camden house since the death of his father. Sam had removed and altered nothing. A coronation mug still sat on the mantelpiece, together with a jewelled miniature of a young woman; they were joined by a small chest, lined in velvet, that held some old coins; there was also a toy music box which, when wound up, played "Underneath the Arches." On a side table had been placed a framed photograph of the three brothers at an early age; they were standing, smiling, in front of the stone pillars of some public building. On the wall above the mantelpiece hung a painting of the Embankment that Philip Hanway had purchased before his marriage. A small bookcase beside the mantelpiece contained a score or so of volumes, among them *Cold Comfort Farm* by Stella Gibbons and *Look Homeward, Angel* by Thomas Wolfe; Roget's *Thesaurus* stood snugly beside the *Penguin Book of Greek Myths*. On the round dining table against the opposite wall was the copy of *The Listener* that Philip Hanway had been reading before his heart-attack.

Sam sat down in the frayed but comfortable armchair which his father had usually occupied. A slight flurry or ruffle of sound caused him to turn his head towards the mantelpiece, where the coronation mug was sliding slowly to the right. The lid of the small chest then opened, and one of its coins jumped out. The painting of the Thames Embankment came off its hook, and sailed across the room onto the circular table. At this moment the strain of "Underneath the Arches," as interpreted by tiny metal keys, could be heard. *Cold Comfort Farm* and *Look Homeward, Angel* flew from the bookcase and landed on the carpet. Sam watched the proceedings with interest and without any fear. *The Listener* rose from the table and hovered in the air. The coins and chessmen now came out of their boxes and began to fly about the room. Some of them fell noisily to the floor but when they collided with Sam they merely brushed past him like feathers. The photograph of the three brothers sailed above his head, accompanied by the *Penguin Book of Greek Myths*. Sam sat there, entranced, as the familiar objects performed their dance.

XIV

Sausage land

E VER SINCE Harry Hanway had become Sir Martin Flaxman's son-in-law he was considered to be, in the words
of one of the night-editors, the "heir apparent"; sure enough,
he was soon appointed as managing editor of the newspaper,
and moved to a large office on the highest floor of the building from where he could see the steeple of St. Bride's and
the dome of St. Paul's. He enjoyed his new eminence in
every sense, and discovered to his surprise that he was capable of malice. He wanted to make sure that the nominal editor, Andrew Havers-Williams, understood who was really in
charge of the enterprise. To that end he snubbed or humiliated him in a number of petty ways. He did not return his
calls; he kept him waiting for meetings; he walked around the
newsroom, selecting items and suggesting stories, without the
editor's knowledge or permission.

"Is my daughter a good fuck?" Sir Martin was standing in
Harry's office, looking over the rooftops of Fleet Street.
  "Sir?"
  "I take it she is no longer a virgin."
  "No. She is not."
  "So you got what you wanted. But I think you are after

much more. Good for you. I like that. You're still hungry. You like to devour, don't you? Money. Power. It's all the same to you, Harry."

"I wouldn't quite put it like that."

"Oh but I would. I am like everyone else, you see. I judge people by my own standards. I wonder what I would do if I were in their position."

"And what is my position, sir?"

"I don't know whether you married my daughter out of ambition or out of greed. Either way, I don't mind. I don't *blame* you for it. I *applaud* you for it. I would have done the same. I am glad that she has married such a dynamic person. I am growing fond of you, Harry."

Harry was driven home that night in one of the company cars. Flaxman had bought the newly married couple a house in Mount Street, just off Park Lane, in Mayfair. It was a good address, and Harry relished the wealth of the neighbourhood. He had always wanted to live in just such a house and in just such a neighbourhood. He woke up each morning amused by his success.

Guinevere was still a social worker in Limehouse. "I'm worried about Sparkler," she told her husband that evening.

"Who?"

"The boy in Limehouse."

"Oh, the pansy."

"I don't think that is a good word."

"All right then. Poof." Now that they were married Harry did not feel it necessary to defer to her sensibilities in every matter.

"He seems so weak. So *weary*. He coughs all the time. I really don't know what the matter is. It really frightens me. I can get benefit for him, I think, but money is the *least* part of it." Two days later she had more news about Sparkler. "The good thing is that a community of nuns lives in the neighbourhood. Poor Magdalens, I think. Poor something, anyway. I was walking past their convent this morning and I thought to myself, I'll just walk in. Impulse. I told one of the nuns that a sick young man nearby needed care and attention. Do you know what she said to me? 'That is *exactly* what we are here for. God has sent you.' Isn't that amazing?"

"Amazing."

There was another matter that concerned Guinevere. "I don't like 'it,'" she had said.

"What is 'it'?"

"You know. The funny business."

"What funny business?"

She pointed at his trousers. "Sausage land. It hurts."

"Why didn't you mention this before?"

"I didn't want to disappoint you."

Harry agreed to abstain. He had not married her, after all, for sex.

He was surprised, two weeks later, to find his mother-in-law sitting alone in the dining room of Mount Street with a glass of sherry before her on the table. "Hello, darling," she said on Harry's entrance. "It is all too vile and uncomfortable."

"Is it?"

"Sir Martin is. He's behaving very oddly." Guinevere came into the room, and her mother stayed silent for a moment. "No. I will speak. Am I a pressure cooker? If you conceal your feelings, Guinevere, you can get lung cancer. Or so I have been told."

"What are you talking about, Mummy?"

"I am talking about your father. And please don't raise your voice to me."

"What is the matter with him?"

"He has become excitable." Harry glanced at her; he had noticed the same change in Flaxman's behaviour. "He jumps whenever the telephone rings. Like a jack-in-the-box." She laughed at her own description. "I hate those creatures."

"They are not real, Mother."

"That's not the point, is it? And then he snaps at me. I said to him the other day, what's happened to Tuesday evenings? He gives me what I can only describe as a very strange look. What about Tuesday evenings, he asks me. You always used to go to the club to play poker, I tell him. He then utters a profanity about poker that will never pass my lips. Wild horses could not drag it from me."

"Did he say 'fuck poker'?" Guinevere asked her mother.

"That is my daughter for you." Lady Flaxman was looking at Harry with an expression of mild satisfaction. "Your wife, I should say. Foul-mouthed. Like her father. I am the first to admit that I am not an angel, but I am not a fishwife either. I do hope that Mrs. A. does not intend to boil something in a bag." Mrs. A. was the cook and housekeeper who had moved from Cheyne Walk to Mount Street, where she now lived in a small self-contained flat in the basement—she had been, according to Lady Flaxman, "practically given away." "During the War, you know, corned beef was a great luxury. We live in a very different world. Guinevere dear, pour your mother another drop of sherry. Just the teeniest bit."

Harry went over to the window that looked out on the back garden, still glowing with the colours of the autumn. He did not know the names of the flowers, or the trees, but he appreciated the spectacle of the golden yellow and the green against the background of the changing leaves. Then he observed a shape emerging from the shade of the trees; it was that of a man standing with his arms apart as if in greeting. Harry saw his father at the bottom of the garden. His father was looking straight at him with that curious piteous glance he had adopted in life. Then he stepped back and was gone.

"Just going outside," Harry said, "to get some air."

He walked down the passage towards the door into the garden and, as he approached the threshold, he felt a curious sensation in his left arm as if he were being held very tightly by a strong hand. A cloud passed across the sun as he walked into the garden, and the shade deepened. His father was standing where he had stood before, but he had changed; he seemed to have become larger, and more fierce. And then he faded.

"He has made his bed," Lady Flaxman was saying when Harry re-entered the dining room. "And now he must eat it."

"Sleep in it," Harry said.

"I will sleep where I choose. And that does not include the bed of my husband. If I do, I will have to wear riot gear."

Guinevere was restless. "I agree with Mummy. I do think Daddy is unwell," she said to no one in particular. "He has a strained look. And he has lost weight. I can tell. Something is worrying him. Is there anything going on at work, Harry?"

"Nothing out of the ordinary." But then Harry remembered an occasion, the week before, when Flaxman had flinched and stepped back when the editor mentioned Asher Ruppta's name in connection with London criminal gangs. "No, no," Flaxman had said. "We don't want to follow that line. Not at all. Stay clear of it."

Harry went to work on the following morning with a sore head; he had drunk too much brandy with Lady Flaxman. When he entered his outer office his secretary was waiting for him. "There is a woman," she said, "claiming to be your mother. I put her in the board room."

"Oh. Good." He did not know what else to say. "I'll go and see her." He felt himself blushing with shame and anger at her sudden appearance. He walked into the board room, where Sally was looking out of the large window over the rooftops of Fleet Street and Ludgate Hill. He stood there without saying anything.

"Good morning, Harry."

"Why are you here?"

"I wanted to see you. Now that your father's gone—"

"—you wanted to come back?"

"No. Not exactly." She still had her back turned to him. "I was hoping that we might talk."

"Talk? Talk about what?"

"Why are you so hard, Harry?"

"I have had to survive, haven't I?"

"No. You always were hard. When you were a small boy, you were tough. You were determined. Nothing like your father."

"How can you call *me* hard? You were the one who left. Sam took it worst."

"Don't."

"I used to hear him sobbing in his room."

"I'm sorry—"

"Is that all you can say? We never really had a proper life. A normal life. We just grew older. Dan hid away in his books. That's what he always did. He would go into a book, if he could."

"And what about you?"

"I'm tough, as you say. You could slam a ten-ton truck into me and I'd survive."

"And I hear you're married now."

"I don't want to go into that."

"Are you happy with her?"

"I don't know. What is it to be happy?" He was silent for a moment. "Haven't you got a business to run, Mother?"

She turned around to face him. "You know about that, do you? Did Sam tell you?"

"No. I never see Sam. I found out for myself. I looked up the court records."

"That was clever of you. I told Sam that your father sent me away after that, but he was too weak to have done that. I left him of my own accord after I came out of prison."

"You left *us*."

"What else was I supposed to do? All the shame. All the guilt of it. I could cope with that by myself, hidden away somewhere, but not with you boys. Would you like to have seen your mother weeping? And the neighbours whispering behind my back? I thought it was better to clear out altogether. To let you all make a fresh start."

Harry was not interested in his mother's explanation. "I saw you in the street." He scratched the side of his face. "You have some interesting clients."

"Have I?"

"Asher Ruppta."

Suddenly she looked fierce. "What do you know about him?"

"He interests me."

"Stay away from him."

"Oh?"

"He is not safe. He is dangerous."

"So why did you visit him?"

"He looked after me once. He's a rich man, you know."

"Yes I do know. What are you trying to say?"

"I have a son by him."

One night, after the three brothers had gone to bed, there had been a bitter quarrel between Sally and Philip Hanway. She had left the house in a rage, and had walked without knowing where she was going. She found herself outside King's Cross Station, in the dirty and dismal forecourt where people loiter before making their way into the main hall of the station. She had some vague intention of catching a train—to anywhere, to nowhere—and so she pushed open one of the glass doors of the entrance.

She thought better of leaving on a train so late in the evening, and instead she went into a cafeteria and ordered a cup of coffee. She sat over it, her head bowed, inhaling its scent, her hands trembling slightly. She hardly noticed that someone had sat down at the next table.

"Where have you been all your life?" The strange question had been addressed to her. She looked up and saw a foreign gentleman, as she put it to Harry, with large hazel eyes that seemed to be oriental.

"I don't know," she said. She was, surprisingly, not at all apprehensive. She noticed the refinement of his voice, and the paleness of his skin.

"It is not usual for a lady to drink coffee by herself in the evening. It is not 'the done thing.'" He put quotation marks around the phrase.

"I was making up my mind what train to catch." It was the easiest excuse.

"You have a husband and children, do you not?"

"How do you know that?"

"You have a ring. And you look tired. You want to escape for an hour or so. Is that not right?"

She was drawn to this stranger with the precise, careful voice. Then, with an elation she could not explain even to herself, she joined him at his table.

She told Harry that she saw Asher Ruppta from time to time after that first meeting. "Your father," she said, "knew nothing about it. He didn't know about a lot of things."

"Such as?"

"I had been on the game before I met him. In Soho. Just for the extra cash, you see. So when we needed the money, after you three boys were born—" She grew silent, fearful that in her desire to tell her son everything she had in fact said too much.

"And when you were put in prison?"

"After I got out, I went to Asher Ruppta. I lived with him for a while."

"That's when you had a son."

"Yes."

"What happened to him?"

"Nothing happened. He's at a good school. A boarding school." She paused for a moment. "Life had been hard, Harry. I always wanted to have money. To be free. But then I met your father."

"I think you ought to go now."

So she walked past him and went out into the corridor. The story soon spread around the office that Harry was not a Barnardo's boy after all.

XV

Don't stick it out like that

"How are you feeling?" Daniel asked Sparkler one morning.

"All right. What's the weather like?"

"Well, it's winter."

"I know. The sun is low in the sky. Like me." Daniel looked down at his friend's pale face bathed in sweat, and at his trembling limbs; he heard his rasping persistent cough. "Is that window open?"

"No."

"I feel a cold breeze. Could you close the window?" Daniel pretended to close it. "I won't go to no hospital. The nun is here, isn't she? The doctor says he has given up on me. He can't find nothing wrong, he says. No cause, he says. What is that supposed to mean? The nun says that there's no earthly cause. She has a funny way of talking. Meanwhile I am burning to death." He seemed to lose consciousness for a moment, and his fingers played listlessly against the sheets. It was as if he were plucking a string. "Well," he said, after a while, "at least I won't grow old." His face was thinner; his eyes were brighter and more protuberant; his voice was higher. Then there was a flash of his old self. "I told the nun that I needed strength to steal again," he said. "So she went down on her knees to pray for me. 'Oh Lord, let him be a thief once more.'"

When Daniel had arrived that morning, he had found a small phial of water outside the door to Sparkler's flat. It had a piece of paper taped to it, with the words "Holy Water" scribbled in biro. One of the inhabitants of the house must have left it there. Daniel put the phial in his pocket, deciding at once that he would not let Sparkler know about it.

When Daniel left the flat that evening, he almost walked into the nun. "Have you been to see your friend?" she asked him.

"Yes. I have." He did not know how to address her, and he could not focus upon her face. It floated in front of him like some bright moon.

"You are anxious, I know," she went on to say. "But there is no need to worry. He won't die. He is being purged."

Daniel was so surprised by this that he took a step back. "Is that so? Are you sure?"

She nodded. "I have come across this sickness before. It is suffering with a purpose." She smiled and walked past him towards the door of Sparkler's flat.

Daniel returned by train to Cambridge in a state of relief close to euphoria but, as soon as he got back to his familiar college rooms, his exhilaration vanished. He had had no dealings with nuns before, but he suspected that they were superstitious to a dangerous degree. There was something about her, too, which had seemed to him to be elusive; she had possessed no strong presence.

He looked from the windows of his rooms, and saw Paul Wilkin walking across the quad; from this height he noticed how bald he had become. To his annoyance he then heard footsteps slowly mounting the staircase to his rooms. He closed his eyes briefly at the knock on his door. "Oh, Daniel, I'm glad I caught you. I thought you might be here."

"And here I am. Won't you come in, Paul?"

Wilkin entered the room and accepted a glass of sherry. The lines were evident upon his face, and strands of hair had turned greyish-white. "I wanted to talk to you," he said. Already Daniel feared the worst, and said nothing. "My editor has left Aylesford & Bunting. Well, retired, actually. And the bastards there don't want to publish my new book."

"Of poems?"

"Of course." For a moment he seemed offended. "Written over the last ten years. Some of them are bloody marvellous. So I wonder if you could put in a word for me with Aubrey Rackham."

"Hanky Panky? I thought you despised him."

"Well, my personal feelings are neither here nor there." Wilkin was blustering. "It's important just to get the work published. Connaught & Douglas is a good firm. I have always said so." No you have not, Daniel thought. "It would be an honour to be published by them again. They were once my mentors. You can tell them that from me." No I will not, Daniel thought.

"You had better give me the typescript then," he said quietly.

"I think it would be better, actually," Wilkin replied, "if Rackham wrote to me."

"You would then avoid the humiliation of seeming to plead."

Wilkin gave Daniel an angry glance. "Something like that. Yes."

"I will certainly mention it to him. I'm having lunch with him on Friday."

"Oh yes?"

"He wants a progress report on my book."

"How *is* the book?" He had obviously decided to treat Daniel with more deference than he had done in the past.

"I'm going to concentrate on the city's popular culture. Music hall. Penny dreadfuls. That sort of thing."

"Barn-storming?"

"Yes indeed."

"Good for you." He did not sound particularly enthusiastic, and he took a large gulp from his glass of sherry. "I might as well tell you, Daniel. I'm having a spot of bother with Phyllis."

"Oh?"

"She found out somehow that I was having a fling with one of the students. She started shouting. And I walked out of the house. Haven't been back."

"I see."

"I suppose it could end in divorce. But how much is that going to cost me?"

Daniel was early for his lunch with Hanky Panky, at the usual restaurant, so he took a walk down Regent Street. He had gone only a few yards when he was suddenly astounded to see Stanley Askisson walking towards him. He had not encountered him since their undergraduate days; they had made no attempt to contact one another. As they met and passed, their eyes swerved away from each other. Daniel quickened his pace.

Aubrey Rackham was already in the restaurant when he arrived; he had his hand on the arm of one of the Italian waiters. "No more than a drop of vermouth. All the rest is gin." He caught sight of Daniel at once. "I always think of Hogarth when I order gin. Gin Lane is in my neighbourhood." He had a surprisingly deep laugh. "What have you been up to? I mean, more precisely, how is *it* going?"

"By next month *it* will be finished."

"You astonish me. You are one of my most remarkable daughters."

"I have become, you know, by bits and pieces, really interested in the London music hall."

"The Crazy Gang?"

"No. Further back. Dan Leno. Harry Champion. Charles Coborn. They are the real heroes of London."

"I really don't know—"

"Do you not? That's a good reason to write about them. Their songs are rather wonderful. 'Why Can't We Have the Sea in London?'"

"Good question."

"'Young Men Taken in and Done For.'"

"Landladies?"

"Yes."

"Hussies."

"'Don't Stick It Out Like That.' That was sung by Bessie Bellwood."

"Lucky Bessie."

"The sad songs are the greatest. 'When These Old Clothes Were New.' 'My Shadow Is My Only Pal.' Far better than the poetry of the period. And then their routines—"

"I suppose their language was *choice*."

"Beg your pardon?"

"Blue."

"Oh yes. Very. Indigo."

Towards the end of the meal Daniel asked, "Do you remember a poet by the name of Paul Wilkin?"

"Of course. I never thought much of him. Dora Dreary. Rather spermy."

Daniel did not know what he meant, but he was reassured by his disdain. "He has a new collection he wants to show you."

"Oh dear. Isn't he a little bit dated?"

"I would have thought so. But I promised him that I would mention it to you."

"You have done. He may have been good at the time. But fashions change. Now what about pudding?"

After the meal was over, Rackham sipped his coffee with evident relish. "I suppose," he said, "that Limehouse comes into your book?"

"Of course. Sax Rohmer."

"I have to go there after this." He put down his tiny cup with a sigh. "A dear young friend of mine has become frightfully ill."

Daniel was surprised by this coincidence with Sparkler's sickness in the same neighbourhood—or perhaps it was not coincidence at all. Could this dear young friend also be Daniel's friend? One of the themes of Daniel's book concerned the patterns of association that linked the people of the city; he had found in the work of the novelists a preoccupation with the image of London as a web so taut and tightly drawn that the slightest movement of any part sent reverberations through the whole. A chance encounter might lead to terrible consequences, and a misheard word bring unintended good fortune. An impromptu answer to a sudden question might cause death.

Flushed by a gin martini and several glasses of white wine, Aubrey Rackham rose majestically to leave. He caught sight of himself, plump and red-faced, in a mirror by the door of the restaurant. "Just look at me," he said. "Not the ruins, but the ruins of those ruins. Silly old *cow*." He put out his tongue at his own reflection.

Daniel decided, at that instant, to travel to Britannia Street. He would wait there and see if Rackham arrived and entered Sparkler's building. "Are you going straight there?" he asked him.

"Where?"

"Wherever you said you were going."

"No. I must pick up one or two things from the office."

When Daniel reached Britannia Street he meditated on where he might conceal himself so that he could watch Rackham without himself being observed. He found a deserted shop on a corner of the street; from here he had a wide view. The wind on this corner was strong, and scraps of paper were being lifted upwards into the air. Suddenly Daniel saw the nun walking along the street; she looked straight ahead, and seemed uninterested in her surroundings. Daniel knew that she was going to see Sparkler. She went straight up to the door, turned the handle and walked in; he surmised that she must have a key. A few minutes later he saw Aubrey Rackham walking along the street; so he had been right in his assumption, after all.

Daniel walked away from Britannia Street, but he decided to wander through the neighbourhood. After a few minutes he heard music and singing; he walked towards the apparent source of the sound, a building of red brick behind a red-brick wall. A door in the wall was partly open, and he could see a small square yard with a statue at its centre. He could now hear very clearly the words of the song. *Veni Creator Spiritus*. The voices were all female. A nun came into the cloister and walked towards him.

"Have you come about the drains?"

"I haven't come about anything."

She looked at him with more interest. "How did you find us?"

"Accident."

"Oh? That's interesting."

"I heard the music."

"I suppose you did. You should be grateful."

"Grateful? To whom?"

"To your good spirit."

Daniel walked out of the courtyard and was just turning a corner when he caught sight of Aubrey Rackham.

"Whoops," Rackham said. "I hope you're not following me."

"No."

"Shame."

"After you mentioned Limehouse at lunch, I thought I'd come."

"Opium dens. Sailors with pigtails. What more could you ask?"

"How is your friend?"

"He is very poorly, I'm afraid." He sighed. "I don't know what else I can do. He won't go into hospital. A nurse comes round in the morning, but—"

"A nun?"

Rackham looked puzzled. "Nun? I don't think you'll find many nuns in Limehouse, my darling."

Daniel visited Sparkler three days later. "Here! I'm here!" Sparkler answered him from the kitchen; there was excitement, even exhilaration, in his voice. Daniel found him sitting at the kitchen table, a plate of biscuits in front of him. He jumped up when Daniel entered the room, and kissed him on the cheek. His face was flushed, his eyes sparkling. "I'm all mended," he told him. "She said I would come through it. And I have."

"What do you mean?"

"Can't you see? I'm better. I've been cured. She did it."

"The nun?"

"Yes."

"How did she do it?"

"I don't know. I have to tell you something, Danny," Sparkler was saying. "When I knew that you fancied me, I thought I could use you. But then I fell in love with you."

"What?" Daniel was seized by panic. He did not want to be loved by him. He went over to the window and glanced down into Britannia Street; he thought that he could see the nun on the opposite side of the road. She was looking up at him.

He returned a week later, and found Sparkler still shining. "I saw him," he said. "The jackdaw. I thought I *would* see him again. It's not a very big world, is it? I was just idling along the Gray's Inn Road, as you do, getting acquainted with the neighbourhood hounds, when I saw him. As large as life. In an old blue coat. Where he got *that* from, I don't know and don't want to know. Then he clocks me. He smiles in a queer sort of way, sticks two fingers up, and disappears down Baldwin's Gardens where the pump is. I follows him smartish of course. He turns left down Leather Lane at a fair rate of knots, and then sort of loses himself in the crowd. There was a market, I'm sure of it. It weren't a market day but there *were* a market. Otherwise where did all the noise come from? Anyway I just keep my eyes on that old blue coat and stick to him. When he gets to the Clerkenwell Road he stops and looks back at me and makes a sign which is too disgusting to repeat. Then he turns right. This is when these ideas just come to me. He's heading for the river, I say to myself. River? What river? Then I think to myself, maybe he wants to hide in the orchard. But there is no orchard, is there?"

"I don't know the area."

"Where can you find an orchard in London? There is no such animal."

"So why did you say it?"

"Most likely my sickness. I am still invalid."

"An invalid."

"That's what I said. So then I thought he was going up Saffron Hill, but he turned left down Herbal Hill. More hills in London than in Scotland. He went into Ray Street and then crossed the Farringdon Road. I stopped at the corner there.

Where the pub is. Coach and Horses. I could hear the sound of running water coming from the grating. Funny what you remember. Sewer probably. Then I'm on the chase again, and I follow him down to Clerkenwell Green. A lot of people were demonstrating there. Flags and such like. So he slides right through them. He's more like a fish than a jackdaw. Off he goes down Jerusalem Passage with me in pursuit. I hear music. I look up and see an old man smiling and nodding at me. What's that all about?

"He scarpers across the open space there and goes towards the old gate. I forget what it's called. I must have been sweating by now, and I swear that the ground felt hot beneath my feet. It was like walking on fire. And then do you know what happened?"

"What?"

"He *vanished*. Just like that."

"He probably turned a corner. Or ran down some alley."

"I know that's what he *ought* to have done. But I swear he just vanished. Well old mate, I said to myself, you are up a gum tree."

"Oh well." Daniel looked around the room incuriously, as if he were simply exercising his eyes.

"You are not really interested, are you?"

"Of course I am."

"No you're not. And I think I know the reason. You're not really interested in me." Daniel stared at him, not knowing what to say.

XVI

An absolute brick

S AM HAD no reason to think that anything was wrong. Asher Ruppta had telephoned the office the previous day, and asked for certain papers to be brought to his house in Highgate.

"I can't go," Julie said. "It's my day off. I've earned it. I'm visiting my sister in Folkestone. Cockles and mussels, alive, alive, oh. I *love* Folkestone."

"I'll go."

"There's a good boy. I'll get the address for you."

"What if he's out?"

"The keys are in the filing cabinet under Q. In case of burglars."

So it was Sam who had the task of delivering the papers to his employer. He set off with them on the following morning, and made his way by bus to Highgate. The road in which Ruppta lived was quiet, lined with large and solid houses of various styles. It was a reassuring, a comfortable, street. He soon found the house, surrounded by high brick walls and two electric gates. Sam pressed the entry button, but there was no response; so he took out the keys and tried each one in turn before eventually unlocking the gates. He walked up the gravel drive, his attention momentarily distracted by a large crow that hopped along the brick wall nearest to him. It was scrutinising him with evident interest.

The front door was locked but not bolted; Sam hesitated before entering it, nervous of entering the private domain of Asher Ruppta. His first impression of the hallway was one of quiet order; flowers in vases, figurines of marble placed on two cabinets of polished wood, a painting of a bridge over a river. A wide staircase, carpeted in scarlet, led from the hall; Sam looked up at the first landing, and saw it. It was lying there in an unusual position, with the left arm trapped beneath the back.

This was the body of Asher Ruppta. His throat had been cut, and the scarlet carpet was soaked in his blood. The rictus of sudden death was upon his face, but it gave him the appearance of smiling. At the sight of that smile, Sam became suddenly calm. He looked around for a telephone, and walked into the room nearest to him. This room was bare except for a long table on which various artefacts had been placed—a flute, an intricately carved casket, a figurine with a long face, a perforated stone, a knife carved out of amber. He looked at each in turn.

When a telephone rang, he walked towards the sound. It was in another room on the opposite side of the hall. He took up the receiver, and heard the voice of someone talking softly in a foreign language. "I cannot talk to you now," he said, and put down the receiver. Then he called the police.

They did not question him for long. His story was consistent and truthful, although he did not tell them about the muttered voice on the telephone. The sergeant had taken one look at the gaping wound in Ruppta's neck. "A sharp knife," he said. "Very neat. Almost perfect, really. You have to take your hat off."

Sam nodded. "There is a knife in the next room." So they

retrieved the amber knife, and placed it carefully in a transparent plastic bag.

When Sam was allowed to leave, he went down the gravel path and found the crow still perched on the high brick wall. He did not know if it was the same crow but he hoped that it was. The bird put its head to one side, and seemed to be listening intently to something that Sam could not hear.

When he had been in the presence of Ruppta's body, he had remained calm and careful; he had not surrendered to panic or alarm. Now that he was outside the house, he felt an overwhelming urge to run and to shout news of the event to anyone he passed. Instead he walked quickly down the road, and then took a bus to London Bridge. He wanted to see his mother as soon as he could. He had to tell *someone*.

When he arrived she was sitting in the back garden, leaning forward, looking speculatively at a patch of soil and considering what to plant there. He bent over to kiss her cheek. "Ruppta is dead," he said.

She fell back in her chair. "What?"

"Murdered."

"Oh my God." She put her hand up to her neck.

"His throat was cut." She put down her hand. "I found him, Mum. I think he must have been pushed down the stairs first. There was blood all over the place."

She stared at him. "Did you say that his throat was cut?"

"Yes. Right across."

"I can't believe it."

"It's true."

"No. I can believe it. When?"

"I've just come from the house."

"From Ruppta's house?"

"Yes."

"Who did it? Sorry. Stupid question." She bowed her head,

and then suddenly she looked up at him with bright eyes. "What about his will?"

"I don't know about that."

"But do you know his lawyer?"

"Julie will know. She's worked with him for years."

"Good. I must speak to her."

"Why should you be interested?"

"I have known Ruppta for a long time. And I have a special reason." Sam could see that she was trembling, and that she did not want to look at him.

"I see."

"You don't see, Sam, but soon you will."

On the following day Sam went into the office very early. He had not been able to communicate with Julie Armitage; he did not have her telephone number, and she had never given him her address. It was likely that she did not know about the death of her employer; she never read the newspapers, and rarely listened to the radio.

She came in at the usual time; her quick step down the corridor was familiar to him, and he stood up before she entered the room. She glanced at him as she put her raincoat on a wooden peg behind the door. "What's up with you, *Samuel*? You're not normally so polite. It makes me feel very ladylike. Very feminine." She was wearing a dress that looked like a dustman's sack. "Tea for two at Claridge's?"

"Ruppta is dead."

She looked at him almost without expression. "I don't believe you just said that."

"He was murdered."

She sat down or, rather, she fell into a chair and put her head in her hands. She remained in that posture for a minute or so, completely still. "Well," she said eventually. "I always knew he would have a bad end. Ruppy's finally had it, has he? My word. Gordon Bennett."

"The police will want to talk to you, Julie."

"And I will want to talk to them. He had a lot of enemies, Ruppy did. They could have been queuing up to shoot him."

"He wasn't shot. His throat was cut."

"That's Ruppy for you. Always goes to extremes." She listened eagerly as Sam went through the story again and again; she kept on asking him to repeat certain details, or remind her of what he had said before. "What colour was his blood?" she asked him.

"Well, red of course."

"You never know."

He was just about to elaborate upon his description of the amber knife when his mother walked in. He was surprised to see her.

Julie looked up at her, puzzled. "Can I help you?"

"Good morning, Sam. Yes. I think you can help me, Julie."

"How do you—?"

"My son told me. Sam told me . . . "

"I didn't know he had a mother."

Sally laughed. "You may know me better as Sally Palliser."

Julie was astonished. "What? Are you here?" She rose to her feet, and then abruptly sat down again. "I never expected to *see* you in all my life."

"And I never expected to be here with you. And Sam. Life has a way of tricking us, doesn't it?"

Sam looked at both of them with curiosity. "Do you want me to wait outside?" He was very demure.

"Not at all," his mother replied. "You have to know this. Asher Ruppta took me in when I was in trouble. We had a child together. A boy. You never knew about this, Julie."

"I *thought* there was something," Julie said. "He used to be driven down to this school. He said he was on the board of governors."

"He is. Well, was. I'm going down there today. To pick up Andrew." She glanced at Sam. "That is why we must find the will, Julie. I want to make sure that Andrew is protected."

Sam sensed the presence of something shuddering in the room, coming not from any one of them but from the three of them in combination.

"If there is a will," Julie was saying, "then George Flom will have it."

"His lawyer?"

"His so-called lawyer, yes. His office is in Gresham Street. Above the shirt shop."

His mother turned to Sam. "Will you go there? Explain everything to Mr. Flom. Tell him to get the papers ready."

On the following day the police questioned Julie Armitage in the office, and took away a stack of Asher Ruppta's files. Julie seemed agitated after the interview, and was strangely abrupt. "You should have told me about your mother," she said to Sam. "What have you got to hide?"

"Nothing at all, Julie."

"Shake the other one. Go on. Ring those bells." She suddenly relented her tone. "I haven't told them everything I know," she told him. She looked him in the face, almost greedily. "What a can of worms."

When Sally explained to him the details of her relationship with Ruppta and the birth of a son, Sam was delighted. He had sensed that there was some connection between himself and Ruppta, but now that had been proved in the most unexpected manner. When he went to see his mother, three days later, he found the house empty. She opened the front door herself. "The girls have gone," she told him. "They understood." She led him to the small room with the blue vase of flowers. And there, to his surprise, sat a boy of thirteen or fourteen years. He was wearing a grey school blazer, and grey trousers. He looked up at Sam with a calm and steady gaze.

"This is Andrew," she said. "Andrew, say hello to Sam."

"Hello, Sam." The boy stood up and gravely shook his hand.

"I'm sorry about your father."

"It *was* rather awkward. Mother and I are in a bit of a spot, to put it mildly. But my chums rallied round. And my housemaster has been an absolute *brick*." He looked calmly at Sam. "Half-brother," he said. He pronounced it very carefully. "My word. It came as rather a shock. Following my father, if you see what I mean—" He burst into tears, but then quickly recovered. "Sorry about that."

"Under the circumstances—"

"I gather that you worked for him."

"Yes. I did."

"Did he strike you as being a fair-minded sort of person?"

"I think so."

"Do you only *think* so?" He did not wait for an answer. "I believe that my father was not properly understood. He was the soul of charity, you know. Grants to institutions and so forth. But he was a little too diffident for his own good. He was, like me, rather an introvert." Sam noticed the boy's hair that consisted of tight black curls, as if his personality had somehow boiled over. "Still, I mustn't gabble on."

"There is something I want to tell you, Sam." Sally sat down at the table behind them, and took out a cigarette. "Asher has left his business to me. To turn it over to Andrew when he is twenty-one. So, you see, you will be working for me. You and Julie will have to teach me all the tricks."

"I don't think there will be any *tricks*, Mother."

"It's just a phrase, Andrew."

"Still, Mother, we must start as we mean to go on. That's another phrase."

Over the next few days Sam, Julie and Sally sat down together in order to go through Ruppta's investments and properties. Sally was intent upon all of the details—who paid through a bank account and who paid in cash? Who paid weekly or monthly? What was the condition of each flat and house?

"You cannot observe and measure at the same time," Sam said to her. "If you measure you cannot observe and, if you observe, you cannot measure. I can measure all the rooms and all the incomes for you. But if I observe instead, I see a picture of human misery."

His mother looked at him in astonishment. "Well, Sam, you have set me thinking. You know how these tenants live, don't you?"

"Mainly they live from day to day. They scrape by. They worry about paying me the rent each week. They struggle."

"I know that Asher made a lot of money out of his flats."

"But that's the point, isn't it?" Julie's eyes were very bright. "We're supposed to make money, aren't we? It's all very well for Sam to say that they struggle. We all struggle. I struggle. If Mr. Ruppta had not paid me a wage, I would have been in the poorhouse. Where did he get the money to pay me that wage? It stands to reason. From the money you collected, Sam." She slammed her hand, palm down, onto the table. Sam was surprised by her vehemence, but he chose not to argue with her. He would speak to his mother privately, to see what could be done for the poorer tenants.

On the following day he was asked to go to the police station for a formal interview about the afternoon he found Asher Ruppta's body. He was questioned by the same inspector who had come to the house. "We have learned a lot more since I last saw you." Inspector Sutherland had a soft voice and tremulous eyes. "We know, if I may say so, a lot more about you." He was polite, almost deferential, to Sam as if he were in some way intimidated by him. Sam sensed this, too, and was bewildered by it. "You are Sally's son, are you not?" Sam nodded. "And your mother had—was close to Mr. Ruppta? Would that be a fair thing to say?"

"I didn't know about that. Until after."

"Naturally not. Very understandable." They were facing each other, across a table, in a small boxlike room without windows. "You were right about the amber dagger, by the way. You seemed to know about it. I was impressed."

"It was the only dagger I could see."

"But how did you guess that he had been killed by that dagger specifically? That was an inspired choice. Hole in one. Was it you who told me that he had fallen down the stairs before his throat had been cut?"

Sam was puzzled. "No."

"Funny. I thought it was you. No. Of course not. How could you know such a thing? As it happens, he fell *after* his throat was cut. Some spatters of blood were found on the wall at the top of the stairs. Did he fall or was he pushed? What do you think, Sam?" Sam shrugged his shoulders. "But if you were a betting man, what would you fancy? Go on. Have a flutter." Inspector Sutherland looked imploringly at Sam; his expression seemed almost comical. Then he laughed himself, as if appreciating the joke. Sam laughed, too, despite the fact that he was not feeling very comfortable with the tone of Sutherland's questions. "I suspect that the deceased—" Here he adjusted his tie. "That the deceased knew his attacker. There is no sign of a forced entry, you see. No sign of a struggle. He might have been having a quiet chat on the landing of the staircase. I can see it, can't you? It's a lovely house, it really is. I've read the will. Your mother gets it."

"She gets the business, too."

"Oh yes. Naturally."

"In trust for her son."

"Not you of course. The other one."

"I also have two brothers."

"Oh?" He seemed interested in this suddenly presented fact. "Do they know—"

"They don't."

"Let sleeping dogs lie?"

"Something like that."

"Well, this has been a most satisfactory conversation." Sutherland rubbed the palms of his hands together and smiled cheerfully before jumping to his feet. "I know where to find you. If I should need you again."

Sam was thoughtful, and a little apprehensive, as he made his way back to Camden Town. A bird fluttered and flew out of a hedge on the road home, startling him. He arrived home at twilight. It was that period, in late October, when the clocks were put backwards by an hour. So the evenings had become darker earlier. He entered the empty house with a sigh, but he did not put on the light. He preferred to sit in the front room until his eyes had become accustomed to the gloom and he could see the familiar objects around him. He did not care for the unnatural light of the electric bulb; it lent a false brightness to the world, and made him uneasy.

Someone knocked very loudly at the door. He hesitated, and then went out. It was his mother. "I thought you must have been in the kitchen," she said. "There was no light."

"I was just sitting."

"May I come in?" He made way for her, and followed her into the front room before switching on the light. "I haven't been here since—since it happened. Nothing much has changed, has it?"

"Dad didn't do much to it. No."

"Still that old radio. It must be an antique by now. Are you still in your old room?"

"I'm in Harry's."

"Treating yourself." She stepped into the kitchen. "It's smaller than I remembered it."

"Sometimes," he said, "I feel the world closing in."

"Sam, that's one of the reasons I'm here. I'd like you to move in with us. Andrew is away at school for some of the time, so you would make good company. You would be much more comfortable in Borough. And we can set up the business there. I've given it a lot of thought. There's no need to be in the middle of town. It's a tiring place."

"What about his house in Highgate?"

"I'm selling it. Andrew wants me to." She sat down at the kitchen table. "Make me a cup of tea, will you?" She was silent as he prepared and poured the tea. "Who do you think killed him, Sam?"

"I think he may have been blackmailing people."

"That wouldn't surprise me." She sipped her tea. "What do you think of Julie?"

"What?"

"There's something odd about her. I can't put my finger on it. Don't you think it funny that, on the day Asher died, she was visiting her sister in Folkestone? She told me that her sister was a bit dotty. Forgetful."

"What are you getting at, Mum?"

"The dotty sister makes a good alibi, doesn't she?"

"Why on earth would Julie want to murder Mr. Ruppta?"

"I don't know. But I'm going to find out."

XVII

Ants in your pants

WHEN HARRY Hanway broke the news of Asher Ruppta's murder to Sir Martin Flaxman, his father-in-law crowed with delight. "The crook has been killed, has he? How was it done?"

"I'm trying to find out the details now."

"Now's the time to go after him. Print everything you've got. Nothing wrong with fucking the dead. You can't catch anything."

Harry Hanway noted, as he put down the telephone, that Sir Martin seemed to have recovered his good humour.

Lady Flaxman came for dinner that night at Mount Street. "Pass me the rat poison," she said almost as soon as she had entered the house. "The kraken wakes."

"What do you mean, Mummy?"

"I mean your father. The old fool has come back to life. Jesus wept." She elaborated on this theme over dinner. "I knew he was getting better when he swore at me. And he kicked out with his foot. With his foot." She repeated the phrase very slowly and distinctly.

"What else would he use, Mummy?"

"Nothing is beyond that man. And he has gone red again. Like a cockataw or whatever the horrible creature is called."

"Cockatoo."

"More like a lobster. Revolting, actually." She looked down at a piece of shrivelled meat upon her plate. "I see we have very slim pickings." Mrs. A. entered the room at this moment. "Ah, my good woman." Lady Flaxman greeted her with what seemed to Harry to be artificial warmth.

"I am not your good woman. I will not be called a good woman in this house."

"Only a turn of phrase."

"There are turns of phrases and there are turns of phrases." Mrs. A. picked up Lady Flaxman's plate and returned to the kitchen, delighted with her sally.

"Your father," Lady Flaxman said, "happened to mention something about retirement." Harry began to listen more intently. "Absolute nonsense of course. Is he a shy violet?"

"He is about as shy as King Kong," Guinevere replied.

"Precisely my point."

Over the next few days Harry found out more about Asher Ruppta's death; he also learned that "Miss Sally Palliser" had inherited the business until Ruppta's son reached the age of twenty-one. He was anxious that her married name should not be published, so he decided to steer the story of Ruppta's death in a more sensational direction. He had not forgotten his discovery of the financial relationship between Asher Ruppta and Cormac Webb. Now, with Ruppta gone, Flaxman had more or less invited him to pursue the story with additional vigour. Harry's enthusiasm had been quickened by the fact that Webb had found himself again in government as parliamentary under-secretary at the Home Office. So Harry called in James Thorn, now chief political correspondent of the *Chronicle*.

Thorn was fatter than before, and had acquired a pretentiousness that might have been mistaken for gravity. He still wore pinstriped suits, and had a rose in his buttonhole. "How can I help you, old boy?"

"What do you think of Cormac Webb?"

"Webb is a coming man. A coming man."

"He may not be coming for very long."

"Oh?"

"He may be going. He's put his hand in the till."

"Is that so?" Thorn was always careful. He knew that Harry liked to disconcert him with a sudden remark or jibe. He retaliated by remaining as bland and as serene as he could manage. That annoyed Harry even more, so that the two men could reach a height of ill temper without either of them betraying the fact.

"I did a story, a few years back, about the connection between Webb and Asher Ruppta."

"That was when you were a journalist."

Harry was not sure if this was simply a statement of fact, or a barb. "It was a good one, too. The story stood up."

"Why was it never published?"

"Pressure from above." He raised his eyes to the ceiling.

"From God?"

"As good as."

"I see."

"But do you see?"

"Sir Martin, I suppose, had 'business dealings' with Ruppta."

"So we couldn't chase the connection between Webb and Ruppta."

"Now that he's dead—"

"It doesn't matter. We can go after Webb."

"You know that Webb is close to Harold Wilson, don't you?"

"Yes. I did know that."

"I don't imagine that the prime minister will be very thrilled if the *Chronicle* makes a target of him."

Harry supposed that Thorn wanted to protect himself, and that he would try at all costs to avoid provoking Downing

Street. The world of political journalism was run on the lines of a mutual benefit society, where ministers and politicians tried to maintain the most agreeable relations.

"Have you ever heard," Harry asked Thorn with a smile, "of the freedom of the press?"

"Of course."

"It's only a phrase. It doesn't mean anything. But you can use it, can't you?"

"I suppose it is an excuse."

"That's it. An excuse."

"People do pretend to take it seriously."

"Do they really? That *is* good news. So I want you to find out if Webb had any more recent dealings with Ruppta. Or with anyone else. I want to find out how bent he is."

Thorn found the remark distasteful, but took care not to show it. "I know his secretary vaguely. Bright young man."

"He wouldn't want his future career spoiled, would he?"

"I sincerely doubt it. If I were to tell him of your previous suspicions—"

"Proven."

"Then he might co-operate."

"What's his name?"

"Askisson."

"Arrange to meet him for a drink."

Thorn did not like being told what to do by a man whom, as he told his friends, he considered to be an "oik." But he really had no alternative. "And then pour poison in his ear?"

"Something like that."

A few hours later, Harry encountered Martin Flaxman in the executive lift; his father-in-law had indeed regained some of his energy. "Is there a bun in the oven?" Flaxman asked him. Harry must have seemed perplexed. "Is she up the spout yet?"

"I don't know. I don't think so." Harry did not want his father-in-law to know that they were no longer lovers.

"You don't *think* so? What has thinking got to do with it? She needs an heir, doesn't she? If you can't do it, I'll get in someone who can." Harry looked at him in amazement. Flaxman chuckled, and held on to his arm with a strong grip. "Just joking." And then he added, "I *think*."

Harry returned to his office quickly. He was practically being accused of impotence. He was startled when the subject of his reverie stepped into the room; he quickly rose to his feet and knocked over his chair. "Ants in your pants?" Flaxman smiled at his discomfiture. "Not much else."

Harry had the urge to blot this man out of existence. But he smiled back at him, and said nothing.

"I want you and Guinevere to come to dinner next week."

"We would be delighted."

"Oh? Would you?" He did not quite believe his son-in-law.

"Absolutely. Guinevere hasn't seen you in weeks."

"But she never did want to see me. Before she was married. Silly cow."

Flaxman went over to the window, and looked down into Fleet Street. It was an overcast day of cold rain. Harry closed his eyes and envisaged his father-in-law hurtling downwards, past the grey and blackened bricks, onto the dark street below. He opened his eyes just as a pigeon fluttered and flew into the obscure sky.

Two days later James Thorn came into Harry Hanway's office or, as he put it, "just dropped in for a chat."

"I had a drink with Askisson last night."

"Oh yes?"

"He is concerned, of course, about your allegations against Webb."

"Not allegations. Facts. Known as 'bribery and corruption.'"

Thorn thoroughly disliked the phrase. "He is worried, quite frankly. He would like to know where he stands."

"And what does that mean in English?"

Thorn, used to dealing in well-oiled platitudes, was annoyed now by Harry's sardonic manner. "Let me put it this way. He thinks that he may be able to help you."

"So he knew about it already."

"I wouldn't go as far as that."

"I would go further. He is involved."

"Now that is going too far, Harry."

"One of your favourite words, isn't it? Far?" He pronounced it with an Harrovian accent.

Thorn glared at him, but Harry regarded him with calm indifferent eyes. "Does he want to meet?"

"I think so. He doesn't trust the 'phone."

"A born conspirator."

They met beside the Thames, in front of the Royal Festival Hall, with Thorn as a somewhat unwilling third party. It was another leaden overcast day, and the river seemed to Harry to be grey and sluggish in the fading light. He could see at once that Stanley Askisson was nervous, but Askisson's first question surprised him. "Do you have a brother called Daniel?"

"How did you know that?"

"I was with him at Cambridge. I was a friend of his."

"Oh."

"I hear that he's doing well there now."

"I haven't seen him for years." He had no intention of mentioning the meeting at their father's funeral. "We've lost touch."

"I'm sorry."

"Don't be. We were never really close. Let's get down to it, shall we?"

"I don't know what you have learned about Cormac. But I had nothing to do with it."

"What is 'it'?"

"You tell me."

Harry looked across the river at the dim northern bank, the water slipping away beneath the level of his vision. "Bribery. Corruption. Call it what you like."

"I know nothing of that." Askisson looked away as he said it, as if his attention had been drawn to something in the water.

"Of course not. But if at some point I were to ask you certain questions—"

"As long as my name is kept out of it."

"I guarantee it."

On the following morning he received a telephone call from Cormac Webb. "We've met before. More than once," Webb said to him. "At Flaxman's house—in the house of your father-in-law, I mean—I knew then that you were on the rise. I have a nose for things like that. You have all the right qualities."

"Oh?"

"Boldness. Ruthlessness. Cruelty. Look at newspaper proprietors, Harry. Bastards." Harry laughed. "In a world like that, we can't afford to be meek and mild. Isn't that so, Harry?"

"I wouldn't know, Cormac."

"Tiger tiger burning bright. That's what you've got to be. In the forests of the night. I don't think you really want to do me any harm, Harry."

"What makes you so sure?"

"What's in it for you?" That was true enough. "On the other hand, if I can help you—"

"What do you mean?"

"Calm down. Nothing illegal. As such. I might give you a lead. I might tip you off. Something of that sort. I could help you, for example, with a story about the prime minister."

"Nothing libellous, I hope?"

"About Harold? Good heavens, no. Whatever gave you that idea?" Webb became more confidential. "It's going to be the biggest story of the year. If I give it to you, then I need something in return. I need a guarantee that you will drop the absurd interest in my affairs. Then I might be prepared to help in future, you see."

"I see."

"If the story I give you turns out to be correct—which it will—then you know you can rely on me. Do you see what I'm offering you?"

Harry Hanway was aware that Webb was desperately anxious to conceal the bribes he took from Asher Ruppta. He could face criminal prosecution, even though Ruppta was dead. "So what is this news?"

"Do you accept my terms?"

Harry was becoming impatient. "Yes."

"The prime minister is going to resign next week, citing pressure of work. But that's not really the problem. His mind is going. There's a word for it. Senility? Is that it? And there may be something else."

"What?"

"We will have to discuss it privately."

Harry, curiously enough, believed Webb. He trusted him to the extent of placing a story in the following day's *Chronicle* in which it was insinuated that the prime minister had come to the conclusion that it was time to leave. Harold Wilson's press secretary denied the "unfounded rumours" the next day. On the day following that, Harold Wilson resigned.

Cormac Webb telephoned Harry that afternoon. "Congratulations. Everyone is saying that you know more than the Cabinet Secretary."

"I have good sources."

"So you do. I have my promise, right?"

"Yes." He paused for a moment. "When are we going to have that private meeting?"

"Whenever you wish."

They met three evenings later, in a small Soho restaurant. "Did you ever read a story by Max Beerbohm called 'Enoch Soames'?" Webb asked him.

"Not that I can remember." In fact Harry had read very little of anything, but he was not about to admit that fact.

"Enoch Soames meets the devil in a Soho restaurant. This is the one."

"Oh?" Harry looked around without interest.

"Soames was a minor poet who, after talking to the devil, made a pact with him. He would give him his soul in exchange for one favour. He wanted to return to life in a hundred years' time—1996—and to find out if he had been remembered by posterity. He would appear in the Reading Room of the British Library and look up his name in the catalogues there. The devil agreed. The deal was done. And this was the point, you see. Enoch Soames had not been remembered at all. His name was absent from the catalogues, except for the titles of two books he had published at his own expense. There and then he is consigned to hell." Webb looked around with satisfaction at the snug restaurant, with its red plush seats and its artfully shaded lamps. "You have to be careful whom you meet in restaurants."

"I've known that for a long time." They discussed small idle things for a while. "You said there may have been another reason for Wilson's resignation?" Harry eventually asked him.

"A very interesting one. There may be a plot brewing."

"What kind of plot?"

"Look around you. Everything is falling to pieces. Strikes everywhere. Unemployment rising through the roof. Inflation going up every month. It can't be sustained."

"You sound like a Tory."

"These are just the facts of the matter. Everyone is aware of them." He leaned forward and lowered his voice. "There are some people who propose a drastic solution."

"What would that be? A general election?"

"Oh no. That wouldn't do at all. The government might be returned. A smaller majority, perhaps. No. That would not be drastic at all."

"What would?"

"A military coup." Webb sat back in his chair and smiled broadly; his eyes widened, and he looked at Harry with evident interest.

"You aren't serious."

"Oh yes. Deadly serious. Harold believed that the army was ready to take over the government. So are others." He leaned forward again, and whispered some names. "That's why Harold resigned. He wanted to ward off the coup."

"How many people know about this?"

"A few. The conspirators, naturally. Most of the Cabinet. Some senior civil servants. Two or three newspaper proprietors have been alerted."

"Among them?"

"Your man? I don't know."

"So what do we do? What do *you* do?"

"We do nothing. We wait. They have already been unsettled by Harold's departure. We watch and wait."

After he had left the restaurant Harry walked along Old Compton Street. For the first time it seemed to him to be drab and unprepossessing, with all the signs of weariness and wear. This is what Cormac Webb had meant by "the facts of the matter." There could be no doubt that the city was in decline; it looked wan and uncared for, its buildings in a bad state of repair, its inhabitants gloomy and irritable. This was a sullen time.

Three days later Harry and Guinevere Hanway were preparing for dinner with Sir Martin Flaxman. "Mummy says she won't be coming. When you two get together you behave like fishwives. That's what she says. Nothing but foul language."

"She is quite good at that herself."

"That's not the point. According to her. A lady should still be treated like a lady."

When they arrived at Cheyne Walk, however, they were surprised by the beaming presence of Lady Flaxman dressed in a low-cut red silk dress revealing the beginnings of the darkness between her scrawny breasts. "I'm so pleased that you could come," she said to them both, "I haven't seen you in an age." She put out her cheek for Guinevere to kiss, but her daughter merely brushed it with her own. "Darling," Lady Flaxman said to Harry, "I do think that you have put on a little weight. It can't be that woman's cooking."

Sir Martin stood by the fireplace, his hands clenched behind his back; he was rocking slightly, backwards and forwards, as if he were about to take a spring. "Here she comes," he said. "The bartered bride."

"Good evening, Father."

"And here is my favourite son-in-law."

"If you can't say anything nice, Martin, don't say anything at all."

"I am nice, Maud. Nice as pie." Sir Martin poured the drinks, and made a point of filling the glasses to the brim. "May I propose a toast," he said, "for the cure of barrenness." Guinevere blushed.

Harry resisted the urge to hit him. "A quick word, sir?"

"Well, darling," Lady Flaxman said to her daughter, "the fighters are in the ring. There will be blood on the floor. I see it coming. And we have ringside seats. Aren't we lucky?"

"I have had a talk with Cormac Webb," Harry was saying. "He told me about a coup. Have you heard anything about it?"

"Coup? As in military coup?"

"That's it."

"What bloody coup? Nobody tells me anything."

"The army against the government. Mountjoy. Hatton. Burleigh."

"Toy soldiers. No lead in their pants. They couldn't arrange a picnic, let alone a coup. Does Webb believe this nonsense?"

"It seems so."

"He is a cunt. Don't trust anything he says."

"I have had some confirmation."

"Oh?"

Harry whispered something to him but, to his evident discomfiture, Flaxman burst out laughing. "They talk about coups," he said, "because they have nothing better to do. They are pathetic. They are just posturing."

"I don't know if there is a word for it," Lady Flaxman said, "but things keep on disappearing in this house."

"What do you mean, Mother?"

"Little things. Handkerchiefs. Earrings. Only the other day I put down a small pair of scissors and, when I turned round, it was gone."

"Daft cow," her husband said.

"Then, yesterday," Lady Flaxman was saying, "it turned up in a completely different place. I was mystified."

"You're going senile."

"No, Martin, I am not. Don't you agree, Guinevere?"

"When I used to live here," her daughter replied, "there were some strange things. Do you remember, Mother, when that little gold pen just went from my desk?"

"Of course. The little gold pen."

"And then two days later it was back on my desk."

"Bullshit." Her father poured himself another drink.

"Where do these things go?" Lady Flaxman asked no one in particular. "That's all I want to know."

"I used to get very tense in this house," Guinevere was saying, "I would become so anxious that I used to lie down. I would imagine the most terrible things. If I had a headache, I thought that I was suffering from a brain tumour. If my eyes ached, I was sure that I was going blind. Whenever I come back here, I feel a sense of panic." She turned to her father. "But things can change for the better. I have a client called Sparkler—"

The face of Martin Flaxman altered colour, and he seemed to choke on his drink. Guinevere watched as her father stumbled and fell against a large sofa covered with red brocade. "Oh Jesus," he whispered, "more trouble." He looked fiercely at his daughter. "Where did you hear that name?" Then he slumped onto the floor. "Why him?" White spittle came from the sides of his mouth.

Lady Flaxman delicately and deliberately put her hand on his pulse. "Don't celebrate too soon, Mr. Hanway," she said. "He is still alive."

XVIII

A comedy sky

DANIEL HANWAY believed the publication party to be going well. It was being held in the board room of Connaught & Douglas, which had changed not at all from the occasion when, three years before, he had attended the "bash" as Wilkin had called it. Even the books, scattered on the small tables, seemed to be the same. Wilkin was here again, as were most of the people Daniel had met at lunch above the Ancient Druids in Soho. Damian Etheridge had lost his job as literary editor of the *Chronicle*, and now earned a more precarious living as a freelance reviewer and literary interviewer. He looked more haggard than before, and had assumed a peevish or dissatisfied expression.

Clive Rentoul was as supercilious as ever. The words seemed to glide from him as if from a great height. "Well done, Daniel. You have surprised me." Daniel concentrated upon his nose; it was narrow, and slightly curved, with large nostrils. It implied superiority; it had a look of perpetual contempt for anything put before it. "We must have lunch," Rentoul said. "When you're next in London."

They were joined by Virginia Crossley. "Now," she said to Daniel, "I expect you to do some serious work." She had the same blustering and bullying manner. "You've got away with it this time. But now we want a masterpiece."

"Would you excuse me?" Daniel went over to Hanky Panky, who was in excited conversation with Graham Maland concerning the literary feud between two middle-aged novelists. Cressida von Stern had given a bad review to Edgar Cowper, in which she had made a veiled accusation of plagiarism. Cowper had retaliated, three months later, with an attack upon a short book written by von Stern on the modern novel. He had accused her of being "ignorant" and "wilful" in her choice of the significant novels of the last decades. None of his had been chosen.

"What he should have done," Maland was saying, "is obvious. He should not have responded to her. Silence is the best policy."

"But I like a good cat-fight," Hanky Panky replied.

"Cressida is a bitch, not a cat."

"Oh that is so *naughty*." Hanky Panky was delighted. "An interesting crowd, don't you think?"

"Well, all people are interesting if you don't really want to know them."

"That is the cleverest remark I have heard all day."

Daniel was about to join the conversation, when someone roughly shook his shoulder. It was Wilkin, who seemed to be swaying slightly. "He never wrote to me," he said, pointing his wineglass towards Hanky Panky.

"I did mention it to him."

"But he never wrote."

"I'm sorry."

"Sorry? Who do you think I am? It is not as if I don't have a reputation."

"You are being orgulous."

"What? What do you mean?"

"Overbearing."

"You're a clever little shit, aren't you?"

Denis Davis came over at that moment. "It's a comedy sky, isn't it?" In the frame of the window pink clouds, inflamed by the setting sun, hovered in a frosty blue sky. "Have you seen the painted sky in the Palladian theatre at Vicenza? Just like that."

Hanky Panky turned round to Daniel. "I spy with my little eye something beginning with 'F.'"

"Filing cabinet?"

"No."

"Fireplace?"

"No."

"Fender?"

"Oh no. That *Fraud* over there." He was looking at Denis Davis.

"Who is *he*?" Graham Maland suddenly pointed to a portrait from the late nineteenth century just beside the window.

"He? He is our founder. A very distinguished old *Fart*." It was a picture of a middle-aged man with side-whiskers and a formidable moustache, bearing the stern and almost marmoreal expression of one who is constantly aware of his duties. "Do you see what is written beneath him? Charles Connaught, Philanthropist and Educationalist. I prefer to read that as Pederast and Hypocrite."

"You are too cynical."

"Oh I don't think you can be *too* cynical."

Virginia Crossley came up to them. "Do either of you happen to know where the phrase 'feasting with panthers' comes from? We were just discussing it."

"Oscar Wilde," said Hanky Panky.

"Jacobean tragedy," said Graham Maland.

At that moment Daniel saw Sparkler entering the room. He became very still as he saw him crossing the room and walking towards Hanky Panky. Why had he come? He must have been invited by Hanky Panky—Daniel had never mentioned the party to him—but for what purpose?

He realised now that Sparkler had seen him, and was raising a glass of wine in his direction. Something had to be done. Daniel stared at him, and walked out of the room. As he hoped, Sparkler followed him.

"What are you doing here?"

"I work here."

"What?"

"Mr. Rackham made sure that I got a job. In the post room. I didn't want to go back to the old game. He asked me to come to a party. I didn't know you would be here, did I?" He put his hand on Daniel's arm. "Aren't you pleased to see me?" Daniel instinctively recoiled from the touch. "Oh? Is that the way it is?"

"I don't know."

Sparkler understood the situation at once. "You're embarrassed to be seen with me."

"No." He sounded hesitant. "Not at all."

"Are they your friends in there?"

"Some of them."

"From Cambridge?"

"And from London."

"And what am I? The abominable snowball?" Daniel shook his head and said nothing. "So why don't you come back inside with me?"

"It's complicated."

"What is?"

"They don't realise."

"That you're queer?"

"That's one way of putting it. I don't want it to be generally known."

"So you put your friends before me."

"It's my career—"

"I was right. You are embarrassed of me."

"I'm confused. That's all."

"You know, once I would have done anything for you. I would have died for you."

"A bit extreme, isn't it?"

Sparkler put down his drink, and walked down the staircase. Daniel felt unwell for a moment, and instinctively put his hand up to his chest. Then he went back to the party, where Virginia Crossley had launched into a violent diatribe against the *Times Literary Supplement*. A young man came up to him. "You are the author, aren't you?"

"Yes. I am the author."

"I'm Tristram Ferry. I'm the senior researcher for *Book Ends*." This was a literary panel show broadcast on BBC 2 every Tuesday evening. "I think you could rock the boat."

"Excuse me?"

"You would be good. You have a natural authority."

Daniel laughed. "I don't think so."

"You're an academic, but you're also a reviewer. Best of both worlds. I've read your work." Daniel presumed that he was referring to his new book. "In the *Post*. How would you feel about coming on to the show?"

Daniel was delighted. "I'm not sure," he said. "I'm not convinced that I could do it."

"I know what you mean. There is an art to television—"

"But I am happy to give it a try. Certainly."

"Do you have an agent?"

"No." Daniel cleared his throat. "But I'll give you my telephone number at college. You can contact me there at any time." Sensing that he may have appeared over-eager, he now frowned slightly. "But what would I be asked to talk about?"

"We'll know that closer to the time."

Wilkin lurched toward them. "I don't give a fuck about any of this," he said. "The fucking publishing scene is corrupt. I despise the lot of you."

"I'm not a publisher, Paul."

"That's beside the point. You're all in bed together." Wilkin leered at Daniel. "In bed with that old queer." He was clearly very drunk. "When a good writer like me is ignored. It's not right, is it?" He stepped closer to Daniel. "There was a time when I was ten times better known than you will ever be. I won the Poetry Council award for my first book. Do you know that?" Then he seemed to lose interest in what he was saying, and walked up to Graham Maland; much to Maland's discomfort he simply stared at him without any attempt at conversation. Having patted Maland heavily on the back, Wilkin then approached Hanky Panky. "Well, old dear," he said, "I don't suppose you remember me. I'm sorry. Am I interrupting something?" Hanky Panky had been talking to Clive Rentoul.

"I am sure," Hanky Panky said, "that you will have something interesting to add."

"Add this," Wilkin said and flung the glass of wine he was holding over Hanky Panky. Wilkin then staggered back and fell heavily against the nineteenth-century portrait of the founder of Connaught & Douglas. His right shoulder broke the canvas, and left a hole where the mouth of Charles Connaught had once been.

Daniel was looking down from the double-bowed window when he saw Sparkler; he glimpsed him walking along New Bond Street. His shoulders were hunched, and his head bowed, as he made his way slowly through the crowd.

XIX

Beginning to rain

I'M JUST popping out," Julie Armitage said to Sam Hanway. "To clear my head. I'm a great believer in fresh air." They were sitting in Sally's house; they had moved Ruppta's business to Borough a few days before. "May I have permission, Sally?"

"Of course."

"You are too kind. Ta very much." In fact she wanted to go outside for a quick snack.

When she had left the house, Sally turned to her son. "We've got five minutes. She took a bag of doughnuts with her. One minute a doughnut. Where did she leave her handbag?"

It was a capacious handbag, wrought out of leather dyed purple and with an interior lining of green silk. It smelled of mints and of nail varnish, and it contained many half-empty packets of nuts and sweets as well as bus tickets, paper handkerchiefs and assorted items of cosmetics. There was also a small diary, the days neatly divided five to a page. "What was the day of his death?" Sam asked his mother.

"Four months ago. April the fourth."

Sam turned to that day. "She's written down an 'F' and underlined it. She did say that she was going to see her sister in Folkestone." Then he noticed, at the top of the same page, what seemed to be some blurred letters that had been unsuccessfully erased. He held the page up to the light, and could distinguish numbers rather than letters. There were seven of them. Sam read them out.

"A telephone number," Sally said.

"I'm going to try it." He picked up the telephone, and dialled the number.

There was a woman's voice in reply. "Sir Martin Flaxman's office."

"Sorry, wrong number." He told his mother what had been said and then carefully put the diary into the handbag, in the position where he had found it; he replaced the bag beneath Julie's desk.

Julie returned a minute or so later. "How was the air?" Sally asked her.

"What? Oh yes. Very fresh." There was suddenly a loud chatter of birds in the garden that distracted Sam's attention, but neither of the women seemed to hear it; they were staring at each other.

The three of them worked on till five, when it was time for Julie to leave. "You've been quiet this afternoon, Sam," she said.

"Have I?" He tried to smile at her but the smile froze on his face; he simply gazed at her with a perplexed expression.

"You look," she said, "like a frowning soup-plate."

When she had left, Sam and his mother sat together in silence for a while. "Let's go outside," she said. "It's a lovely evening."

There had been a brief shower earlier that day, and the air was heavy with moisture and perfume all the more intense for lingering in the dust and shadows of the city; the generally overheated atmosphere now seemed languorous and restful.

"So now we know," Sam was saying, "that Julie has been in touch with Flaxman."

"Or Flaxman may have contacted her."

"What did he want? What did she want?"

"What do you think?"

"Money of course."

"And Flaxman?"

Sam was silent for a moment. "Information. Either Flaxman offered her money for something, or she approached him. I never told you about the letter, did I?"

"What letter?"

"I was asked to deliver it to Flaxman."

"Who asked you? Asher?"

"Pincher Solomon."

"I told you never to get involved with him."

"That's why I didn't mention it to you. The letter really upset Flaxman."

"Do you know why?"

Sam shook his head. "Not really. There was something about Tuesday evenings. Wait a minute. There was a little book. At least I think it was a book." He rubbed his forehead violently. "I think," he said, "that we should go back to Highgate."

"Why?"

"I don't know. But we're missing something."

The house was exactly as he had seen it on the day he discovered the body, except that a "For Sale" board had been planted neatly in the garden. It now belonged to Sally and to Andrew, but it still retained the personality of Asher Ruppta. Sam wandered into the clean and modern kitchen, where a fly was hurling itself against a window above the sink; with some difficulty he opened the door into the garden and allowed the fly to escape. When he went back into the hall, where he had seen the body lying on the first landing of the stairs, Sally had gone. He called out to her, but there was no reply. He walked into the living room that looked over the gravel drive in front of the house, but then suddenly turned around when he sensed that someone had entered the room behind him and tapped him on the shoulder. There was no one, of course: he had imagined it. Yet he knew now that Ruppta had been murdered by Flaxman.

He left the room and began to climb the staircase, when he heard his mother scream. He ran up the stairs and into a bedroom on the first floor; she was standing at the side of the room, close to the wall. "I almost trod on it," she said. It was a dead crow, its black plumage still glistening in the sunlight. "How did it get in here?"

At that moment the bedroom door closed with a thud, startling them both.

"Open the door for me," he said. Then very carefully he picked up the dead bird and, carrying it in both hands, took it down the stairs and out through the open door into the garden. He put the bird in the earth, and then covered it with fresh soil. He looked down at the spot for a minute or so.

"I think I know what happened," he said to his mother as soon as he re-entered the kitchen. "Julie gave Flaxman a key to the house. She kept three sets in the office. Flaxman was looking for something. I think it might have been the little book I once saw. He was looking for something that had to do with his Tuesday evenings."

When Julie arrived on the following morning, she seemed distracted and ill at ease. She made herself a cup of tea, and munched disconsolately on a digestive biscuit. "Are you feeling all right?" Sam asked her.

"Bad dreams. Funny how they affect your mood. They're only ghosts, after all."

"What are?"

"The people in dreams. They're mostly dead, aren't they?" She spoke with her mouth full of biscuit. "Do you know that song? 'You meet the nicest people in your dreams. It's funny but it's true, that's where I met you.' I can't remember the rest."

"How's your sister?" Sally had come into the room.

"What sister?"

"You know. The one in Folkestone."

"Oh. She's still very poorly."

"I am sorry to hear that."

Julie looked at her suspiciously. "What is that supposed to mean?"

"Nothing." Sally looked at Sam, as if asking his permission. "Except I don't believe you have a sister. I think you made her up."

"And why would I do a stupid thing like that?"

"To give yourself an alibi. On the day that you met Martin Flaxman. The day Asher was murdered."

Both women looked pale and strained, their eyes larger than usual, their lips white.

"You don't know what you're talking about."

"Yes I do."

"Do you really think that I did him in?"

"No. But I think you gave Flaxman the key to his house."

Julie's face was suffused with a sudden flush, and she realised at once that she had betrayed herself. "You can't speak to me like that. That's slander, that is."

Sam could not bear the tension and animosity between the two women; he got up and, leaving the room, walked up the front path of the small dusty garden where grew roses and geraniums. He could hear their voices rising and falling in counterpoint. There was a silence and, just as their quarrel resumed, Sam went back into the house.

"Flaxman said he wanted a notebook," Julie was saying. "A diary. I agreed to help him find it."

"Why did you do that?"

"Why do you think? Money. Ruppy wasn't exactly a philanthropist. Anyway, I couldn't find it. I looked everywhere. I was sure that Ruppy had put something in the safe, but it wasn't there."

"What's in the book?"

"How am I supposed to know? I wasn't Ruppy's keeper."

"You're shouting again."

"I have a right to shout. You have been accusing me. Threatening me."

Again there was a pause, both women becoming quickly exhausted by their argument that seemed as if it might have no end. "So then what happened? You couldn't find the book. What did you do?"

"Flaxman arranged to meet me at the north end of Battersea Bridge. Funny spot, really. Very windy. A lot of traffic. Maybe that's why he chose it. No one could hear him. He was a strange one. Dressed like a tailor's mannequin, but with the face and manners of a navvy. He had very small hands. I remember that."

"Why did he want to see you?"

"Why do you think? He wanted my help. Where did I think the book might be? That kind of thing. I told him that it was more likely to be in Ruppy's house than anywhere else. That was my first thought."

Sally glanced at Sam, as if divining his thought. "So you decided to give him the key."

"It seemed like a good idea at the time."

Sally was indignant. "How could you betray him like that?"

"Don't use that word to me, Madame Palliser."

"So you gave Flaxman the key," Sam said in a voice that he hoped was without blame.

"He knew the address already. They had some some kind of business in the past. Something dodgy, or I'm a Dutchman."

"And he went there to look for the book."

"I assume so."

"This was on the morning that Ruppta was killed."

"So it seems."

"Assume? Seems?" Sally went over to Sam, and held on to the back of the chair in which he was sitting. "You know what happened, Julie."

"Do I?"

"Ruppta surprised Flaxman, and he was killed. Simple."

"Is anything ever simple? Do you know the reasons for anything you ever do, Sally? Do you understand the consequences? I don't. I don't think anyone does." At this moment Julie appeared to Sam to have acquired some kind of power; it was as if he had seen the blue vault of heaven open above her. She moved towards the door. "Would you like your son to know how his father behaved? Arson. Beatings. He set dogs on some of his tenants. I am sure Andrew would like to read about that. And would he like to learn about his mother? Don't you think I know all about you, Sally? Silence might be the best policy."

"I don't accept that." Sally's voice was uncertain, and she looked towards Sam for a response. He sat with his head bowed.

"Well," Julie said with an expression of triumph. "There we have it."

"We can't leave it like that." Sam raised his head. "Something has got to happen."

"Hasn't enough happened already?" Julie got ready to leave.

"You can't work here any longer," he said.

"Why should I want to? I don't really fancy working for a whore." Sally walked over to her, and slapped her hard upon her right cheek. Julie put up her hand to her face, and laughed. "Listen," she said, "it's beginning to rain." Sam also heard the sound of a swift and sudden shower. But when he walked over to the window, there was no rain falling.

XX

A happy shagger

As long as her husband still lived, Lady Flaxman was in charge of the company; only on his death would it pass to her daughter. "Of course," she said to Harry, "I would prefer to be the merry widow. But not everything is possible." Her care for her husband was exemplary; she had installed a team of three nurses in the house on Cheyne Walk. Whenever she referred to her husband she called him "Sir Martin" and spoke almost in a whisper. "I am tiptoeing," she told Guinevere, "through the tulips."

All decisions about the *Chronicle* were now directed to her. Harry was at first dismayed by her ascendancy—thinking that he would only ever have to deal with a more compliant Guinevere—but slowly he began to adapt to the situation.

"You know, Harry," Lady Flaxman said to him one evening as they sat alone in the office that had once been her husband's, "he could go on for a long time. Modern medicine is absolutely wonderful. Have you thought about that?"

"Surely you could hand things over to Guinevere?"

"Guinevere hasn't got a clue. She is a social worker. She's practically brain-dead. But you know that, don't you?" She smiled sweetly at him. "She would need a big man behind her. Are you big, Harry?"

"You must ask Guinevere."

"Why don't I find out for myself?" She gave a harsh laugh when she saw his expression of horror. "I won't eat you, you know. Or perhaps I will. Would you mind that, Harry?"

"You're Guinevere's mother."

"What has Guinevere got to do with it? Have you got something against mothers?" He shook his head. "I should hope not. Well, we will be very discreet."

"No. I mean that I can't do this, Maud."

"Lady Flaxman, please. Think of it as business." He waited solemnly for her to continue. "The boss is always right. Isn't that what he used to say?"

"Are you threatening me?"

"Not a threat. An opportunity. I can do things that Guinevere cannot even imagine."

He closed his eyes for a moment. "I am not sure what you mean by that."

"In the sphere of business, Harry. I have plans." She outlined to him her scheme for an *Evening Chronicle* and a *Sunday Chronicle*, making use of the same building, the same presses and the same staff. "We won't just be printing newspapers," she said, "we will be printing money. Does that excite you, Harry? Will you be a happy shagger?" She came over and grabbed his cock. "I think something is stirring."

So began the affair between Lady Flaxman and Harry Hanway. Harry was surprised how quickly he overcame his initial reluctance; she was Guinevere's mother and he began to notice, or to emphasise to himself, the ways in which physically she resembled her daughter. She was not desirable, but she was not altogether repulsive. He was in any case strangely excited by her schemes for the future; he had not believed that he could be aroused by the idea of profit, but had that not been one of the reasons for his attraction to Guinevere?

Lady Flaxman was very eager in her lovemaking, although she often expressed horror at her husband's treatment of her in bed. "In the past," she told Harry, "I have been a common field system for that man. He has ploughed me and fertilised me. It was medieval. I might have been laid out in strips." "He would handle me," she said on another occasion, "as if I were a church organ. Pushing bits in. Pulling bits out. And all the time paddling with his feet."

She was not insatiable, but she was demanding. There was a small attic room in the house at Cheyne Walk, where she frequently took Harry; she called it "the blue lagoon."

Harry was relieved by the fact that Guinevere was more than ever detached from married life; or perhaps she was simply more distracted by her cares as a social worker. In particular she seemed to be worried about Sparkler; as far as Harry could gather from her comments, the young man had been dismissed by his publishing employers for petty theft, and was now descending into a state of bored and listless drunkenness. "He used to be so cheerful," she said to her husband. "Now he can't be bothered to get up."

"You can't help someone who will not help himself."

"If I hear that again, I will scream. It doesn't absolve me."

Guinevere seemed unaware of the relationship between her mother and her husband. She still invited Lady Flaxman to the house in Mount Street, where she half-listened to her complaints about the business, the state of her husband and of the world in general. "How's Dad?" was her first question one evening.

"Well, he is not tap dancing. And he's not getting fat on a drip, I can assure you of that." At this moment Harry entered the room. "Ah, Mr. Hanway. My partner in crime." She smiled sweetly at her daughter. "Don't you think your husband is looking well these days, dear? He has such a spring in his step. And I'm sure he's lost weight. How do you do it, Harry?"

"Healthy living, Maud."

"That's what I like to hear. I don't doubt it for a moment. Do you, Guinevere?"

"What? No. Harry is always good to me."

"I gather from Mrs. A. that you have a healthy appetite. Even for her food. You are very brave."

"He eats carefully, Mummy."

In fact the Hanways remained polite and good-natured in each other's company; they had so few mutual interests that they found it unnecessary to quarrel. They shared the house. That was all.

Harry always took a shower after he had returned from an encounter with Lady Flaxman, and then climbed into bed smelling only of almond-scented gel. He felt no guilt about the matter. It was, as Lady Flaxman had said, business. Already he had been promoted to the post of chief executive, with a large rise in salary; the more money he earned, the more fervent became his lovemaking.

One evening Harry, on a visit to Cheyne Walk, heard the sound of high-pitched laughter from behind the closed door of Martin Flaxman's sickroom. He put his ear to the door, and made out the voice of Lady Flaxman. "Look at you, you old tart," he heard her say. "You're all knocked up. Finished. I just wanted to let you know that I am spending your money and fucking your editor. Or whatever he was. Enjoying myself, sweetheart, I really am. That's never happened before. Oh, one other thing. I always hated you touching me. I despised you. But I don't want you dead. Oh no. I want you to be a vegetable. While I'm having fun. Now look. You're dribbling. Does that mean you can hear me? Is that your new way of crying?"

Lady Flaxman was always capable of surprising Harry. "That day is coming," she said to him at the beginning of March, "the holy day."

"What day is that?"

"Mother's Day. It has always been a sacred day in my book." She had in fact consigned her ailing mother to an inexpensive care home in Bromley, and had never visited her there. "Is it for you, Harry? Is your mother that special person in your heart?"

"I have told you that my mother is dead." He looked back at her impassively.

"Oh yes. Sorry. I forgot." She put her hands upon her hips and began to sing. "'Sally. Sally. Pride of our alley. You're more than the whole world to me.' Lovely old song, isn't it? Wartime. Gracie Fields. Our Gracie."

He looked away.

Lady Flaxman began to inflict on him little humiliations. She once handed him his tie neatly cut in half. "I do hate that colour," she told him. "It makes you look like a cinema attendant." On another occasion she ordered him to gargle with an antiseptic. "The smell of drink on your breath is so vulgar."

The resentment, and the instinct for revenge, were by now deeply planted in him. At night, while lying beside Guinevere, he would entertain fantasies of following Lady Flaxman and striking her down unseen and unknown.

One morning he went into the drawing room of the house in Cheyne Walk, and found her standing beside a small and highly polished oval table. "I've had enough," she said. "I have decided to tell Guinevere. She ought to know what kind of husband she has. How can I keep a secret like that from my own daughter?"

He looked at her curiously, not clearly taking in what she had said. "I don't understand what you mean."

"It's very simple, Harry. I intend to tell Guinevere about us."

Slowly he comprehended the fact that his life was about to change for the worse. "Why do you want to do that?"

"What can I tell you? Life's a bitch. And so am I." She paused to consider. "Why does anyone want to do anything? I do it because I *can*. I do it because I *like* it. I like you, Harry, hard though it is to believe." He stepped towards her, but she looked at him defiantly. "Have you ever wanted to do the one thing you know you should not do? Wouldn't that be a great relief? To press the button that might destroy you? And then it becomes more like a need. The need to fling yourself off the cliff. It would not be right, of course. But what are right and wrong anyway? Just words." She shook her head. "I can't explain. I just want something to happen, Harry."

"You can't do it."

"I can do anything. Watch." She picked up the telephone on the oval table, and began to dial a number. So he went towards her, snatched the telephone from her hand, and began to wrap the cord around her neck. She seemed not to resist, or perhaps he did not notice her resistance. He pulled the cord tight and watched her eyes as he throttled her; they soared upwards.

He shook her, enraged by her weak response, and then pushed her violently to the floor; the telephone fell upon her left shoulder, but she was no longer moving. He stood over her for a minute or so, waiting patiently for any sign of life so that he could extinguish it. He realised then that she was staring at him in surprise, almost as if he had made a sudden and unexpected remark.

He left the house and, closing the front door very quietly, he walked across the street towards the Thames. As he approached the river he stopped, and looked around. It was a dry clear day, and the air was very still. A small flock of pigeons, animated with one purpose, landed on the green that lay between the house and the river. He started walking on the embankment road, thinking of nothing. His mind was completely clear and untroubled, doing nothing more than receive the impressions of the world around him.

When he reached Battersea Bridge he was invaded by a sudden fear; he fled in panic. Although he did not know who his pursuer was, he did not dare look over his shoulder. Then it occurred to him that he was trying to run away from himself. At that point his panic subsided; he stopped, his shirt damp with sweat, when he came up to Vauxhall Bridge. He did not think about what had happened. It held no meaning for him.

There were sounds all about him—horns, whistles, bells, shouts and cries surrounded him. He might have drowned in the clamour. Yet he had the strangest sensation that all this noise emanated from himself. He was the source of the commotion. He sat down on a bench beside the river. Wait and hope. Wait for what? Hope? He could see only darkness for him; darkness behind, and darkness ahead.

He was coming up to Westminster Bridge, where the landing stages for the river-boats lined the bank. Ticket sellers were calling out "Kingston!" and "Richmond!," "Greenwich!" and "Kew"; for a moment he contemplated the choice of one of these destinations. One would be as good as another. But then he changed his mind. He walked onto the bridge. As he approached the rail overlooking the river, he wondered what Sam and Daniel were doing at this particular moment. He tested the rail with his hand, and as Big Ben tolled midday, he eased himself across it and jumped into the water. A dog barked somewhere. It was just an ordinary day.

XXI

Surprisingly good

D ANIEL HANWAY approached the television studios of
Shepherd's Bush in a state of terror. What if he could
not master or remember his words, or sweated uncontrollably,
or said quite the wrong thing? He had been asked to partici-
pate in a panel discussion on a biography of Mary Shelley, a
new novel by Graham Greene, and a history of New York.
None of these subjects remotely interested him, but he had
forced himself to concoct opinions on all of them. He wrote
these opinions on small pieces of paper, and then memorised
them.

As he approached the reception desk he felt a curious light-
ness in his head. He allowed himself to be conducted into
a lift, and then into a passage, and then into a small room
where he was greeted by a young woman who called herself
a researcher. "I'm Camilla," she said, "you're the first. Tea or
coffee?"

He was in a kind of trance. "Yes," he said, "that will be fine."

"Tea or coffee?"

"Neither, thank you." He did not believe that he had the
strength to swallow anything.

The two other guests, on the book panel with him, were
a biographer and a journalist who had been the New York

correspondent of the *Chronicle*. Daniel knew both of them by reputation, such as it was, but had not met either of them. They seemed to him to be making every effort to appear calm and casual at the prospect of the ordeal.

The biographer was an easy-mannered middle-aged man who seemed to be the very epitome of bland equability. Every word was correct, every expression and gesture measured. He purred his words, and gently chuckled at his own wit. Daniel did not trust him. The journalist was sharp and, even to a stranger like Daniel, a little acerbic; his words came out in a volley, his voice rising and falling in continual exasperation. Daniel was wary of him. He did not pause to contemplate, however, what impression he was making on them.

They were led into a studio, a brightly lit room chill with the air of vacancy; it was unreal, with an abstraction of two sofas and a bookcase. There was a coffee table with a neat pile of books and four glasses of water upon it. A small microphone was being clipped to the lapel of his jacket as the presenter of the programme walked onto the set. Daniel had seen Helen Gurney before, as a participant in various documentaries connected to the arts. She had short dark hair, and wore a large pair of glasses that seemed to magnify the earnestness of her gaze. She spoke forcefully in a low voice, carefully modulated, but seemed to be half-apologetic about introducing anything as vulgar as a book panel. Her favourite phrase was "it seems to me . . . ." "Do you not think," she asked Daniel as the camera turned upon him, "that feminism has changed the terms of the debate on Mary Shelley herself? It seems to me that her narratives must be deconstructed with much more care."

How he managed to survive the half-hour of filming he did not know. His voice sounded forced and clumsy in this airless room; he believed that he was talking nonsense, despite the fact that he had carefully memorised most of his lines. It had been an entirely meaningless exercise, in which all of the participants were in some way degraded. "Yes," he said at the end, summarising the study of New York, "surprisingly good."

"And on that note we must leave it. Goodbye from everyone on *Book Ends*."

When he came out onto the street on the west side of Shepherd's Bush Green, he welcomed the cold wind as it cleansed him. The Green itself was largely grey, the earth getting the better of the grass, and unlovely. Daniel did not know this western part of London well; it did not have the freedom and the airiness of Camden Town and the rest of North London. It seemed intimate and over-familiar. This was the effect that certain areas of the city had upon him.

He passed a small boy in the street, muttering to himself, shrugging his shoulders, raising his hands into the air and gesticulating wildly. "What am I supposed to do?" the child was asking with such a look of misery and helplessness upon his face that Daniel turned away. But then he felt the pavement beneath his feet, and the obduracy of London began to enter him. He decided to go underground at Holland Park, and travel to Liverpool Street where he could take the Cambridge train. The lift took him down to the east-bound platform, the sound of its metal gates following him as he walked through the passage. He did not know the Central Line well. He was accustomed from his childhood to the Northern Line, which seemed always to carry with it the sensations of the northern heights of Hampstead and Highgate. The Central Line was closer and more intimate; the platform was warmer, and the sound of the train as it entered the station less harsh.

He settled in the carriage with a sigh of relief. It was already midday, when the majority of people were at work, and there was a sense of illicit pleasure about the journey. It was almost luxurious. He passed through Notting Hill Gate and Queensway, when the train came to a sudden halt before it reached Lancaster Gate; the brakes shrieked and the train slid a few feet before becoming still. Daniel looked at one or two of the passengers, but there was no sign from them of disquiet or alarm.

He remained still, and looked out of the window at the darkness all around him. This tunnel had been bored through the London Clay, laid down some forty million years before. He was travelling within prehistory, held up by the remains of an unimaginable past. There was a noise as of sudden thunder ahead of the train. He imagined a vast invasion of water or, perhaps, a reawakening of some prehistoric life. But the noise passed; it was that of another train entering a tunnel.

He left the tube at Liverpool Street and made his way along one of the white-tiled passages that conveyed travellers to various parts of the world above-ground. A mild breeze surprised him. It seemed to have come up from the depths and, at the same time, he heard the sound of drums being played somewhere in the distance. It was clear that this was the work of a busker, but that did not lessen his unease; he always felt a slight tremor of anxiety when he passed such people, and he avoided looking at them.

The drums were beating out a recognisable tune in the confined space, where they mixed with the sound of hurrying footsteps. He walked along the curve of the passage, and saw the busker halfway down; he was leaning against the white tiles with the drums strapped around his waist. It was an oddly casual or capricious stance. As Daniel came closer he sensed something familiar about the man. He looked more carefully, and saw that it was Sparkler. His instinct was to turn and run back down the passage, but that would draw attention to himself. He walked on, holding himself rigidly erect; he did not look at Sparkler directly, but he knew well enough that Sparkler's eyes were following him. He expected him to speak, or to call out, but the only sound was that of the beating of the drums. They were beating more loudly as he walked on.

The two young men had been so close, so intimate in the past. Now Daniel had not stopped, had not spoken. He had glanced at Sparkler, and then walked away. Sparkler had seen him—he was sure of that—but had made no attempt to call him back.

The drumming stopped, and Daniel was suddenly convinced that Sparkler had decided to come after him; he fled down the passage and bounded up the stairs, two at a time.

When he stopped at the gateway into the vast expanse of Liverpool Street Station, fighting for breath, he felt an uneasy sensation within his heart. He felt its unnatural beating. He walked more slowly across the concourse to the platform from which he knew the Cambridge train departed. Now he had the luxury of turning round. Sparkler was not to be seen. Yet still Daniel flushed at the thought of their previous intimacy.

A week later, on the same day that Harry flung himself into the Thames, Daniel was feeling more refreshed than he had been for some time. As he prepared a pot of tea, he allowed himself to savour the luxury of his isolation. His first supervision was at ten o'clock, on the symbolism of *Bleak House*, and the second at midday was on the poetry of Tennyson; he took down the appropriate volumes from his shelves, safe once more among his books.

"What we have to explain, in *Bleak House*, is the imagery of the prison." The first supervision had begun on time. "It is perfectly obvious that, in most of Dickens's novels, the city itself becomes a form of penitentiary in which all of the characters are effectively manacled to the wall. If it is not a cell, it is a labyrinth in which few people find their way. They are lost souls."

"But what then," the young man in spectacles asked him, "do we make of the continuing use of coincidence?"

"That is the condition of living in the city, is it not? The most heterogeneous elements collide. Because, you see, everything is connected to everything else."

The undergraduate left the room, and Daniel placed his copy of *Bleak House* on the shelf and took down *The Idylls of the King*.

When he heard the sound of drums, coming from the courtyard beneath his rooms, he was seized with an alarm so great that he almost lost consciousness. He knew what was happening, but he felt the need to witness it. He was in pain as he limped to the window. Sparkler was on the lawn beneath, entirely naked, slapping the small drums with his right hand.

He was looking up at the windows and, now that he could see Daniel, Sparkler let out a wild cry of recognition.

Daniel staggered back, his hand to his mouth, and fell into an old leather armchair. He found it difficult to breathe, and gasped for the air around him. But then the room itself began to tremble. "This is it," Daniel said.

The next undergraduate, a few minutes late for his midday supervision, found him dead in the leather chair.

XXII

Anything is possible

As soon as Sam was awake, earlier on that same day, he sensed that Sally had already left the house. He was always aware of the presence of his mother; he felt more settled then, and more assured. Why had she left at such an early hour? When after two hours she had still not returned, he grew more alarmed.

Some days before, Sally had been discussing matters of business with her two sons. "I will be happy to take up the reins," Andrew had said. "When I'm a bit older, naturally."

"But will you enjoy it, Andrew?"

"I think, Mother, I have a pretty good head on my shoulders."

"Do you know what I want to do?" She was addressing them both now. "I want to set up a fair rent scheme. And I want to house some of the homeless. In return they would refurbish the flats."

"May I put my oar in, Mother?" Andrew seemed perplexed.

"Of course."

"Aren't you being just a trifle idealistic? I know your intentions are good, but are you sure that these homeless types will *want* to refurbish their flats?"

"What do you think, Sam?"

"I don't really know." He scratched his face. "I'll soon be moving on, anyway."

"Don't say that."

"I'm a wanderer, Mother. I can't stay still. I don't know what I'm going to do, or where I want to go. Something will happen soon enough."

By the early afternoon he had become seriously alarmed by her absence. Sally had left him when he was eight years old, and now he returned to that time when he wept for his mother under the cover of London fog and darkness. He sat by the window all that afternoon, looking into the street, caught between fear and indecision. To whom could he turn?

He had to go out. He had to walk through the streets in search of her. So in the waning light he went towards London Bridge. The street lamps shone on the crowd, casting long shadows across the brightly lit hoardings and shopfronts. It was a procession in torchlight, celebrating all the haste and fervour of London. He walked into the middle of the crowd, and slowly his anxieties began to subside. The touch of the stone beneath his feet, and the presence of the people, calmed him. He could feel the forgetfulness of the city rising within him. It was as if individual fear had no place in this concourse, where the great general drama of the human spirit was being displayed in the light of the street lamps.

He walked on across London Bridge and into the City. He soon reached Spitalfields where, in front of the old church beside the market, he saw the man he had once met in the local park at Camden; he was the one to whom he had given Tizer and packets of crisps. He had grown older and greyer, but Sam still recognised him. He looked up at Sam, and then put his forefinger to his forehead in a gesture of salute.

Sam walked further east through the dark streets, surrendering himself to the city. He realised that it had grown cold, and so he made his way towards the first pub he saw. It stood on the corner of Bethnal Green Old Street, as sturdy and as grimy as the street itself with three baskets of plastic flowers hanging above its entrance. He walked inside, enjoying the sensation of sudden warmth and the sour-sweet smell of beer and cigarette smoke.

He had gone over to the bar, and ordered a Guinness, when he became aware that he was being watched. He turned his head, and met the eyes of Sparkler.

"Hello, Samuel, fancy meeting you again." Sam, in the sudden excitement of seeing him, embraced him. "Hang on. The locals might get the wrong idea."

"What have you been doing? Where have you been?"

"I've been wandering. I'm the liberty boy."

"Where are you living now?"

"Here and there. Everywhere."

"You lost touch."

"I suppose I did. But I still see Guinevere. You remember?"

"Of course."

"She's started a housing charity in Hackney."

"She'll never change."

"Oh yes. She has changed. She don't look young any more. I don't think she likes her husband very much. Harry. That's his name. I don't think she trusts him. I think she despises him. I can't be sure. I never met him, did I?" A shadow of a scowl passed across Sparkler's face. "And her mother's a right old bitch. So she says. I feel sorry for Guinevere, and she feels sorry for me. So we're quits." He seemed to Sam to be in a strangely excitable mood. "Guinevere told me a funny story. Not so much funny as weird. She arranged for this couple to move into a council flat on the corner of Britannia Road. Near where I used to live. She said they were a strange couple.

But devoted. Then the husband goes and dies. The woman is in a terrible state, breaking down and crying at the funeral. He was *cremated*, by the way. She goes back to the flat and to her job. As an office cleaner. She is too poor to move anywhere else, do you see? And then one day there is a knock at the door. When she answers it, there is her husband. As large as life. He doesn't say anything. He just walks in and makes himself a cup of tea. Just as if nothing had happened. She was glad to see him again. Of course. She doesn't want to ask no questions. She doesn't want to upset him. And they've been living together ever since. What do you think of that, Sammy boy?" Sparkler smiled and put out his hands, as if he had just performed a trick.

"I suppose," Sam said, "that anything is possible."

"You can believe it. Guinevere says that the neighbours have just accepted it."

Sam pointed to the pair of small drums that Sparkler had placed on the counter. "What are they for?"

"I'm doing a bit of busking, aren't I? Keeps me occupied. And I earn a few quid. Do you want another one?" In the surprise of meeting one another, they had drunk their beer very quickly. "I saw your brother this morning. Daniel. Danny boy."

"You know each other?"

"Oh yes. We go way back. Or we *did*. He looked out of the window. Danny boy. It's a long time since I've been in Cambridge. I was afraid the porter would come after me. But, you know me, I'm *invisible*." He tapped the drum. "They seek him here, they seek him there. I was back in London before you could say—whatever people say."

As soon as Sam returned home, drunk and weary, he knew that his mother was in the house; characteristically she had left her high-heeled shoes at the bottom of the stairs. She did not want to damage the carpets. In his dreams that night, the three brothers were sitting in a darkened space that had no palpable boundaries; then they began to disintegrate, like clouds, and to become part of the darkness.

His mother was already in the kitchen when he went down. "Sleepy-head," she said.

"I didn't get in till late."

"What were you doing?"

"I was looking for *you*."

"Were you?"

"Where had you gone?"

"It's a long story." She turned away for a moment towards the sink, and pretended to arrange some dishes. "I wanted to find Julie." Sam waited for her to continue. "I wanted to confront her. I wanted to lay out the charges against her. That sounds very official, doesn't it? I had no real evidence. And what good would it do? I have to protect Andrew, you see. But I wanted her to admit that she had done wrong. Do you want a cup of tea?" Sam shook his head. "She lives in Camden. In Cooper Crescent. Near where we—Anyway, I waited for her until she came out. She surprised me by going into the church round the corner. The one where you saw me. Ages ago. I was going to walk up to her. I don't know what I would have said, but I would have said *something*. But she knelt down and started to pray. I didn't have the heart to interrupt her. I don't know. She may have been praying for forgiveness or something. A woman came out from the room beside the altar. She was wearing a blue coat. One of the cleaners, probably. She went up to Julie and put her arm around her. Julie looked up at her, and I could see that she was smiling."

Sam misheard the word. "Crying?"

"No. I don't think so. But I didn't want to talk to her any more. When I left the church eventually, I just wandered through the streets. I never knew that you were looking for me." She turned back to the sink. "Well, that's the end of that. I should get your lunch ready. It's nearly midday."

"It may not be the end," he said. "What was it Dad used to say? Wait and hope."

"That reminds me. A letter came for you."

He picked up a slim envelope from the kitchen table, addressed to him. He took out a small piece of white notepaper with the heading "Our Lady of Sorrows." The letter was very brief.

"Dear Sam, We appreciate all the work you have done for us. Come back at any time. We have been waiting for you."

A Note About the Author

Peter Ackroyd is a master of the historical novel: *The Last Testament of Oscar Wilde* won the Somerset Maugham Award; *Hawksmoor* was awarded both the Whitbread Novel of the Year and the Guardian Fiction Prize; and *Chatterton* was short-listed for the Booker Prize. His most recent novel is *The Casebook of Victor Frankenstein*. He is also the author of *London: The Biography, Shakespeare: The Biography, Thames: The Biography, Venice: Pure City, London Under,* and the Ackroyd's Brief Lives series.

A Note About the Type

This book was set in a version of the well-known Monotype face Bembo. This letter was cut for the celebrated Venetian printer Aldus Manutius by Francesco Griffo, and first used in Pietro Cardinal Bembo's *De Aetna* of 1495.